Praise for the work of
Annette Blair

BEDEVILED ANGEL

"A very clever, entertaining, and humorous addition to the uplifting Works Like Magick series." —*Fresh Fiction*

"A magically enchanting paranormal romance that readers will find hard to put down . . . Richly enhanced with well-drawn, charismatic characters, an enthralling and imaginative plot, humor, scorching-hot love scenes, and a perfect ending, this story is absolutely bewitching." —*Romance Junkies*

"Annette Blair is a master at sweeping you from one emotion to the next with the flip of a page. Her humor mixed with life challenges always give you characters with dignity and laced with fun streaks." —*The Good, The Bad and The Unread*

"Annette Blair successfully creates a convincing world where the paranormal exist among everyday humans . . . The story is driven by the dynamics and interactions between the two [Chance and Queisha] and convincingly takes the reader on their personal journey . . . It is hard not to be carried away by the humor, emotion, love, sex, and mischief." —*Romance Novel News*

NAKED DRAGON

"Blair's unusual paranormal . . . features charming characters, rich relationships, an inviting community, and sensuous lovemaking, all rolled up in a rollicking good read." —*Booklist*

"Forget the vampires and demons, give me the dragons! Full of suspense, humor, and romance, this novel is sure to please any paranormal or fantasy fan." —*Huntress Book Reviews*

continued . . .

SEX AND THE PSYCHIC WITCH

"Sassy, sexy, and sizzling!" —Reader to Reader Reviews

"A sexy, hilarious, romantic tale with fun characters, snappy writing, and some super-spooky moments." —Fresh Fiction

THE SCOT, THE WITCH AND THE WARDROBE

"Sassy dialogue, rich sexual tension, and plenty of laughs make this an immensely satisfying return to Blair's world of witch-craft." —Publishers Weekly

"Snappy dialogue can't disguise the characters' true insecurities, giving depth to Blair's otherwise breezy, lighthearted tale." —Booklist

MY FAVORITE WITCH

"Annette Blair will make your blood sizzle with this magical tale." —Huntress Book Reviews

"This warmhearted story is a delight, filled with highly appealing characters sure to touch your heart. The magic in the air spotlights the humor that's intrinsic to the story. A definite charmer!" —Romantic Times

THE KITCHEN WITCH

"A fun and sexy romp." —Booklist

"Bewitching! Full of charm, humor, sensuality . . . An easy-reading, reader-pleasing story that makes you feel good all over." —Reader to Reader Reviews

Vampire DRAGON

A Works Like Magick Novel

ANNETTE BLAIR

BERKLEY SENSATION, NEW YORK

THE BERKLEY PUBLISHING GROUP
Published by the Penguin Group
Penguin Group (USA) Inc.
375 Hudson Street, New York, New York 10014, USA
Penguin Group (Canada), 90 Eglinton Avenue East, Suite 700, Toronto, Ontario M4P 2Y3, Canada
(a division of Pearson Penguin Canada Inc.)
Penguin Books Ltd., 80 Strand, London WC2R 0RL, England
Penguin Group Ireland, 25 St. Stephen's Green, Dublin 2, Ireland (a division of Penguin Books Ltd.)
Penguin Group (Australia), 250 Camberwell Road, Camberwell, Victoria 3124, Australia
(a division of Pearson Australia Group Pty. Ltd.)
Penguin Books India Pvt. Ltd., 11 Community Centre, Panchsheel Park, New Delhi—110 017, India
Penguin Group (NZ), 67 Apollo Drive, Rosedale, North Shore 0632, New Zealand
(a division of Pearson New Zealand Ltd.)
Penguin Books (South Africa) (Pty.) Ltd., 24 Sturdee Avenue, Rosebank, Johannesburg 2196,
South Africa

Penguin Books Ltd., Registered Offices: 80 Strand, London WC2R 0RL, England

This is a work of fiction. Names, characters, places, and incidents either are the product of the author's imagination or are used fictitiously, and any resemblance to actual persons, living or dead, business establishments, events, or locales is entirely coincidental. The publisher does not have any control over and does not assume any responsibility for author or third-party websites or their content.

VAMPIRE DRAGON

A Berkley Sensation Book / published by arrangement with the author

PRINTING HISTORY
Berkley Sensation mass-market edition / April 2011

BERKLEY® SENSATION
Berkley Sensation Books are published by The Berkley Publishing Group,
a division of Penguin Group (USA) Inc.,
375 Hudson Street, New York, New York 10014.
BERKLEY® SENSATION and the "B" design are trademarks of Penguin Group (USA) Inc.

PRINTED IN THE UNITED STATES OF AMERICA

10 9 8 7 6 5 4 3 2 1

Dedicated with love and thanks to:

Diane Haynes
for welcoming me to
SOME ENCHANTED EVENING,
A New Age Shop where magic comes to life
and hope fills the air with charm and possibilities.
Diane, may you carve your niche in mountain rock
with pen and ink.

And to the friends who make my every visit to
SOME ENCHANTED EVENING
a tea-party delight,
rich with friendship, laughter, and joy.

Here's raising my teacup to each of you.
Brightest Blessings!

DRAGONS TO MEN AGAIN

A Roman legion, Killian the dark witch did change into
    dragons and banish.
To the Island of Stars, on a plane beyond ours, they did
    vanish.
Wondrous beasts who might well be dead,
But for Andra, guardian witch, from whom hope never
    fled.
At the rise of the moons when all went black,
She had turned the first to a man with mild flak,
So for this and future spells, her rhyme stayed intact:
"Shed horns, spines, claws, and webbed wings. Shrink
    scales, spade, and tail—"
Killian countered with a fiery bolt; Darkwyn writhed as
    he took the jolt,
While Andra missed not a beat or a mote:
"Warrior to beast, now back again. Send this man to the
    plane he began."
Darkwyn twisted to shift, from dragon to man, in the
    steam from the rift,
An elder stood by to share the gift.

ONE

Darkwyn Dragonelli tucked and rolled into a damp, pungent alley and came to a forced stop against a pair of well-turned ankles, one of them about to puncture his shoulder with the spike at its heel.

"What have we here?" she with the spikes asked. "A naked acrobat? Don't kneel there hiding your assets. Stand and introduce yourself."

Darkwyn ran his slow gaze upward, along a set of curves that could make a dragon man weep. She wore boots of a sort that ended at her thighs, slick-black leg-huggers with the supple, sturdy texture of leather, though he could see himself in them.

On her face, her horned mask of the same sheen revealed a striking pair of bold violet eyes. Eyes that met his, head-on, no backing down, a gaze that brought his heart to life, and, oddly, to beat in time with hers, a heart of flawless beauty.

Darkwyn took pause. How would he know how fast her heart beat, how beautiful it was? Unless—

No. Per Andra, his guardian, he must *seek* his heart mate—the single female in the universe whose heart he could see for its undeniable beauty and whose mind and emotions spoke to his.

Heart mates did not stand waiting at the threshold of the veil, destination side, no matter how tempting and extraordinary their hearts.

Did they? Did *his*?

As if to prove his argument, the stunner's valor yielded to hesitant confusion, and she stepped back, boots squeaking when they rubbed together. She seemed as perplexed as he. Except, she did not have the Goddess Andra's counsel on seeking heart mates, nor would she be of a mind to find hers, in the way he must seek his own.

Without another word, she quit the dim alley for the sunny outdoors, her long violet hair bouncing off her perfect backside with every sultry swing of her hips, in the same way the door bounced behind her.

She'd made an escape of sorts, but why?

The action concerned him, as if she refused to succumb to her own inner thoughts, an attitude that might concern her life quest, soon to be his . . . in the event she *was* his heart mate.

Absurdly, as he watched her go, Darkwyn sensed he wanted more from the enchantress, but what exactly? Besides seeing behind her mask. Why show courage one moment and run the next?

He sensed her unease and did not feel mistaken in that. Did the violet-eyed wonder have the sight like Andra? Could this splendid earthling who braved him in the present expect to fear him in the future? A question not to be answered until, if and when, at some point in time, they met once more.

Case closed. Perhaps.

Darkwyn took a moment to appreciate the quiet after his erratically raucous passage through the ether, avoiding clawed, wailing felines and the colorful mockery of a dive-bombing bird. Magickal creatures all, per Andra's invisible assurance.

Those caws and mews filled the distance, still, but Darkwyn saw nothing of their owners as his cramped legs forced him to rise to his surroundings.

Ah, he'd not been crouched in an alley but behind a half wall. And judging by the sea of gape-jawed patrons, he stood in a publick house and must appear to have risen as if from the ether. Close enough.

Given his lack of dress, Darkwyn appreciated the waist-high flat-topped divider between himself and his watchers.

He took in the sweet-sour scents of fermented grapes and roasting meats. He observed the wary, hostile whisperers, clear tankards in hand, and found this to be an extraordinarily ordinary world, much like the one he left centuries before, when Killian of Chaos turned his Roman legion into dragons in an evil act of spite.

"Civilization," Andra might call this. But given the expressions on the human types watching him, "civil" did not fit the mood. Nevertheless, Darkwyn firmed his spine, thinking he might, after all, *prefer* drowning in lava to standing *here*. But Andra's words rang true: "No going back."

His throat rusty, he had yet to form a word. A dragon, silent for centuries, now a man again, he firmed his lips. Telepathy and dragon speak he knew well, with but a rudimentary grasp of English, thanks to Andra.

He employed it attempting a telepathic call for help, but no one replied. So he raised his chin, revealed no fear, and regarded his watchers as steadily as they did him.

Astonishing, women sitting with men in an alehouse. Neither serving wenches nor prostitutes, they drank the fruit of the vine wearing less than dancing girls. Another world, this, where camp followers lived equal to men, and a bird squawked in the distance.

Ah, his magickal companion, sent to breach the veil, perhaps, because magickal supernaturals journeyed at different speeds.

Cranky bird would enjoy the hostility here—wherever here may be.

Darkwyn looked from one to the other of his watchers and felt the need to grab a nearby flask by its neck, while in his left hand, he hid a fist-sized island diamond, rough and raw for "she who would acclimate him," from Andra Goddess of Hope.

Raising that flask warmed local expressions, their amusement giving him hope. Not as hostile as he surmised.

Thankfully, Jagidy, his sea green guardian dragon, arrived, and flew about, emitting a faint air-shivering whistle as he smoke-tested the area. Green smoke meant neither good nor bad, but an inability by the guardian to detect malice or kindness, likely a result of general surprise. He'd caught them off guard, of course.

Darkwyn opened his thoughts to the miniaturized elder, now a pocket-sized dragon. *Jagidy, methinks we stand in Rome no more, even the Island of Stars is a memory.*

Fortunately, no one could see Jagidy but him.

A man entered the narrow alley beside him, bearing on his shoulder a shiny silver barrel, on his face, a small mask. "What's this?" said he. "Inebriated entertainment?" He'd come in the door through which the violet-haired beauty left.

Given the man's affability, Darkwyn lowered the flask.

"Only the bartender, and that's me," the masked man said, "belongs behind the bar, though I'm not sure you want to step around it advertising that fancy Johnson of yours. The ladies of Salem will follow you like rats to the sea."

"What?" a female patron asked, stepping closer. "The 'Jock in the Box' is *entirely* naked? In that case, I'll take one of *him*, to go."

"Or come," another said, while another moved in. The three leaned over the bar, all but popping their breasts from their clothes—and his eyes from their sockets—as they grinned at his man lance, shaped like a dragon tail, their attention making the thing misbehave.

Jagidy flew by, got an eyeful of bosom, and hit the far wall—splat—like a buzz-bee in a beaker.

"Will ya look at that," one of the camp followers said, her gaze pinned to Darkwyn's rising soldier. "I gotta get me one of *those*."

Unsure of his next move, Darkwyn backed into the rows of flasks on the wall behind him, knocking them against each other, their banes and toxicants swishing precariously. He searched his mind for the language and dared give it a try. "Where am I?"

A large, bright, airborne creature appeared and dive-bombed him. "Bite Me, peckerhead." The bird squawked as it perched on his head, talons closing to get a painful grip. Then the cock leaned forward and stared upside down into his eyes. "Ride in a coffin, drink some blood. It's Bite Me at the frickin' Phoenix. Run for your life!"

The bartender kicked open the screen door and tried to slap the bird with a towel. "Get lost, Nimrod."

Darkwyn backed away, to protect his wily cohort, talons or not.

"Wanna buy him?" the bartender asked. "As far as we can tell, Puck has all the markings of a Catalina macaw. Showed up a few days ago. Seems like forever. He's brilliant, if off-color. Quotes Ambrose Bierce, according to one customer, jokes until you want to shoot him, and cusses like a sailor. I'll give you a great deal."

Puck squawked. "Hypocrite: One who—professing virtues he does not respect—secures the advantages of seeming to be what he despises." He ruffled his feathers. "Also known as a douche bag."

The bartender scowled. Darkwyn felt oddly uplifted.

Jagidy smoke-tested the bird while Puck fake coughed and waved off the smoke with a wing. *Definitely* his magick traveling companion. In which case, Darkwyn supposed it didn't matter that Puck the cock *could see* Jagidy the guardian dragon, smoke and all, as long as the bird didn't give them away.

Yellow smoke meant Puck didn't have a malevolent bone in his bright body.

Relieved, Darkwyn noticed a resolute female human— not the goddess he'd rolled into—sweeping into the pub, headed straight for him, her black-spotted, white cloak flying behind her. The cat at her side, spotted the same, stood taller and more slender than most felines.

The female bore a crown of tiny, fast-flapping air snacks, a whirr of red and green hummers and a purge of bony black pingers flitting about her head. *My name is Vivica Quinlan*, she said in telepathic dragon speak. *I'm here to acclimate you.*

Quite the task, acclimating him to this odd place, he thought while the brightest of yellow smokes dissipated around her and she placed on his shoulders a cloak, black as his hair, and long as his overtall body. "For my acclimator," he said, placing the island diamond in her hand. "From Andra, for Dragonelli expenses. She said you would understand."

"That I do," Vivica said.

He ducked several of her fluttering entourage until Puck held a wing straight out. From the corner of his eye, Darkwyn saw several of Vivica's critters perched on, or hanging from, that wing.

"Don't mind them," Vivica said. "The bats are as harmless as the hummingbirds."

Fine, Darkwyn thought, *but which is which*?

"Follow me, Dragonelli," his acclimator said. "Your brothers are on their way."

Her air snacks quit their perch and hovered around her head, moving with her, like a wreath of living flowers.

If someone says something you don't understand, Vivica communicated, *say "okay."*

"Okay," he repeated. "But my heart mate?"

"Right," she said, "your mandate on earth, among other tasks, is to find your predetermined heart mate and assume responsibility for her life quest, correct?" Vivica scanned the room and frowned. "Is she here?"

Darkwyn studied one female after another.

Their hearts varied as much as they. Hearts for money, Darkwyn saw in several. Hearts for lust. No kindness, no softness, a closed heart, one dark, one clouded, two as empty as the cloth-flicking bartender. "No heart mate here," Darkwyn admitted, though he couldn't forget the violet-eyed beauty with the cautiously shrouded heart.

Vivica nodded. "Fine. Let's go. Give the man the bird."

"No way!" the bartender yelled. "I'm giving *him* the bird. Literally."

"Well, Puck me," the bird said.

TWO

"*Air,*" *Puck said, at the door.* "*A nutritious substance* supplied by a bountiful Providence." And like a fair-weather friend, Puck paid homage to Providence by making a break for freedom. But the bird's defection fell by the wayside as Darkwyn became distracted by the woman who seemed to own the sidewalk.

She stood in front of the building he exited, at the base of its wide porch, that tall violet-haired goddess, not twenty feet distant, her breasts raised by a torso-cincher as black as her horned mask and leg boots.

Watching her controlled movements, her command, men doing *her* bidding, held him captive.

"Bronte," Vivica said as they embraced. "I'd hoped to see you before I left today."

His vision's name slipped off the tongue, seductive as a song, and it matched her heart for beauty. *Bronte.*

Caught by the aura of mystery surrounding her, Darkwyn's heart raced, his hands began to sweat, and his inner dragon stirred.

Bronte glanced up, as if she knew. "Secure that cloak," she said. "I *joked* about seeing your assets."

Vivica gave him a quick, telepathic translation *with* sarcasm.

He caught his cloak tighter. "Okay," he said, and wished he could speak Bronte's language as well as he could think like a dragon.

Bronte had just diffused their taut attraction—mutual, he believed, however much it seemed to frighten her—by making another joke. Did she do that, always? Use humor to lighten serious moments? Whatever Vivica planned for him at Works Like Magick, he would eventually return to Bronte to learn as much about her as he could.

Despite her misgivings, he felt her reach out to him, in some nebulous way, her interest driven by an unwelcome anticipation and a longing that surprised, almost angered her, and how could he know so much about how she felt? "Vivica?" she asked in the same tone she'd use to give her workers their orders. "Do you know this man?"

"Darkwyn's a friend," Vivica said. "He lost a weird bet. Bronte McBride, meet Darkwyn Dragonelli. Darkwyn, Bronte."

They reached with more than their hands—a moment in time. Fingers touched, held, silk on silk, no more than the brush of a flutterby wing.

Their eyes met, too, their hearts as well.

He read her confusion, her yearning, and answered with his own.

Vivica cleared her throat. "Sorry I didn't bring his cloak sooner."

The spell dissipated as Bronte quick-claimed her hand

as if from a flame. "What weird bet? A drinking bet, I suppose," she said with disapproval. "That figures."

Vivica chuckled. "Don't *run* a café with a bar if you don't want the results."

"I don't *run* Bite Me. The bartender does," Bronte said, a possible evasion.

Vivica nearly smiled. "But you own the Phoenix, the building that houses the bar and grille, do you not?"

"Yes." Bronte looked miffed. "Zachary and I own the Phoenix and every business in it."

Zachary? Darkwyn caught his breath. The knowledge landed like a blow to his solar plexus. Who in floating starfields was Zachary? "You already have a man?" he asked.

Bronte's head came up, her gaze snapping to his. "I beg your pardon?"

"Darkwyn," Vivica said. "You're getting ahead of yourself."

He turned to the right, the left, then checked behind him. "I don't see how that's possible. I can only stand in one place at a time."

Bronte chuckled, a marvelous sound, though she composed herself as if she'd broken some rule.

"Ignore him," Vivica suggested.

Ignore? Ignore? What did that mean? Darkwyn swore to learn this woman's language, and well. Still, he believed Bronte understood his interest and returned it.

Vivica examined the huge three-story brick building behind them. "Bronte, below the word 'Phoenix,' in granite, which seems part of your building's structure, you added a sign that says: A PLACE FOR VAMPIRES. Why not call it 'Dracula's Castle' for clarity's sake?"

"There's already one in Salem, so I named my second-floor vamp nightclub Drak's Place."

Vivica half nodded. "Wait. You give public day tours of your nightclub?"

"No, no, no." Bronte's denial took on a whole-body move, graceful and man-hardening. Darkwyn followed each curve with his hungry gaze.

The violet-haired vixen indicated the line of people at a far side door. "They're waiting to get into Fangs for the Memories, our vampy fun/horror house tourist attraction. It starts in the hall beside Bite Me and continues through the entire basement level, exiting into our fairgrounds."

"Ah, so Drak's is a *private* club?"

"Members only." Bronte nodded. "We cater to real vamps and vamp role players."

Darkwyn wanted "vamps" defined, but Jagidy claimed his attention, because the tiny dragon blew purple smoke Bronte's way, which meant the guardian was captivated.

Join the club, Darkwyn thought.

Thank the stars Jagidy remained invisible, because he hovered in Bronte's line of vision, patting her lush breasts with both happy little dragon hands.

The receiver of Jagidy's misplaced attention, Bronte shivered, stepped back, and crossed her arms, catching a tiny green hand exactly where Jagidy wanted it, smack between those luscious globes.

The pocket dragon glanced back at Darkwyn and gave him a "Look what I've got!" grin.

Jagidy! Darkwyn scolded, telepathically. *Lady breasts are not for your pleasure. They are for mine*, he thought, and wondered how to bring *that* about.

Bronte's were breasts to feast on, feed on, with his gaze and more, pleasure for a closer acquaintance, so for now, he made an attempt to disregard Bronte, the way she tried, and failed, to ignore him.

For her protection, and because jealousy held him in its

grip, Darkwyn yanked the pocket dragon away, not allowing himself to touch Bronte's cream-silk skin, despite his itchy fingers and a distorted man part attempting to hard-mend itself.

"What are you doing?" Bronte asked, which made him check to see if his cloak remained closed.

"Bee!" Vivica said, having witnessed Jagidy's obsession. "You were about to get stung."

From Darkwyn's shoulder, Jagidy nodded enthusiastically.

Feisty old dragon, Darkwyn thought, holding the elder back so he, himself, could concentrate on the beauty, her cloak, crimson as blood, thrown over her shoulders, her attention now called upward.

She opened her arms, as if she could catch a man-sized box—like an uncarved sarcophagus—being raised toward a window on the second floor. The private club level, Darkwyn remembered.

He wanted to see her face, wondered why she and Vivica—he looked around—and many of the women in his view wore on their feet objects that resembled spikes.

Mostly, he wondered why his violet-eyed vision dressed in costume. Face covered, legs covered, arms gloved to the elbow, a black cincher at her torso, a black skirt long in the back but high in the front. Black, the color of shadows, paired with violet, symbols of mourning.

There was so much more to this woman than met the dragon eye, and Darkwyn figured himself as the man-beast to uncover each layer in every way possible.

From the moment she stopped his forward roll in that alley, she'd worn the demeanor and posture of a masked queen who towered over her subjects, tall, slender, regal, in command.

He had never stood eye to eye with a woman—nor

man, nor dragon—at any point in his hulking lifetime. But Darkwyn suspected if he stood as close to this woman as he wanted, they would be of a height, all parts at the ready, and the invisible connection between them would spark and flame.

With her willingness and permission, his hands might always be busy about her person, but her breasts, he would leave to his mouth.

He had scanned the hearts of the women in Bite Me long after Bronte had left. Most were smallish, protected, dim, brittle, and self-focused. Now he turned his mind to scanning Bronte's in earnest, though he realized—after those first women and the ones in the crowd around him—that his connection to Bronte, and hers to him, transcended the norm.

What he saw beating in Bronte's breast stole his breath. A huge heart, open to great love, yet shrouded by fear. In each beat, he saw a protector, a nurturer, a woman who would sacrifice life and limb for those she loved. He saw so much, *felt* so much, he nearly backed away.

She turned and, at her back, her hair fell from her shoulders and down her spine, almost into one long curl—violet; even her hair was in hiding—pointing to the wonder of her form. And though she struck him as stellar—struck in the way lightning strikes, awaking his inner dragon—nothing, but nothing, in his considerable life experience, touched the splendor of her heart.

So, did that make Bronte McBride his heart mate? As unlikely as it seemed that he would meet her on arrival, a thrumming yet invisible cord connected them. Taut. Unbreakable. Everlasting.

He believed in his head and heart that he'd found his mate. The trick? To convince Bronte that she belonged to him.

He understood her heart, like no other, and though she radiated loyalty, a fierce defense against injustice, and a vulnerable openness—especially to him—she saw her vulnerability as a weakness she should fight.

It wouldn't be easy breaking her down, helping her achieve her goals, because that task required access to her secrets.

Yes, Bronte McBride harbored a world of secrets, and a powerful resolve to keep them.

Yet, despite these many barriers, his heart beat in time with hers while his wings ached to slip free of their muscular sacs and encircle her with a lifetime's worth of protection.

THREE

Vivica's spotted feline raised a paw to stroke Bronte's skirt for attention, the greedy cat.

"Isis, you magnificat, you," Bronte said as she stooped and nuzzled her face in its fur, scratching it behind its ears, Bronte's soft coos calling to the man beast in him.

"You've grown so pretty, Isis. I'd love to raise one of *your* kittens."

The cat almost laughed, or so its response seemed.

Vivica mimicked the sound. "No kittens for her. Bronte, don't you have an orange tabby?"

"Hoover's cleaning crumbs on the rainbow bridge, these days. Old age won."

Isis pawed Bronte's hair, as if consoling her, while Bronte continued to cuddle her, the feline's human reaction a surprise.

"I'm so sorry to hear it," Vivica said. "Get another. You love cats."

Darkwyn ached to stroke Bronte the way Isis did, but he went with an instinct that said he should not . . . yet.

"I miss Hoover so I haven't had the heart. Maybe. Someday. Still, it's hard to stay on the move with a cat." Bronte sighed heavily.

Move? Darkwyn wondered. *Move where?*

Vivica studied her. "Are you leaving Salem?"

The barest pink color washed over Bronte's cheeks. "Not at the moment."

Darkwyn's heartbeat slowed with hers.

A shout from the second floor drew their attention.

"A new casket?" Vivica raised a brow. "Bright for death. Is red a special order color?"

"Not at all. Bereaved families may not choose it, but vamps do; they're glorious in candlelight. Drak's has a Music Room, a Green Room for live action role players, or LARPers, and now the Crimson Room, with red and salmon coffins, for real vamps. The two factions tend to vie for prominence when sharing space. So much hissing and exposed fangs. Green means eco-friendly, by the way. Lightweight six-sided caskets like old pine boxes, each a unique work of art. Zachary, my brilliant inventor, turns some of them into sofas."

Zachary again. If he was so important to Bronte, where was this man of hers?

A boy stepped before her, and she embraced him from behind, her love for him lighting her features. She had not only a man but a child? She could *not* be his heart mate, then.

Darkwyn tried not to roar his disappointment.

The boy had yellow hair striped green and blue, and wore a red mask. "Hey," Bronte said. "Here he is, Zachary Tucker, wonder boy, my brilliant inventor."

Zachary? A boy, not a man.

Tingles ran up Darkwyn's arms and legs, and his inner dragon stood down. He had *not* lost the woman whose true heart spoke to his. Neither had he won her, he must remember. Not yet.

A longing to transform Bronte's expression with his presence marched in Darkwyn's mind beside a need for her to welcome him with an enthusiastic embrace, though he envisioned her welcome to include her supple body moving with his.

"Wearing your Spider-Man mask today, I see," Bronte said, kissing Zachary's head, square between her breasts.

The lucky boy gave an exaggerated shrug. "Yeah, 'cause my Einstein and Churchill masks are in the wash."

Bronte's eyes danced, and Darkwyn fell deeper beneath her spell.

"Zachary was born an old man." She ruffled his hair.

"Why are you both masked?" Darkwyn asked.

Whoa, Bronte's inner fortifications rose like one of Killian's dragon traps. "Vamps attend my club masked. It adds to the anonymity and allure of our vampiric profile. Tourists are exempt, though most embrace the masks we offer as part of the charm, hence my employees also wear them. Masks extend the enchantment."

Darkwyn tilted his head as if he were satisfied, knowing her truth had been stretched. "But the boy?" he asked.

Zachary's own chin went up. "I work for Bronte as an inventor, so I follow the rules of the establishment. I turn coffins into sofas," the boy said. "A universal bit of poetic justice."

He spoke telepathically to Vivica. *First lesson: "poetic justice," please.*

Don't worry, Vivica said. *I'm as confused by that remark as you are.*

Slight consolation, he replied.

Unaware of their exchange, Bronte beamed at the boy. "Zachary does the real magick around here, despite my botched attempts to learn the craft."

"Mine is hardly magick," the boy said, sounding wiser than his years.

Bronte pointed, guiding their gazes to a fenced area at the right of her building, music and laughter sailing on the air, where a huge wheel rose skyward. "Kid," she said, "you invented the coffin wheel. Not many twelve-year-olds can say that."

Zachary shrugged. "I didn't invent anything. I like Ferris wheels so I made a few modifications."

"Zachary can modify anything," Bronte said, turning to Vivica. "Sweetie, you *have* to find me a host who can play Master Vamp to my Vampiress. Right now, Ogden, up in the window, there, is doing too many jobs. I need to cut him a break."

"Workin' on it," Vivica said.

In that moment Darkwyn released the spirit of his bold dragon and took Bronte McBride's arm to escort her down the sidewalk. "I can tell you're in hiding," he said, stopping her from pulling away.

She nearly tripped over her spikes, but she stilled. "What do you mean?"

Because his heart raced, he knew hers did. Fear, he sensed in her. "Hiding inside yourself, I mean. Keeping your emotions to yourself."

Heart race, full stop. "Oh," she whispered.

"Let me help."

"What?"

"My ability to speak in your tongue is limited, but you, too, are a creature of few words." He couldn't petition her love—impossible on short acquaintance—so he appealed to her alarm and need. "Let me explain. I am strong. I am fearless; I can be *fearsome*. I would make your goals mine. I would be loyal to the death. I would."

"We just met."

Killian, his enemy—she who would stop him from winning his heart mate—would laugh at so bumbling an attempt as this. He'd showed his hand too soon. "You employ workers. I could get your—what did you call those boxes?"

"Caskets," she said.

"I could get them to the second floor with no effort." He'd fly them up, under cover of night, if he must. He patted her hand and turned them back toward Vivica. "Call upon me, if you will. I can help."

"How?"

"Protection. I am stronger than you can imagine. You are also strong. Together, we could be doubly so." He released her. "Think on it."

Zachary tilted his head and gave her a half nod.

Bronte appeared thunderstruck, by his offer or the boy's reaction Darkwyn couldn't tell. Then she looked from him to the man in the window and back. "Mr. Dragonelli, do you faint at the sight of blood?"

FOUR

A terrible fear gripped Darkwyn. Suppose Killian, An-
dra's sworn enemy—she who turned his Roman legion
into dragons—had disguised herself as Bronte? Andra
had warned him that Killian, determined to defeat him,
might turn to using a disguise, after his brother Bastian had
bested Killian as herself.

Andra, he pled, sending his prayer into the universe,
*please don't let her be Killian, because Bronte already owns
my soul.*

He considered her request. Did he faint at the sight of
blood? In any other situation, he would laugh. As a dragon
he'd chased his prey and tore it to bloody edible shreds. "I
have no problem with blood," he replied.

Bronte brightened, a sight that could bring him to his
knees.

"Darkwyn has a prior commitment," Vivica said,
"which will keep him busy for two weeks, at least."

I do? he asked telepathically.

Vivica wore a militant expression. *You must be acclimated to this plane like all chameleons of the universe. Magickal supernatural ancients are not simply transformed on arrival. They need lessons, papers, time. You can't help Bronte unless you're acclimated properly.*

So you know my intent?

Vivica shot him darts of ire with her gaze. *I have been standing here watching you, have I not?*

He bowed Bronte's way. "I will be available in two weeks' time, Miss McBride."

She nodded, hesitant, almost but not quite opening to him, fearful but wishful. "I'll keep that in mind."

Look away from her, Vivica chided telepathically, *or she'll read your interest. Is she your heart mate?*

I'm surer by the moment, he silently answered.

She's a friend of mine, Vivica said, *but a mysterious one.*

No surprise, he responded. *I believe that is her intent, to remain a mystery.*

Vivica nodded wisely and turned to Bronte to change her thoughts. "You have a flood of Halloween tourists. Great for business, I'm sure."

"Yes," Bronte said, "these are the days the Phoenix gets busy. Bite Me serves more food and drink. Fangs for the Memories gives more tours. The fairgrounds stay open later.

"As for the private club, it's a year-round safe haunt, if you will, a lounge with vamp drinks, smokes, and peer socializing, for Salem's vampire community. The LARPers act out original skits written for each evening's entertainment," Bronte said. "Zachary writes some. They enact war games, jousting tournaments, blood sports—setting wolves, dragons, shape-shifters against vamps. It's done mostly in fun, though some take it too seriously. People come to play from all over the country."

"A safe haunt," Darkwyn repeated.

"Check it out some time," Bronte said, issuing a personal invitation, but she must have caught her slip, her back going ramrod straight. "Our VIP room, Vampires in Play, is the learning connection. After newbies graduate, they can role play seamlessly. We had to get the question-askers out of the game, before there was more blood in the Green Room than in the vamp drinks."

Bronte's smile reached her eyes, and Darkwyn stepped away from the intense spark, a flash as tangible as fire or lightning. *Too soon*, he told himself, though he had never been a patient dragon.

Without his permission, a lusty roar formed in his throat. He had lived centuries with "kill or be killed" engraved in his essence, and survived. On earth less than a day, and he was felled by a woman.

He fought the sensation of falling and warned Vivica not to tell his brother dragons about Bronte's effect on him.

What happens in thought stays in thought, she pledged.

Something tickled Darkwyn's bare foot, so he scratched one with the other, and knocked two fur balls into the sunlight from beneath his cloak.

Ah, likely his journey's feline companions. They had finally landed . . . on his feet, somewhat in the way he had landed *beneath* Bronte's.

She spotted the kittens immediately and made that man-hardening come-hither sound she employed with Isis, charming the magickat hitchhikers her way.

One kitten, a pure white, bore lavender gray ears, face, feet, and tail. The other had a triangular-shaped head, almond eyes, its fur a red brown near its body and black at its tips, as if charred around the edges, head, and back, but with a full-singed black tail.

Darkwyn glanced at Vivica. No doubt those kittens came through the veil. They were as otherworldly as cats could get. Winged from another plane, they glowed, despite the sun.

Bronte could not possibly see their glow or flutterby wings, because she petted them as if the appendages did not exist, her hand slipping through the wings like air, before she scooped them into her arms and cuddled them at her neck.

She closed her eyes in a façade of ecstasy, enough to make him imagine her at an intense height of rapture, caused by his attention. A fantasy both intimate and sexual.

Sick bastard!

While Bronte coddled the kittens, and he wished she would toss him a quick gaze, the sun played tricks with his vision, so it looked as if she, or one of the kittens, cast a beam toward the hauling rope, a trick of light that even his keen dragon vision could not confirm.

The rope snapped.

Ogden shouted.

Darkwyn leapt forward and tossed Bronte from harm's way.

With the kittens safe at her neck, Bronte flew over the corner of her property toward the body of water to the left, and—magick—he wrapped her in a bubble, invisible to the naked eye, to cushion her water fall, and spare her the pain of body-slamming the surface.

All as if in a blink, the freeze she must feel as she sank into the icy arm of the sea, inch by slow inch, ran up *his* legs and spine, causing him to shiver as the casket slammed into *him*. Pain jolted his inner dragon with bone-rattling retribution, which brought the beast to life, and his dragon wanted out, badly.

His wings began to emerge from their muscle sacs. He fought them, and after a hard-won inner battle, they retreated beneath his cloak back into his body.

His roar did escape, however, a wretched cry of pain, reverberating in an echo that only water could magnify to such a level.

The fury of his inner beast gave him the added strength to withstand the blow. And though his knees buckled beneath its weight, the casket gave, cracked, and shattered.

One piece flew through the pub's large window; the rest scattered like ash from a volcano.

"I'll call 911," Vivica said, her meaning flying as high over his head as Bronte had flown toward the water.

Bronte screamed. Darkwyn ran.

He covered her property in one dragon leap and cut into the water beside her.

She grabbed him like a lifeline, while fighting him at the same time, and he couldn't help but enjoy their first physical contact, for which he should be pierced at short range with a throwing spear.

Nevertheless, when he lifted her in his arms, the kittens got slippery, and while he carried Bronte toward the beach near her building, he lost his grasp on the felines while trying to keep his cloak together.

Vivica and Zachary approached at a run, Vivica's Isis stopping by the water's edge to howl until the kittens emerged on their own—slick and ugly as porcupigs. Isis took to mothering and grooming them.

The black and red narrowed its almond eyes and hissed at Isis. The white kitten abandoned the magnificat's attention to run in circles, her coat quick drying in a puff like a bunhopper's tail.

Vivica cleared her throat. "The white looks like she stuck her paws in a light socket."

Bronte, still in his arms, shivered, eyes full, lips aquiver, likely as much from happiness over the kittens' safety as her own. "Ogden," she shouted, seeing her worker help people to the curb. "Anyone hurt?"

"Nothing major missus. Stay there, take care of yourself. I've got it covered, ambulance and police. My brother's on the force. You all right? Need the ambulance?"

"I'm fine, thanks."

Ogden nodded and went back to his task of settling the injured on the Phoenix porch steps, though they all stood when the ambulance arrived. Darkwyn was relieved he'd taken the brunt of the blow along with the part of the building in which he'd landed.

He examined Bronte's face for injury, the worst being her blue lips, which he'd like to kiss warm.

He realized, then, that being a man, again, made you want . . . well, man toys . . . like women whose hearts opened to yours, whether they wanted them open or not. Women who might be evil incarnate. Please not.

True, Bronte did not appear evil, but neither did Killian, unless she wanted to.

On purpose, he believed, Bronte slapped him in the face with the icy wet cape she wrapped tighter around herself, dousing his longing and distracting him until he nearly dropped her, the hellcat.

Maybe he should rethink the evil bit.

She tried to kick him. "You tossed me in icy Salem Harbor in October, Neanderthal! Me and two cats in Cat Cove, of all places. What a sick sense of humor."

Despite Bronte's bruises and her foul mood, Darkwyn held her tight and liked it. His dragon liked it, too. Maybe too much.

A lesson: his inner beast rose to attention and sought release when he was wounded *and* in lust. The two must be equal.

He didn't care what Bronte called him, but he cared a great deal when the spikes of her heels made sharp contact with his man-parts. She brought him to his knees, a feat the heavy sarcophagus failed to do.

He shouldn't respect her for that, but he did.

She took the opportunity to roll free, spread her cloak on a bush to dry, and turn to stand over him, arms crossed, while *he* tried not to die in front of her.

She wrung out her skirt over his head. "My boots!" she screamed, while he tried not to enjoy the length of her legs.

Bronte examined a gaping hole in the knee of one boot, while he blew a bit of warm air her way, not enough to make him smoke, just enough to dry her off.

Scumduggers, he guessed he would stroke this woman, this cracker of man parts, in any way he could.

Jagidy blew purple smoke directly at her breasts.

The pocket dragon must have warmed her, as well, because Bronte raised her gaze and fast, then she scowled down at him as if she saw the real him—horns, scales, wings, and fire, except he wasn't using them. "Are you out of your mind?" she asked.

He frowned. "What mind?"

"Ex-actly!"

Her ire shot through him while his middle finger throbbed. He held it up to examine and saw Bronte's was cut, *not* his. Also, his right knee smarted where hers, behind the boot tear, dripped blood and bruised blue. He'd felt the icy water as she . . . He felt what she felt? Was this some unknown dragon magick, dragon torture, or the work of an evil sorceress? If the latter, in which of the forms around him did Killian the sorceress hide?

Did she know he made it to earth? Did she stand before him in violet hair and eyes? Could ruining those boots cost him his life?

"What were you thinking?" she asked. "How far can you throw, anyway?"

"I was saving you."

"Saving me? You nearly drowned me. And don't go giving me the finger. Do you know how much these boots cost? Puck you, too."

Darkwyn lowered his throbbing finger.

"You rang?" Puck landed on his head with a squawk. "Siren," the bird said. "Any lady of splendid promise, dissembled purpose, and disappointing performance."

"I don't like that bird," Bronte snapped.

Darkwyn realized, as he moved Puck to his arm, that he did like the bird. It amused him. Except when it perched on his head.

He regarded Bronte. "Your boots matter more to you than your bloody bruised body?"

"My clothes and hair will dry. My body will heal. My *boots* will do neither!"

Earth women: a puzzle he must learn to solve. Well, he wouldn't try to learn all women. Just this one, Goddess help him.

"Bronte," Vivica said. "Darkwyn kept you from getting crushed by the falling casket and got hit in your place. If he hadn't pushed you from harm's way, you could have been killed. As far as tossing you such a distance, he simply doesn't know his own strength." Vivica gave him a pointed look. "And *that*, he has to learn, among other things."

"More to the point," Zachary said, his eyes narrow, making him look wiser than his years, "why didn't the casket kill him, instead of *him* killing *it*?"

FIVE

This Darkwyn Dragonelli guy—he who'd oddly offered her his protection, she should remember—didn't look like a casket fell on him, Bronte thought. "Are you hurt? Headache? Anything?"

"A few bruises," he said. "*You* caused the most damage."

Bronte's face got warm. She would have preferred to put his nuts in a vice at the time. Rather late to be sorry.

Zachary scoffed. "Who are you? *Super* Dude?"

Bronte caught Vivica giving Darkwyn a warning look. "He works out," the owner of Works Like Magick said.

Bronte nearly laughed. That sounded like a lie, yet she was surprisingly inclined to let it pass, as inclined as Zachary seemed. She could tell by the tension leaving the boy's shoulders that he'd found a spark of hope in this man— bad, very bad, to count on a stranger—but not surprising given Dragonelli's obvious strength, his formidable rescue, and the offer of help Zachary overheard.

She regarded Darkwyn, the man who'd saved her, who'd sensed her need to hide—chilling thought—and offered his help, to the death, a slow route to a certain end, if only he knew it.

And yet he'd touched a chord in her, a burgeoning sense of trust she couldn't shake. Hope, long abandoned, and a glint of faith, came to life despite her knowing better, all stirred by a cloaked stranger's actions.

She should *not* trust him.

He'd saved her, albeit brutally, offered his help, appeared like a god from the sky, naked and gazing up at her with his otherworldly savior's eyes, violet, like hers. She'd never seen the like, except in her mirror. A grand reminder. She was no saint, and despite his gallantry, neither was Darkwyn Dragonelli.

Human, the both of them.

Humans did stupid things.

She so did not want to make another stupid mistake, like trusting this man. But he'd kept her from being crushed by a casket—some kind of universal prank, given her appalling karma. He'd saved her by tossing her in Cat Cove, then by rescuing her, *again*. Neither a saint nor a savior, just a gallant, perceptive man who saw her disguise for what it was.

Pray the goddess, he would never see past it to the real her.

"You saved me twice," she said. "I owe you my sincere thanks. Not that I do humble well, but I appreciate . . . everything." Yes, being indebted, even in thanks, rubbed her the wrong way, but she said it, and swallowed the bitter aftertaste.

She'd declared her independence years before with no intention of going back. Not even for a man who touched her on every level, especially the emotional and physical. Of course, if they'd had a meeting of minds—if he saw into hers, which, praise be, was impossible—she'd have to abandon ship, take Zachary, and run. Again.

"Humble?" he questioned, mocking her?

She'd lowered her standards for him, but no smile marred his square cut features, not even at her admitted conceit. Actually, only the icy purple scar across his cheek and the curved scars, like humongous claw marks, that ran up his neck from beneath his cape marred the perfection of his features.

Perhaps he *would* fight to the death. Perhaps he had already done so. Physical trust she could manage, but never emotional, which is why she'd give him a job, nothing more.

Curiosity rode her. Where did his scars begin and how did he receive them? Did others mark his robust physique?

Sudden prickles of fear rushed her. Could Darkwyn Dragonelli be one of Sanguedolce's henchmen? Had she and Zachary been found, despite all their best efforts?

She hadn't thought it through, given her near drowning, but Ogden could have severed the rope, if Darkwyn's appearance, as a fellow mobster, had been a signal to proceed. This was crazy. She'd never doubted Ogden until this moment. Who to trust? She never knew.

Hot buttered blood, she was getting paranoid these days, suspecting everyone. She supposed that meant it was time for her to act.

Vivica had done an extensive background check on Ogden Canby, Bronte reminded herself, before she hired him. He didn't have a blemish to his name. She knew because Vivica's queries ran FBI/CIA deep. On the other hand, Bronte didn't think the Canadian mob or the RCMP, The Royal Canadian Mounted Police, leaked much to the U.S. feds.

Bronte clasped her hands behind her, so no one could see them tremble.

Life for her and Zachary, since their narrow escape from Montreal, had been a lot like tumbling into the bowels of a mine shaft and rolling aimlessly downhill in a rickety rail-car on incomplete tracks. Yes, *Journey to the Center of the Earth* gave her the familiar creeps. Oh, there was a bit of light now and then—from live wires that arced when least expected, electric current that could fry them to cinders at a wrong move.

Sure, she had street smarts, and she'd used them, bending the letter of the law, if not breaking it outright. Anything to keep Zachary safe, until they got to Salem. Here they'd found *old* Zachary Tucker's building, as *young* Zachary Tucker said they would, and set up housekeeping, more or less. Sure, they lived vampire-style, hiding in plain sight, daring to advertise while living in fear, a suitcase always packed, but *living*, however they could, beat the alternative.

Her suspicions ran rampant; trust being a luxury she couldn't afford. Even the two kittens connected to this odd, bare-footed mangod made her wonder.

As the child of a psychic and empathetic father, who died young of cancer, she had little control over the nebulous and erratic psychic gifts she'd inherited from him, and she did not do risk well.

Frankly, if she were any kind of empath, why would she not sense the danger in him? Why sense a kindred spirit, a possible error of huge proportions.

Idiot her, running from the mob, yet jolted out of composure by a weird, huge, drop-dead gorgeous intruder from whom she pulled her gaze *only* because his *kittens* circled her.

Was theirs a dance to determine the alpha between them? Or a challenge, kitten to kitten, to turn one of them into a prime bit of mouse pudding? Silly thoughts to ease the soul. These were kittens of the cuddliest kind, no more.

Bronte shook off her unease. "Do you know that your cats are purebreds?" she asked to turn her thoughts. "They're show cats, Mr. Dragonelli."

"You mean they perform, like in an amphitheater?"

An image of them dancing with top hats and canes brought a rusty giggle to her throat. The shock in Zachary's eyes made Bronte compose herself. "Your white with lilac points and pink paw pads here is a Birman, and the scorched-looking ruddy with black paw pads and almond-shaped eyes is Abyssinian. Though both kittens' eyes are the same intense blue."

The kittens appeared to subtly stare each other down, some cat ceremony taking place behind their kitty masks, an encounter that looked rather *out of this world*.

"They're not mine," Darkwyn said. "I don't know where they came from."

Bronte turned to Vivica. "Did they come with the cloak?"

"No. They're strays, doomed to begging food on the streets."

"No," Bronte said. "We can't leave them to the elements. They're not outdoor cats, which you know, Vivica dearest, my supposed friend, playing on my sympathy."

The red/black charred kitten with black paw pads leapt into Darkwyn's arms. Stating her preference, Bronte wondered.

Darkwyn set the kitten on the ground, stating his.

Ms. Almond Eyes climbed Darkwyn's cloak and perched on his shoulder.

He removed the persistent cat, claw by claw, and handed the stubborn thing to her.

"Thank you, I think," she said, stupidly proud that he trusted her to care for them.

"Congratulations," Vivica said. "You've just replaced Hoover."

She shouldn't do it. Pets helped root you to mother earth. The need for a hasty departure would be delayed in finding them homes, and yet . . . Bronte sighed. "The lilac point, I'll call Lila, and the charred, almond-eyed beauty is Scorch."

Lila celebrated her adoption by springing for Puck the parrot, minding its own business on Darkwyn's arm, the cat becoming something of the bird's hunchback, Puck being thrice her size.

"Cat," Puck said, flying to the ground. "A soft indestructible automaton provided by nature to be kicked when things go wrong." Puck kicked the air, and turned, kicked, and turned, until he made a full and worthless circle, but he couldn't shake the cat.

"Oh, no you don't. You won't be kicking my cats," Bronte said, removing Lila, at which point the bird flew up to the safety of Darkwyn's head.

"Darkwyn," Bronte said, fluffing her drying hair and dress. "You have a bird on your head."

Puck squawked and Darkwyn bowed solemnly. "Ouch. Yes. Thank you."

Vivica gasped. "Darkwyn, your cloak fastening looks as if someone's holding a magnifying glass over it. It's . . . smoking."

The owner of Works Like Magick barely finished her warning, Bronte noted, when hunk man's cloak quitted his shoulders, revealing a brawny, "take me baby" physique, a fine waist, and washboard abs that made her itch to explore them. Which she might do, if it were not for the phoenix tattoo on his chest that wholly unnerved her. The symbol of her rise from danger on his chest. The bird's favorite quote leapt to mind: *What the Puck?*

The universe, Bronte feared, had been playing tricks on her since she set eyes on this gorgeous man. Deceptively gorgeous.

And yet, what a shame, she thought, that the cloak stopped falling at the place she most wanted to see.

"Uh," she said. "I think your cloak is caught on something."

"My interest, dear Bronte. My cloak is caught on my firm interest."

SIX

When she understood how Darkwyn's interest kept his cloak from falling to his feet, a wash of warmth rose up Bronte's breasts to her face, while a smile, however foreign, hovered below the surface. Unwilling to embarrass either of them further, she firmed her lips, gratified and a little frightened to discover a case of *mutual* interest between them.

Providentially, one of the two men on the Winter Island Road Bridge, separating Cat Cove from Juniper Cove, at the corner of her property, whistled.

His companion chuckled. "Nice ass," he shouted, viewing Darkwyn from behind and making Bronte wish she dared circle him.

"My brothers," Darkwyn said, "are, I believe, approaching from behind me."

"Literally." Vivica bit her lip.

"Brothers?" Bronte looked from him to them. "You look nothing alike."

"Except for our eyes," Darkwyn said. "Dragonelli eyes are violet, like yours, minus the clarity of a diamond."

A compliment. She had no idea what to do with that. So Bronte fluffed her hair and smoothed her skirt, both dryer than her corset and squishy boots.

"Let me guess," Darkwyn said. "Jaydun whistled, and Bastian complimented my backside, right, Vivica?"

"Correct you are." Vivica removed her black on white, polka-dot lady cloak to place on the shoulders of "Mr. Do Me and Do Me Again." *He doesn't look ridiculous enough in cloak and bird*, Bronte thought. Now he stands in drag and bird, his damp man cloak finally landing on his big bare feet.

Darkwyn Dragonelli; a great sport. Magnificent and manly despite all, alpha to the core, he gave the impression of having a hard candy shell and a chocolate truffle center. You didn't grow up in the mob without calling that a rare combo in a man. Rarer still, retaining your dignity, while making a fool of yourself . . . without a gun in your hand.

He could likely stand up to a demanding vampire, both the Aristos with pinstriped suits, regular manicures, and high expectations *and* the Gothics in black rags, heavy metal, and pallors to mimic death.

Sure Darkwyn had a tree trunk for a body—a redwood—but in much better shape, which is exactly what you needed in a "vampire/bouncer/maître d'." He'd make her a great bodyguard, too, if Vivica's background check came out clean. She'd give him the front-facing apartment across from hers, *if* he earned her trust beyond the moment.

His full, sculpted lips would be cool against hers, then warm, then hungry, hot, and . . . *No!*

Thank the Goddess he couldn't read her. And though she might be somewhat empathetic, she couldn't read him, either. That rankled.

He fanned himself, the hot sun as much a dryer as a steam bath today, thanked Vivica for the cloak as he adjusted it, no more or less serious than since she met him.

Okay, she was mesmerized by the man, and more shaken, in a womanly way—one who hadn't been touched in forever—than she had a safe, sane right to be, but she'd cope. "Mr. Dragonelli, are you, by any chance, seeking employment?" Talk about insanity . . . She'd just taken one big damned step beyond "Do you faint at the sight of blood?" and almost wished she could take it back. After all, she said she'd give him a job. She *wanted* to give him one. And her insecurities and fear were annoying her.

At the question, Vivica turned from waving his waiting brothers over while Darkwyn sent his doubtful gaze *her* way. Bronte felt the heat of it melting her clothes and tantalizing the skin beneath.

Vivica shook her head. "Darkwyn needs to take a few courses before he's ready to enter the workforce. When he's passed them, if you're still hiring, and you still want *him*, I'd be glad to send him. But don't make any rash decisions, Bronte."

Appreciating Vivica's good sense, Bronte, nevertheless, locked gazes with Darkwyn, him oddly pleased, like she'd tossed him the sun and he kept it despite the burn, because it came from her. "Let me know when he's ready," Bronte said. "And I'll consider him." She wished secretly that he'd hurry. She'd almost be willing to wait for him, perish the hasty, dangerous, insane thought.

Darkwyn gave her a half nod, as if he read her mind. Heat raced up her cleavage, which he noticed, which made her hotter and more interested. As *firmly* interested as he once again seemed, judging by the shape of the smaller cloak, but that could be a play of sunlight.

Vivica took his arm. "Bronte, I'll find you a Master Vamp, whatever happens."

Darkwyn pierced her with a look. "I will hurry."

Shivers clawed at Bronte. Drat her scrabbled psychic gifts; she should be able to read him, not the other way 'round. In light of his response, her possible exposure—hers and Zachary's—bore a deeper, more frightening weight.

Vivica looked from him to her and back.

Darkwyn bowed. "I will come next week, so you can show me around."

"Abrupt!" Puck snapped from Darkwyn's head, ruffling his wings for attention. "Sudden, without ceremony, like the arrival of a cannon shot . . ."

"Yes," Bronte said, agreeing to Darkwyn's offer *and* the bird's definition, not quite in her right mind, or soul, or emotions, and jolted by the fact.

A subtle change took place around Darkwyn's eyes, an inner smile, perhaps. Hope? Desire? A vague sentiment aimed her way.

"Please," Bronte whispered, though she dare not count the reasons and ways she meant it. *Forget it, don't listen. Don't come. Hurry!*

SEVEN

Darkwyn saw Bronte do a trick with her eye before she turned and headed for the crowd in front of her building's porch steps, near a giant wheeled thing in the road, a red and blue bubble spinning on top.

He touched Vivica's arm as they turned to greet his brothers. "What does it mean?" he asked, "when a woman closes one eye?"

"She winked? It means she's attracted to you. Are you attracted to her?"

"Does her name not sound like a song?"

Bastian belly laughed, and Scorch leapt into Darkwyn's arms.

"Kill the cat," Puck snapped. "Kill the cat."

"Shut up, chucklebird," Vivica snapped before she took the kittens to Bronte. "According to the paramedics," she said, returning, "no injuries, but the police are taking names, in case of whiplash, that kind of thing."

"Is Bronte keeping the kittens?" Darkwyn asked.

Vivica scratched Isis behind her ear. "She was glad to have them back."

He and his brothers embraced while their guardian dragons reunited. Jock the blue, Koko the tan, and Jagidy the sea green, dragon elders all—now small as the palm of a human hand—puffed red celebratory smoke in an air dance that would draw a crowd were they visible.

Darkwyn walked with Vivica and his brothers along a street with crisp red, yellow, and orange leaves beneath their feet. "My heart mate likes animals," he said, still thinking of Bronte and the kittens. "That is good, yes?"

"Yes," Bastian and Jaydun said, elbowing each other.

"Do not mock," Darkwyn said. "I am younger and stronger than both of you."

Vivica raised a staying hand. "Darkwyn, don't you think it's a little too soon to tell that Bronte is your heart mate?"

"I tell only you and my brothers, and I wish to go back soon. *Now* would be good."

"You need Works Like Magick. It's more than an employment agency, it's where I acclimate the chameleons of the universe."

"Chameleons sound like they should have fifty legs and bite. Do they itch?"

"We are not a disease." Bastian shoved his shoulder. "Do you itch? *You* are a chameleon. We all are."

Darkwyn stopped. "We sound like a scourge."

"I know a journalist who would say you are." Vivica shoved his arm. "Chameleons acclimate to their surroundings. They fit in wherever they must. They change. Adapt. Sometimes they're called shape-shifters. You all shift shape, from men to dragons and back. In my business, chameleons are universal travelers who move between the planes and slip through the veil into our world."

"I see," Darkwyn said.

"They—you—don't know how to live on earth, or speak our language at first. You must learn those things so you can earn a living—at the Phoenix, if it's meant to be. But you will need to be more like one of us, which should take at least a week's worth of *concentrated* lessons, usually two weeks, while I make you legal."

"Will it hurt?"

"A casket just broke over your head," Vivica said. "I'm thinking you have a high pain threshold."

Darkwyn raised his throbbing middle finger knowing Bronte's must be killing her. "This hurts."

Bastian and Jaydun barked unfamiliar laughter.

Vivica curled that finger down again. "You're not even injured."

Bastian cleared his throat. "Bronte hurt the corresponding finger," his brother said. "So Darkwyn hurts there, too, proof that she is his heart mate. It's classic for the Dragonelli Brothers. I still hurt when and where my McKenna does, so I really hate that time of the month."

"What time?" Darkwyn asked.

"Women are not kidding when they say that PMS is brutal."

"We are so *not* the weaker sex," Vivica agreed. "Darkwyn, you will learn everything in the unfolding of time."

Jaydun knuckled Vivica's cheek. "Acclimator, be warned. Darkwyn's never been good with lessons or rule following."

Vivica gave him a hard look. "Darkwyn, you have to learn our ways if you want to be legal. Bastian and Jaydun are so legal that Bastian is married."

"I am," Bastian said. "The first of our legion on earth and the first to marry. You will visit our bed-and-breakfast, the Dragon's Lair, Darkwyn, to meet my wife and my son,

Seb. Glad to have you here, by the way." Bastian gave his arm a fist shove. "Why do you wear Vivica's cloak?"

"To hell with that," Jaydun said. "Why was he still naked?"

"My wet cloak fell off," Darkwyn said. "Bronte and I went for a dip in Cat Cove. A little matter of life and death, but I saved her."

"That's bad," Bastian said. "Anyone in water with you absorbs some of your magick, and can see things, like your fire and whatever you brought through the veil. For me it was the faery Dewcup and Jock, here."

"I brought in Puck the bird and two winged kittens that glow. I feared one of them, or Bronte herself, might have cut the casket rope with a light beam and burned the clasp on my cloak. I feared Killian might have taken over Bronte's body, but since she didn't retaliate when I tossed her into the Cove, I know better. Besides, Killian doesn't want Bronte, she wants me. Bronte is safe."

"For my money," Vivica said, "Bronte is too strong to have let Killian in, but then her background is a mystery, and she likes it that way."

"Bronte is safe from Killian only until Bronte means the world to *you*," Bastian warned. "Killian came through with me," he added, "though not in disguise, and she did not set her sights on McKenna until McKenna became my world."

Jaydun nodded his understanding. "I've been having trouble with a leaf pixie on and off. Lightning and scorched tree branches above my head, that kind of thing. I've thought on more than one occasion the pixie might be Killian."

"Manipulating the weather is one of Killian's strengths," Bastian said as they walked between buildings.

As if they'd summoned Killian the evil sorceress, the

alley turned dark, while raindrops became hailstones, arriving at growing speeds and sizes.

"Some are big as baseballs," Jaydun shouted, settling his jacket around Vivica's shoulders. He protected her from the pelting, until a bolt of lightning raced through the alley, one sunny end to the other, raised them off their feet, tossed them around, and left them lying in puddles.

All except Bastian, who watched, grim and helpless.

As fast as the storm came, the sun returned to warm them.

"It only stormed on us," Darkwyn said. "Look, it's sunny and dry everywhere but in here. What must people think?"

"Whatever you do, Darkwyn, don't tell anyone about—"

"Killian's ba-ack," Bastian said, stealing their attention. "I'm dry, because when you best Killian, it's done. I've won my final battle with her. Unnatural air, wind, rain, hail—sent by her—all went around me. I saw what happened to you, but her malevolent magick can't touch me anymore."

Darkwyn shivered in his polka-dot cloak, dreading the prospect of fighting their enemy, as they emerged from the alley into a world where everyone was dry but them.

Darkwyn rubbed the new-grown stubble on his face, a sign of his humanity. "If I don't best Killian—I mean if she bests me—she also steals the magick I drew from Andra to get here, and Andra can't turn our brothers back to men and send them."

"You got it," Jaydun said. "They'll die in a sea of boiling lava." He whipped the water from his hair. "Besting Killian hasn't yet been my burden to bear, though it will be, in time."

"For now, Jaydun is my bodyguard," Vivica said, "while I acclimate you, and your brothers after you, so I think Jaydun's task will ultimately be longer lived and harder won."

"I hate when you explain my mandate that way," Jaydun told her.

She shrugged. "I tell it like I see it."

Darkwyn assessed their proximity, Jaydun's covertly protective stance, his hand at Vivica's back. "So," he said. "Jaydun watches your body and you watch his?"

EIGHT

Vivica squeaked and Jaydun removed his hand from her back as if from a flame. His brother straightened. "If Vivica and I had a connection, it would be our business, Darkwyn. She connects us, protects us, teaches us earthen ways, and she respects us and our mandates. We owe her the same courtesy. She is our mentor, our guardian here on earth, acting in Andra's stead," Jaydun said. "If not for Vivica, we would be charging around on all fours or getting shot from the sky. Subject closed. Now, as for that masked, violet-haired girl, what do you think she knows of us?"

"Jaydun, the *girl* is Bronte, and she is my heart mate. Therefore, please give *her* the courtesy of respect."

Vivica nodded her approval. "Good beginning. You must continue to act like a man of earth, and after you're acclimated, you can go back and discover for yourself where Killian fits into your new life."

"I suppose," Darkwyn said, reluctantly agreeing to his lessons. "I will return to Bronte in due course. I did not *want* to leave her. Her heart is wondrous beautiful and speaks to mine. Her emotions speak, too. I do not think she saw the magick in me. She did not mention Jagidy nor the kittens' wings."

Bastian frowned. "Are you certain? Having been in the water with you, she did not catch your magick?"

"She pets the kittens as if their wings do not exist. Her hand cuts through them, and when she holds them, her face is framed by wings. For some reason she supersedes their wings."

"Like when you walk through a ghost," Vivica said.

Jaydun looked doubtful. "But you say Bronte sees the cats, themselves?"

Darkwyn sought patience. "I believe the cats *want* to be seen."

"It's true," Vivica said. "They practically made a red-carpet entrance."

"Like Dewcup the faery," Bastian muttered. "Irritating brat. And when I first got here, Killian wanted me to see *her*, as well. I understand what you're saying about the cats wanting to be seen. Could a kitten, or the bird, be Killian?"

"I suppose. The bird is irritating enough, yet I feel a kinship."

"Trust your instincts," Bastian said, then he snapped his fingers. "I know why your magick did not infect Bronte like mine did McKenna when she was in the lake with me. Cat Cove is off Salem Harbor and the Atlantic. An ocean is too vast a body of water to hold magick intact. It probably got splintered into a trillion tiny glistening shards worth no magick at all. While in McKenna's tiny lake my magick remained whole."

"That makes sense."

Bastian gave a half nod. "So, you landed at the Phoenix. Less public, I hope, than landing naked on a thorn bush in a circle of chanting women."

"More public," Vivica said. "Darkwyn was practically up for bid when I got there. Oh, and now that we're alone, Darkwyn, I'll sell the raw diamond you slipped me and bank the money for you and your brothers."

"Minus expenses for the three of us, Andra said to tell you. When Bastian came, we did not know the rocky shores of our beaches were valuable on earth, so he took nothing. Jaydun, I heard the pouchful you tried to bring was torn from your hand on the journey. So the secret is for each dragon to bring one raw diamond, firmly grasped in the palm of his hand. And, yes, three women peeked over the bar and wanted to take me home."

Jaydun slapped him on the back. "You make a decent man, if a little tall, though *we* still see you as a dragon."

Darkwyn flicked one of Jaydun's wings. "The way I see you."

Vivica led them beside buildings, along which odd wheeled boxes rolled, which Vivica called cars, trucks, trolleys, and buses. "Supernaturals see each other as they really are," their acclimator said. "An angel coming down the road is probably not the angel of death; don't freak. He looks human to everyone else. As do you."

"I appreciate the warning. What I see is not what humans see."

"Don't mistake me, humans will be in costume. It's Halloween, and even when it's not, we're a magickally theatrical city, but I think you'll be able to tell the supernaturals from the workers and trick-or-treaters.

Whatever the obstacles, Darkwyn intended to enjoy this new world.

"I still sense the warrior poet in you," Jaydun said. "You have always balanced the cruelty of life with a higher purpose better than most."

Darkwyn frowned, unsure. "We were all taught as much by the ancient tradition of our Roman leaders."

"But you excelled," Bastian said.

"Andra called me her black ice dragon. I would rather be hard-hearted than a thinker."

"Our sorceress bolstered our egos." Jaydun chuckled. "Did you never catch on?"

"No, he's right," Bastian said. "Darkwyn was one of the fiercest dragons, as unpredictable and dangerous as black ice. Andra meant it. She told me so."

"Now I don't believe either of you," Darkwyn snapped. "I am on earth, Andra is on the Island of Stars, and I do not know what I meant to her."

"We all meant the world to her," Jaydun assured him. "She sustained us on a dying island, protecting us from Killian at every turn for centuries."

"She did, and well," Darkwyn agreed.

"Speaking as a man of earth," Bastian said, "I understand Andra's meaning of black ice. Warrior men and dragons are often called upon to harden themselves against emotions. We then think our hearts are dead, but they are not. Bruised perhaps, and so hollow they echo like empty casings, but still there, beating faint and steady. The good news is the right heart mate can heal you, bring you back to life. I know this for a fact."

Darkwyn's rude feathered friend landed on his head, but Darkwyn removed him. "You may sit on my shoulder." He regarded his brothers. "A warrior poet, really?"

"Little bit." Bastian shrugged. "But as a dragon you are also huge, dark, and hard as black ice."

Darkwyn growled low in his throat. "I do hope, Bastian Dragonelli, that you pierced your ass, but good, on that thorn bush you landed upon."

Bastian firmed his lips against amusement. Jaydun and Vivica did the same.

His brothers' temperaments had improved. Darkwyn appreciated being with them again. "So I landed at the Phoenix, tattooed with a Phoenix, though the two are hardly the same."

"Glad to hear that your roman tattoo survived dragonhood," Bastian said.

"A memory from the past I am glad to embrace. Tell me, has Bronte's building risen from the ashes? If not, why the name?"

Vivica led them through a set of glass doors. "Bronte's Phoenix lives up to its name. It housed an inn, The Phoenix Hotel, until about forty years ago, then fell into decay. Bronte brought it back to life. It is now simply the Phoenix. Many towns in this country are named for the mythical creature tattooed on your chest."

"I chose it to help me rise from the ashes of battle."

"And so you did rise, from a battle of dragons on a plane far from ours." Jaydun indicated that Darkwyn should precede him.

Puck flew inside. "Bite Me at the frickin' Phoenix. Ride in a coffin, drink some blood."

NINE

In what Vivica called "Solitary Confinement," alone in his apartment at Works Like Magick, Darkwyn sorted his DVD lessons. "Vivica said that I am an undisciplined, disruptive dragon, Puck," he told the caged bird. "I am supposed to put these DVD lessons in my computer in order of number, yet I find myself choosing according to subject."

The discs slid in an unruly heap on the floor. As he picked them up, he found one about Salem. "Tonight I'll sleep with this one."

His first day, he'd gotten thrown out of a public lecture for "snoring and snorting like a pen of porcupigs" and disturbing the class.

On the second day, he was barred from taking computer lessons in the big classroom beside Vivica's office. He'd instigated a mutiny by getting every magickal supernatural student to abandon their lessons and compete in a computerized intergalactic war game.

So far, the only course that held his attention, even here in "solitary," explained women's bodies, their sexuality, and how he could enhance a woman's sexual experience. After learning those mysteries, he wanted nothing and no one but Bronte McBride.

His brother Jaydun, who lived here, too, his apartment next to Vivica's, to guard her from a mean-spirited journalist, said he should bide his time.

Darkwyn tried. He believed Jaydun had found his heart mate in Vivica, though neither would admit as much, perhaps not even to themselves.

Darkwyn opened a window to gaze in the general direction of the Phoenix. Not one for sitting still doing paperwork, or lessons, he'd agreed to a compromise. He slept wearing earphones and woke smarter in the morning. At roughly midnight, he started his night's lesson, *Everything You Ever Wanted to Know about Salem*, before he settled into bed, arms behind his head.

Sleep became a strong taskmaster as he followed the lesson's words and wandered Salem in twilight, allowing Morpheus, God of Dreams, to lead the way.

In a sleep state, rest gave way to awareness until panic slammed him to action.

Though he knew he slept still, he ran through foggy city streets, evading ghosts, ghouls, gray-faced zombies, and a floating red casket with Bronte inside.

A surge of strength and energy shot through him.

He reached the Phoenix in record time, but the brick building had spires and stained glass, with firelight dancing behind one peaked window.

"Bronte! Zachary!" Darkwyn shouted, while dragon-leaping from one metal balcony to the next, gaining hand-and footholds on granite bands and blocks.

On the opposite side of the firelit window, cool to the

touch, came a destructive commotion. He broke the glass with a fist, blood spiraling down his arm as he leapt inside.

No fire, but moving light swept the room, blinding colors disturbing the shadows.

Everything appeared as if in reality, though he floated somewhere between sleep and awareness, between life and death.

He took a blow of powerful magick to the chest, hard, breath-stealing, his attacker burning a raw path down his cheek.

"Is anyone here?" he asked, then he identified his assailant, a glowing kitten, but which one? Lila or Scorch?

Stumbling across the room, he tripped over lamps, walked into caskets, grabbed the cat and dropped it into a salmon coffin, her growl fierce as a wildcat's.

A lightning bolt came straight for him.

Darkwyn ducked, and the wall behind him glowed and cracked, the sound reverberating in an endless echo.

Darkwyn turned a dial where a light switch should be, throwing a chaotic jumble of bold, bright, and painful colors into a now pitch-black room. In this hellish light, or the odd black lack of it, the kitten glowed blood-garnet red and evil, its threat more acute and frightening, every hair delineated, almond eyes and paw pads amber with negative promise.

He turned the dial again, this time to light the room, and read the markers. ON, OFF, and BLACK LIGHT.

He retested the black light, and the kitten's eyes glowed gold, again.

Scorch the Abyssinian, her evil revealed. Killian had not taken Bronte's form, a thought he'd dismissed, but the almond-eyed cat's. Scorch. How appropriate for a lightning thrower.

Darkwyn ducked a second bolt, and turned on the light.

The cat had trashed the room. It meowed now, curling around his ankles—looking cuddly, innocent, sounding less like the cat from hell, so he tried black light, again, and saw a pure white kitten glow.

Killian, the evil sorceress, must sometimes abandon the cat to do her dirty deeds elsewhere, perhaps as a leaf pixie with Jaydun.

Darkwyn took the kitten in his arms. "Let's go find Bronte."

He climbed the stairs toward the third-floor living quarters, apartment doors to right and left, four on this hall alone. Going by instinct, he chose the door to the far right and stepped into a red, white, and black apartment, mostly white, lights on, like reality inside a dream.

A boy's bedroom, he found. A woman's. Both empty, but he followed his instincts up a round staircase to a library, wonderful and ancient with knowledge, went straight to the door at the far end, and opened it. A closet. Empty.

Darkwyn stepped inside, the bare lightbulb in its socket doing no good. He needed it to shed light on his quest. He made sure it was screwed in properly. As he turned it, the back of the closet slid upward.

There Bronte sat on the floor; Zachary huddled against her.

She pointed a gun his way. "Do you know Sanguedolce?" she asked without recognition and without removing her finger from the trigger.

"I do not, but if you hum the tune, I might be able to follow."

Zachary sneered. "Sanguedolce is a name, dork. Italian. Deadly." The boy stood and attempted to pry the gun from Bronte's hand. "Geez, let go already. Vivica researched and bonded this guy, for Drak's sake. He's innocent, true of heart, and healthy. What more do you want?"

Bronte came out of her freeze and released the gun to the boy. It went off and Darkwyn felt the blow to his heart.

He jumped from his bed, Bronte's scream lost to the dream, and turned on his light. He was still at Works Like Magick, as he should be.

Dream be damned. That had been *reality* inside a nightmare.

All too real.

He touched his cheek, and his fingers came away covered in blood.

Bronte!

TEN

The dream had been a call for help.

But who wanted him to go to the Phoenix? Killian or Bronte?

A knock at Darkwyn's door startled him. He slipped into his jeans to open it. "Vivica."

"You shouted Bronte's name. I heard you clear at the end of the hall. What happened to your face?"

He covered his cheek with the palm of his hand to heal it while she watched. A moment later, the wound had disappeared.

"I won't kid you," Vivica said. "Every time I see you or your brothers heal using magick, it freaks me out. Was it the bird?"

Puck squawked. "Contempt: The feeling of a prudent 'bird' for an enemy too formidable to be safely opposed. Simply put: 'Bite Me.' "

Darkwyn ignored Puck. "Did I wake you?"

"It's three AM. What do you think?"

"I think . . . I have to go. Bronte needs me."

"But you're not ready."

"I am. I can speak human, read, write, do math, and find my way back to the Phoenix. Was it ever a church?"

"Before a fire in the nineteenth century, yes. But let me clarify something, you can speak *English*," she said, "not human, and I don't think you know your way out of this building."

"I do. I have a Google map." He produced it and waved it in front of her.

Vivica took it from his hand, examined it, and nodded her acknowledgment. "You did ace computer science, but do you know biology, sociology, psychology?"

"I learned about vampires and tonight I tried to learn about Salem, but I dreamed a bit of scary reality. I have looked up the history of the Phoenix. It was rebuilt—now I understand why—by thirty-year-old Zachary Tucker more than a hundred years ago. That would make Bronte's young Zachary a hundred and thirty years old? Is that suspicious, or what?"

"Not in my line of work. You, yourself, a former Roman warrior, are older than dirt. Besides, humans tend to name their children after parents and grandparents. Zachary is Bronte's nephew; they *inherited* the building from another Zachary Tucker, likely a son or grandson of the man who rebuilt the place. You're *too* suspicious."

Of a cat, he thought. "I've been locked in the body of a dragon for centuries, looked after by a white witch, stalked by an evil witch. Suspicious? Me?"

"Bronte is also suspicious," Vivica said. "Do you think she'll buy into your *dragon* background? Seriously?"

"Your point?" Darkwyn asked, slipping stacks of black jeans and T-shirts into his duffel bag.

Vivica handed him an open book. "You haven't learned enough, yet, not to stumble over your own weird truth. Knowledge would make you less clumsy about your past."

Darkwyn zipped his bag. "With age comes wisdom?"

"One can only hope."

"I already have enough wisdom to wonder why Bronte doesn't have a man." A grating unease ran through him. "She's too beautiful not to have a protector."

"I would have told you if she did when you claimed her as your heart mate. By the way, never call yourself her protector. She would be insulted on so many levels. Having a protector is, in some cultures, the mark of a kept woman."

"I intend to keep her."

"You tread dangerously. At least learn about how to treat a woman of today." Vivica handed him the right DVD, and he took it.

Vivica nodded her approval. "Bronte is free to be yours, if she wishes."

"She does." Truth was, he did not know as much as he should, but he planned on-the-job training. Yes, he read every night, quite fast, and found pleasure in what he learned in those books. Computer lessons, not so much. "I will catch up with your culture in my own way in my own time."

Vivica raised her hands in defeat. "What are you planning?" she asked. "I can practically see your mind racing."

"Does that mean thinking while running?"

"Darkwyn, you need enough knowledge to get past your own weird truth. You're scaring me. Leave too soon and someone could get hurt."

"I will apply wisdom to new and old truths."

"I mean that *Zachary or Bronte* could get hurt, because of what you do not know."

"I would never let that happen."

"I don't worry about you. You have the strength of ten, heightened hearing and sight, the powers to heal, read minds, and shape-shift, to flee skyward in an extreme emergency. Mind you, try to fly, and you'll be shot down like a UFO, but that's beside the point. I'm not sure you would know how to stop if your inner dragon took control, though you do have a keen instinctual insight."

"Exactly. I sense when someone's in trouble. Bronte is in trouble."

"I won't argue that. What other lessons do you take with you?"

"The basics to live by on this plane. I liked biology, especially the reproductive system, but not theory. I need hands-on experience." He opened and closed his fists like claws.

She swatted his arm. "You're such a man."

Puck made a clucking sound from his cage. "Bronte practice. Grab, grab, grab. Kiss, kiss, kiss." He squawked in the trumpeting way that announced a pending quote. "Weakness: Certain primal powers of a Tyrant Woman wherewith she holds dominion over the male of her species binding him to the service of her will and paralyzing his rebellious energies."

Vivica gave the bird a thumbs-down and turned her back on his cage, brow raised. "The cock's opinionated."

Darkwyn scoffed. "Do humans eat parrot?"

Puck squawked. "Well shut my mouth!"

Vivica opened his portfolio. "Incredible, you aced the art course. These pictures—Whoa. Provocative. Bronte in a red corset dress, a black mini."

"I copied them from her website. It says she's the 'Vampiress' who runs Drak's."

"True." Vivica shuffled through his sketches. "You didn't get *these* off her website."

He snatched them from her hand. "Sorry, no. Those came straight from my imagination."

"She's nearly wearing clothes, but I can see how you'd get there so fast. Her costume is meant to draw customers, and yes, those customers are *mostly* male. Do you think you can watch Bronte interact with other men who enjoy her body as much as you do? They ogle her, you know."

"'Ogle'? I have to look that up. Is it sexual?"

"Almost. Stay a few more days, Darkwyn. Read a dictionary or ten. What's the rush?"

"Bronte's in danger."

"From what? Her customers? Outside sources?"

"I wish I knew."

"Know your friends and enemies. Did you open this DVD on vampires and witches?"

He packed that lesson as well.

"Witch," Puck said. "An ugly and repulsive old woman, in a wicked league with the devil."

Vivica gasped. "Shut it bird before I roast you on a spit, or worse, before I take your voice. *I'm* a witch. No devil."

Puck fluffed his feathers. "Rewind. Witch: a beautiful and attractive young woman."

Vivica nearly smiled as she opened Darkwyn's door to leave. "Stay," she begged one last time, but she did not expect him to listen, because, as she'd often said, he rarely did. "If you go," she added. "*When* you go, take your lessons and your cell phone, and call if you have questions."

"Will do."

"Please remain circumspect about your situation." Slipping her business card into his T-shirt pocket, his mentor stood on her toes to kiss his cheek. "I'll be here when you need me, because you will."

His bedroom door closed as he opened the bird's cage. "Puck, remind me to look up 'circumspect.' Now, I'll hear the rules, please."

"Don't sit on your head." *Squawk.* "Don't poop on the girl." *Squawk.* "Don't kick the cat."

ELEVEN

Bronte surged up and out of her nightmare with a scream trapped in her throat.

Her room, she saw, not the pitch-black inside of a closet.

Silence, she heard, not the approach of a killer.

Alone, she thought. No Darkwyn with a bullet in his chest.

She released her breath and fell against her pillows, hand to her thumping heart. "Blessed be."

The Phoenix had looked different, like a church, Scorch the cat, at first evil, turned tame. A threat, but not to her. Yet.

Another phoenix rose up in her mind's eye. Darkwyn. Nearby. His heart beating with worry beneath a tattoo that, to her, symbolized victory. If only . . .

Her tricky psychic gifts in play, Bronte rose to put on her mask and wrap, and she went to the balcony, her emotions at war.

Joy trumped anxiety, layering her fears in an odd sort of way, anticipation at the base of it all.

Opening her mind, she sensed Darkwyn's yearning as she watched him hesitate when he saw her.

She stopped fighting fear to give him a sense of her positive reaction to seeing him. And how did she know he'd catch either nuance, unless he was as empathetic as her. Well, more empathetic, hopefully. He must be.

Darkwyn Dragonelli could make her open to him, a stranger who should frighten her, though he seemed more like a friend. Odd, his affect on her. Troubling.

Everything she'd experienced in life—including a mother who'd been battered before and after her birth—trained her to hide in every possible way, emotions included. The more mysterious she remained, she believed, the more power *she* wielded. Yet this invader coming her way turned determination to dust scattered like dry leaves in the autumn wind.

She should . . . see a psychiatrist first thing in the morning, which wouldn't help her now.

Maybe a twenty-four-seven Internet shrink would do, but did she close the French doors and go find one? No.

She waited on her balcony for *Darkwyn Dragonelli*— tall drink of stud-sculpture, atypical Greek god, broad, straight-spined, regal bearing. Interested in helping *her*; the paradox.

His effect: mouth-drying, knee-weakening, womb-pulsing, so stimulating, she must try not to pounce.

She should grab her stash of vibrators and lock herself in the bathroom, though she'd probably still emerge wanting *him*.

As he came closer, taking a breath became an act of will: inflate lungs, deflate. *Heart, don't stop pumping now.*

Her flowing white wisp of a robe billowed around what

must appear to be her nakedness in the chill predawn air, this pink baby doll nightie, her least substantial item of night clothing. She'd worn it for a reason she hated to admit, though she didn't know why exactly. Yet here he came.

Finding her waiting here on her balcony at the hush of the hour, her yard in shadow, should give Darkwyn the impression that she, and the universe, welcomed him.

A swirl of leaves waved him closer, the ripe scents of apples, pears, and pumpkins, as the earth prepared for a winter sleep, welcomed him.

On this amazing night, she'd try a bit of magick, utilizing the witchcraft she'd been trying to learn from her friend Vickie Cartwright and Vickie's triplet sisters to help protect herself and Zachary.

In her room, she lit a candle to raise a flame, and set it on the floor of the balcony. She sprinkled salt around herself, protection, as she hoped to open to a man she knew nothing about, though Vivica approved him. Even now, Mother Nature brought him on a current of sea air and a swirl of winged maple seeds.

"Earth, air, water, fire,
Pure of heart, make him aspire.
Match his needs to my desire.
One in flesh, two go higher.

Bless this man ringed in fire,
Sent by fate as head vampire.
Crazed in doubt, I am mired,
Ease my mind as I require.

This I will, so mote it be.
And it harm none.
Bring him to me."

Fizzle and *hiss*! Her spell tossed bullets of bright light that popped at Darkwyn's feet. She just didn't have a witch's talent. But at least her magick hadn't turned him away. If anything, he closed his fists and proceeded more determined.

He skirted the bright blighted fireworks and kept coming, despite her half-baked spell. She could only hope that he ached for her as much as she did for him.

The steady crackle of crisp leaves beneath his feet told her that the closer he got, the faster he walked.

No more doubt then. She would attempt to trust the universe, trust requiring a superhuman effort on her part. Then again, she awaited someone that seemed rather superhuman himself.

Yes, she was going to do this.

Goddess bless them both, somehow his heart matched hers, both of them pulsing in the air around them, thumping a sexual beat.

He set his bags down and began climbing up the building, toward her balcony, taking the direct route, as if a door and stairs would be too much in his way.

But oh, if she had known how vulnerable the Phoenix was to being climbed, she would have locked her balcony door from day one. So why did she believe that with Darkwyn around, she would never have to lock them again? Why did she believe he'd stay, Goddess help her, when few people ever did?

Empathetic instinct, she had it in spades, when she had it, unlike the magick that failed her time and again. Then she heard that dratted bird squawk somewhere nearby.

"Woman," it proclaimed. "An animal usually living in the vicinity of Man and having a rudimentary susceptibility to domestication. A species . . . lithe and graceful in her movements . . . can be taught not to talk." *Squawk.*

"Shut it, Puck," Darkwyn grumbled. "I'd like to teach you not to talk."

"Don't touch her, dragon. She'll drink your blood!"

"Fly away, bird. I'll eat *her* for breakfast," Darkwyn said, eyeing her, his words having to do with promise not threat.

Gazing on him, she knew she was lost. Or found. Saved, perhaps, however improbable, her psychic instincts right on the mark, in this case. No second guessing needed.

With him outside the railing, lit by the moon, she examined his five o'clock shadow, the violet of his eyes, his yearning literally stroking her in the most intimate places. "I had a nightmare," she admitted.

"So did I," he whispered, and with forethought and purpose, he took her hand in his.

His confidence, rare for her, probably stemmed from being so big. As for her letting him take her hand, chalk one up to extraordinary circumstances, and chemistry.

He jumped the railing. "I dreamed the Phoenix looked like a church." He stood before her, kissing close, without lowering his head, learning her fingertips with his thumb, moving it over the tips of her nails and back, the silk of his skin against hers a wonder.

"It was a church first, a long time ago."

"And in my dream, you were in danger, past or future, I couldn't tell." He slipped a hand to her waist.

"I know. It's like—We dreamed past and present mixed together," she suggested.

"We?"

She touched his cheek. "Scorch the kitten was evil and struck you with lightning. I was with you every step of the way, even before you found me. Zachary didn't mean to shoot you. I half expected to find cat scratch marks on your cheek."

He covered her hand on his face. "I came to save you, even if it meant getting shot."

"I need no saving at this moment."

"Then I will have to make love to you, instead."

Her legs turned to jelly and he had to hold her up. "You are safe then?" he confirmed.

"At the moment. Am I safe from you?"

"No."

"Fair enough. Darkwyn, do you believe in destiny or karma? You see, I have always believed it existed and that mine blows."

" 'Blows'?"

"Sucks," she clarified, delighting in his eye twinkle.

"We shall see which of us wins the sucky karma prize another time," he said. "Despite your past, I am here to prove you wrong."

"Do you know my past?"

"I know from Vivica that you will be a good employer, and that is all I need to know, in addition to the way you affect my man parts. You should know about them. I am flawed. You already know that I want to be more to you than a bodyguard."

"I'm flawed, too," she admitted. "Your flaws don't bother me. Mine do."

Darkwyn raised a hand to trace her lips, and Bronte shivered, first on the outside, then deep at her core.

"You have a generous mouth kissed by nature's reddest berries and sculpted by an artist's hand," her blind knight said.

"I am too tall."

He ignored that, she noticed, in all but expression. "I like the way your brows curve like a seabird on the wing." He stroked her top lip. "The way your lips rise in the center like a heart. I would make turning them into a smile my life's work."

"Goddess help me, I would let you. But be warned, I arrived on this earth wearing a frown."

"As did I. You were there. You saw me arrive."

She tilted her head, confused, but inclined to let it pass so as not to break the spell. "I barely know how to smile," she admitted.

"I will teach you."

"So *you* do know how, then?"

"Not really. Let us teach each other."

The red sheers at her French doors embraced them, gently forced them closer together, dancing and wrapping them in a cocoon of the North Wind's making.

The wind of death blew from the north. Death of the old meant new beginnings.

Death courted her, yet Darkwyn's presence let hope flicker, though only a miracle would allow her to see hope bloom.

"Your nose turns up the least bit. I know because I have been sketching you to keep my sanity until I returned."

"Returned," she said. "Yet we barely know each other."

"I know your heart is open to mine. You, Bronte Mc-Bride, are my heart mate."

"I should be afraid," she whispered, her lips against his, against her good judgment. "Is heart mate anything like . . . employer?"

"In this case," he said. "Yes."

"In for a penny," she added, having revealed her fear. "Do you know Sanguedolce?"

"No, but I remember that you mentioned him in our dream."

She tried to pull her hand from his. "Why do you suppose we had the same dream?"

"As a way for the universe to bring us together?"

"I suppose that's as good an explanation as any, but it smacks of destiny, and you know how I feel about that.

And bring us together with a positive force or a negative one? I mean, where did it come from?"

"I do not know. I am not from this country."

She tried to step away from Darkwyn, but he wouldn't let go of her hand. "Neither is Sanguedolce," she said. Neither was she.

"I know four places, Rome, Scotland, an uncharted island a million miles away, and Salem, Massachusetts, for nearly a week."

She stepped closer. "Name your island."

"The Island of Stars. Who is Sanguedolce?"

"Never speak his name."

Darkwyn took her chin between his thumb and forefinger. "You spoke it first. I am going to kiss you now."

Her amusement was lost to the supremacy of his kiss, his cool lips authoritative, his open mouth ravenous, his hands and body vigorous and greedy for hers.

She didn't know him, she reminded herself. But she wanted to.

"You know me," he said, devouring her lips, scary appropriate in his response. "You are my missing center." He lifted her in his strong embrace, and she wound her legs around his waist, mostly so she wouldn't fall when she fainted, and he crushed her in an openmouthed kiss so wild, so filled with rapture, that she became more helpless to resist.

As they stepped into her bedroom off the balcony, Lila and Scorch raised their sleepy heads, quick to observe her riding Darkwyn like a breathless spider monkey. "No man has ever stepped foot in this room."

"No man belongs here, but me." He shooed the cats out with a directive hand and they obeyed.

She placed her head on his shoulder as he carried her—all parts touching, flawed or not. She breathed deeply for the room to stop spinning before she could speak. "You're pretty sure of yourself."

Disproving her theory, he had a one-handed fight with the bedroom door, mumbling something she didn't quite catch. "Jagidy?" she asked. "Who's Jagidy?"

"Imaginary friend. Don't want him watching."

"Have you seen a shrink?"

"Shrink. I looked up this word. Vivica said I needed one. It means to make smaller. But tonight, since I saw you from outside, I have experienced a continued enlargement; no shrinkage at all."

He lowered her to the bed so she lost interest in word games, though she got his meaning loud and clear. How could she not, given its pulsing presence? She kept her legs around Darkwyn when he would straighten and yanked him down on top of her. She could tell from the befuddled look on his face that he hadn't expected to lose his control or his breath.

"Bemusing Bronte, you're quite the seductress."

"What? My clothes didn't give me away the first day?"

"I saw only your heart."

"Hah! Tell me another." She shoved his shoulder. "Before we do anything," she said. "We do have a couple of big problems."

"No, I have only one. If I had two, I might not have come here tonight. Would two feel twice as good, I wonder? Or would the extra just get in the way?"

Bronte raised herself on her elbows. "What?"

He seemed to come back to himself. "Oh, you think *you* have problems?"

TWELVE

"I do have a problem," she said, *"and it's a biggie."*

Darkwyn didn't care. "Is it because you're ugly? I mean, I don't care, but—"

Like being splashed with ice water, she rose on her elbows. "You think I'm ugly?"

"I think you're the most beautiful woman in the universe, but you wear a mask, so either you are scarred or you think you're ugly."

She shoved him so hard he fell from hovering above her to bounce against the red striped wall beside her bed. She hoped he sprained his perfect head.

"I'm not ugly," she snapped, getting up. "I'm *old*. Years older than you, more than a decade, maybe fifteen years older. You're about twenty-three, right?"

"Give or take a millennium or twenty." He grabbed her hand and pulled her down on top of him, then he tilted his head to nibble and lick that spot low between her breasts.

"A decade is ten years, yes?" he confirmed, peeking up at her.

He'd come up for air when she least wanted him to, leaving her nipples standing and shouting, "Here! I'm over here." *Slow on the uptake much?* "Yes, a decade is ten years. You don't have to rub it in."

His head came up fast, his eyes wide and eager. "Rub? What would you like me to rub?"

She huffed, horny and achy and frustrated as hell. "Stick to the point!"

Darkwyn did what she wished but not what she wanted. He didn't explain his point about being millenniums older but raised his hips so they met at exactly the perfect place, and if she'd stopped sniping she might have a big surprise in store. She ground her hips against his generous offer. "You have a pretty impressive point there."

He fingered her hair, brought it to his lips, romantic and sweet, and getting her hotter. "Ah, my impressive point," he said, sliding her hair against his cheek, then tickling her chin with it. "My impressive point is our *other* big problem."

"I don't think so. It's more than hard enough, quite thick, incredibly long—"

"And incredibly deformed."

"You jest."

"I do not know how to jest. I will take lessons if I must, but—"

"Not 'joust,' 'jest.' "

"That is what I said. One problem at a time, please. You are decades older than I am, you *think*. Wrong. I am centuries older than you."

"Be serious," she said. "I was born the day man first walked on the moon."

Darkwyn dropped her hair and furrowed his brows,

making him look that much more yummy. "An earth man walked on its moon?"

"What, you don't watch the news? Never mind. You hadn't been born yet, but surely in American history, you learned—"

"American history!" he said, snapping his fingers. "Vivica said I should not skip that, but I did, to get here faster."

Bronte rolled off her frustrating boy toy and sat with her back against the wall. "You talk in circles."

"Well, this earth of yours is a convoluted place."

"Hah!" she said, pulling her favorite throw over herself, holding it up to her neck. "Tell me about it."

He stroked the bottom of her left foot.

"I'm not ticklish."

"You are not a 'tickle-me-toy'?"

She tilted her head. "Well, I am, actually, but you sound as though you just came from kindergarten."

"I learned that on television. I never watched kindergarten."

She crossed her ankles and rested them in his delightful lap. "You're the strangest man."

"And the most desirable?"

"Certainly the most confusing. I'm worried about our age difference," she said. "You should be, too."

He reached for her mask. "Take it off so I can see what an old crone you are."

She slapped his hand. "Stop that. Everyone who works here wears a mask. It's the rule. I never, *ever*, take mine off." Except when she slept, or had a minute alone in her room, behind closed doors. "Neither does Zachary. What our employees do on their time is up to them, but when they get here, they're masked."

"You are a bossy *old* woman."

"I will be your boss if you take the job as Master

Vampire, which encompasses the jobs of bouncer and maître d'."

"I might be too old to be a vampire."

Bronte ran her fingers back and forth against the stubble on his godlike face. "Real vampires are ancient."

"Shall we discuss our ages, our jobs, and even vampires, after sex?" he suggested. "Your elders walked on the moon, mine discovered fire. It is, as humans say, a wash. You will never be as old as I am."

"Now you sound like Zachary."

"He is a child. You are a woman. One who is young enough to have sex with me *without* breaking a hip?"

"I'm not that old."

"Too old to appreciate a man in your bed?"

"You really don't care that I'm old enough to be your—"

"*Lover.* You are the perfect age to be my lover. Whereas, I am older than dirt and have a trick dick."

"Is it magick?" she asked, getting hot all over again. "Sounds tantalizing."

"It is magick, as am I, but it is also not like any you might have seen."

"Your magick also bears discussion," she said. "Don't worry. I haven't seen that many dicks."

"Neither have I, except in pictures. You will be disappointed if you like the average everyday type."

"Are you . . . longer than average?"

"Too long."

"That's what I'm talkin' about." Bronte felt a foreign urge to grin, maybe, but she fought it as she rose to her knees. "Is it thicker?"

"Afraid so."

"It probably does magick better than I do, I hope."

He knelt to face her. "According to my brothers, magick in the bedroom *is* a specialty of ours."

She shuddered with anticipation but his manner distracted her. "Your vocabulary is decidedly odd."

"I never learn what I should in the order I should. I found a book of sex slang in the Works Like Magick library. That is how I learned 'trick dick.'" He shrugged. "It seemed to fit. A man's sex has many meanings, but historically speaking, I also thought that 'battering ram' fit."

"Oh my."

He cupped her at her center, caught her by surprise, and found her pulsing. "You like that idea."

Intrigued by his description of himself, she did rather enjoy his word play, the weirdest foreplay ever.

"Unfortunately, I read the meaning of it out loud," Darkwyn said, "and the bird remembers more than I do."

"Oh, no, not the bird? He'll ruin the mood."

"He's not here now, and when he is, he'll stay in his cage, unless he takes what he calls 'a road trip for a bit of tail,' though he never does use the road. Do not worry, though, he will come back. And never with a tail to spare."

"Lucky us," Bronte said, instantly regretting her sarcasm as she went for Darkwyn's zipper. "Lucky us, we're taking trick dick out for a test spin."

Darkwyn reared back. "It is supposed to spin?"

"I'd settle for that battering ram."

"Coming up, and I mean that in the truest sense."

"And up," she agreed watching some tantalizing super action beneath his zipper. *Yowsa!* But far be it for her to question a well-endowed stud who had the hots for her.

She unzipped his fly and—"Holy battering ram, Batman!"

THIRTEEN

"Wait," Bronte said, raising herself on her elbows. "That was a compliment, not an insult. Don't zip up. We haven't played hide the salami yet."

Mortified, Darkwyn tried to stow the frisky thing, but, no use. "I cannot put it away. It takes up too much room when *not* this ready, but having appalled you, it will not stay hard for long." He turned away from her and got off the bed.

"Fool," he called himself. Mad bad dragon man, angry because the sex object of his choice did not like the look of his beastly erection.

Bronte came around to face him, not a sex object, he reminded himself, but his heart mate, causing further indignity, because his shrinking Charlie did not yet fit into its mouse house. "If you do not wish to see it, stay behind me," he snapped.

She cupped his face between her hands.

He huffed. "Your nearness does not help shrink it, Bronte. It may be deformed, but it is no slacker."

"You misjudged my exclamation as that of disdain. A better shout would have been 'Yowsa, baby, give it to me, now.'"

He frowned. "It would never be this big on a baby, not even a baby dragon."

"You *are* from a land far away."

"'A distant galaxy,' dare I quote. Vivica made me watch movies. I was first inclined to call it a 'light saber' in your language. It does more than the saber in the movie, except that it does not glow. Oh, I should not have brought the tricky thing up, if I want it to go down."

"Great pun."

"Define 'pun.'"

"Strange man."

"Yes, well, I may be a pun, but I am definitely not a bargain. I have no experience of women, and I come with a deformed member, as you saw."

"That's the problem. I didn't see well enough. I want to hold it in my hand and learn everything about it."

"Stop," he said. "You are making it grow."

"I know." She winked, again, and unlaced the skin-colored top on her filmy night wisp, so her breasts fell nearly into his hands. He reached for one of her breasts, and with a finger at the wide outside edge of one, he began tracing a circle, raising his finger higher, making the circle smaller, until with her silent permission, he got near to capturing a nipple. He stopped. "You are *trying* to seduce me."

"Ya think?"

"I will take that as permission to continue." He cupped a breast, noting that Bronte's breathing sped up, her eyes nearly rolling back in her head. His sex quickened and rose to the occasion.

While stroking his length through his jeans, and driving him happily insane, she caught her breath. "Tomorrow, remind me to ask how you got this way"—her nipple grew hard beneath his palm—"but tonight," she said, "we will work the sturdy thing until it faints, yes?"

"Yes. Tomorrow I will explain," he said, glad she did not step back for getting stroked exactly where he wanted to put himself—bull's-eye. "Tonight, I will show you how it works. There are several variations."

Her wide-eyed sigh nearly made him ejaculate. From what he understood, that would be in bad form before Bronte experienced her own rapture.

"Let's get naked," she said, and his part danced.

"Hey," she said, playfully. "Careful, you'll put an eye out with that thing."

He understood now that her jokes lightened the mood, that playful sex, especially with Bronte, could be fulfilling, that cavorting with her could be the ultimate sex play for man or beast.

Instinctively, he reached for her mask.

"No, Darkwyn, the mask stays on, a story for another day, but no. I wore a mask when you met me. Please accept me as I am."

"Of course. We must accept each other. One worry: I learned sex from books, Bronte, but I would make it good for you, so you will please tell me what you like?"

"There is a god," she whispered, unlacing her nightie to her waist to give him better access to her body. "Let's do something erotic," she suggested. "Let's face each other on the bed and kiss but don't touch."

"Oh, that will be hard," he said. "My hands, they want you as much as my dick does."

"Just for a few minutes to give us a slow start, like stoking a fire."

"Ah," he said. "Chapter three. Foreplay. You should know, however, that my fire is already stoked, but then the next step would be to touch each other in one special place, yes?"

She fell against him, making a muffled sound against his shirt like a little baby porcupig.

"Are you mocking me?" he asked, standing straighter.

"Darkwyn, I am having the time of my life, but . . . please don't make me fall in love with you."

"I do not know how." He wished he did.

"There's the danger. Artlessness coupled with gentleness, kindness in the midst of unbridled sexuality. I'm not strong enough, I tell you."

FOURTEEN

"*No falling in love,*" he said. "*Eventually, though, you will* touch this big boy begging for your attention, will you not? You are not repulsed by it? You are certain?"

"Darkwyn, given the fact it doesn't have a battery, it's the largest, most ingenious sex toy to hit my bed in . . . forever."

"I did not *hit* the bed, Bronte. When first we got on the bed, before we got off, you pulled me down. If I hit it, you made me."

"Yes," she said, wrapping her hand around his arrow-tipped beast. "This is hard and ready. I see we will have to give it the old 'fast and furious' before we can do a slow burn, because you are so far ahead of me, you might finish on your way to the mattress."

He groaned as she pushed him, and he let himself fall backward. "This means you will have your wicked way with me, does it not? Thank you."

Before she got wicked, she got curious, for which he thanked the universe. "This beastly thing of yours is more than a battering ram or even a trick dick. It's shaped like a dragon tail. You said something about a dragon that I took as a comparative description; what was that? Never mind," she added. "This is fascinating and exotically beautiful, not to mention stimulating times infinity."

Bronte's excitement seemed to double with his size, and Darkwyn rose so fast toward rapture, with her hands all over his cock that way, he didn't know which of them would reach completion first. He tried to wait for her, but this close to the edge, any hope for his staying power became laughable.

"Is this a result of plastic surgery?" she asked, stroking every facet of his dragon-tail.

"Magick," Darkwyn hissed, still holding his breath.

"Ah," she said, "someone else's magick backfires."

"Clashing spells," he said, jaw rigid, "white magick versus black."

"Note to me: add clashing spells to future discussion. Right now, Darkwyn, *shh*, I'm exploring new territory. Enjoy. Let yourself go and come if you want to. Your first ejaculation will not be your last. We'll both come, alone and together, over and over again, all night, I swear. I'm that horny."

With little thought beyond the permission granted him, Darkwyn clutched the back of Bronte's nightie and tore it away, laces flying, breasts in his face for his delectation, more stimulation than he could take, and take, and take, and he came, cresting so hard and high, he couldn't have done it with anyone *but* his heart mate.

As he came, he claimed her with his gaze, eye to eye, heart to heart, in a way she couldn't deny, then he rolled against her, nestled his temporarily sated sex between her knees and placed an arm around her to pull her forward to claim a breast.

Starving for her, he suckled her hard, enough to make her writhe and whimper, and gasp her release, a sight that revamped his sex, so he insinuated it between her knees like a heat-seeking missile.

She clamped those knees tight.

He pulled on her nipple and let it pop from his mouth.

She gasped and shuddered again, as a result. "Darkwyn, you do know how to rev my womanly engine."

"Yes, but I do not understand the meaning of closed knees."

"Find me a man who does. I simply cannot get enough of your superior and unusual self, and find I want to explore the amazing thing one last time before my body swallows it whole."

His heart palpitating, Darkwyn rolled to his back, deep joy rising in him, a foreign sensation, nearly comfortable, and wholly attributable to Bronte McBride, heart mate.

"May I have it to play with for another short while?" she asked.

Truth to tell, he could easily sleep, which wouldn't last long with his cock in her hand.

"Come anytime you want," she said. "In between, I'll make its acquaintance."

"Get to know each other. I will just close my eyes for a bit."

"I admit that I let your presence rush me the first time, so now I am ready to explore. Because I noticed that this tricky thing has what might be called scales beneath the skin. As I slide my hand along your length, the hidden scales appear to move in the direction my hand does. The scales stand for a minute beneath your skin, then flip to the opposite side. That must feel amazing from the inside—when you're the overcoat."

He opened his eyes, his contentment unbound. "You are confused, my masked lady. You would be the overcoat," he said, his breath coming in short gasps as she intentionally manhandled him. "I would be in"—he caught his breath—"inside you."

"There, I would be wet, Darkwyn, and warm, and pulsing. I would pull you deep, and deeper, kneading your finest asset, its scales, its arrowed tip, your ability to—is this prehensile? This sucker has a mind of its own!"

"This is bad," he said, once again on the edge of completion. "I can barely hold back while you talk like that, while you—with both word and action—toy with me."

"You *can* come again so soon?"

"Since I began to practice, while thinking of you, I have noticed no time gap in my ability for pleasure."

Bronte's eyes twinkled with delighted mischief. "I am so keeping you."

FIFTEEN

"You are keeping me*?"* he asked, his delight rising and infecting her. "Keeping me happy is what you mean, right? Or," he added, looking disappointed, "keeping me for the sake of employment?"

"Guess again," she said, enjoying her seductive torture.

"I prefer to hope that you would keep me as your plaything. Please say yes."

She laughed. *Laughed!* And amazed herself for the first time in longer than since the last time she had sex.

As if by mutual agreement, they settled into her bed facing each other, their lips meeting, their no-touching rule dissolved the minute she stroked his chest.

His tongue mated with hers in such a way as to make her think him experienced. At nearly the same height, even their feet stroked each other. And she'd thought she was too tall.

His arousal created action, traction, and a reaction of

its own, as his sex appeared to knock at her warm, willing center. He craved entry so well, she answered by moving her hips his way, and together they mixed one hell of a chemical cocktail.

He attempted to memorize her shape with his hands, but they were experts at finding certain spots—unknown to her—that drew pleasure with a skim or a stir of warm air. His mouth couldn't possibly be in the same place as his hands, and yet, warm breezes, everywhere, raised her nipples and warmed her top to toe as he removed each slip of fabric between them.

She caught his hand. "Not the mask, remember?"

"I forgot. It is beyond cruel to see every place but your face. It is cold and human."

"Are you not human?" she asked.

"I am now."

"Shelve that for further observation," she said, thinking she should worry but she couldn't, not when there was such rich pleasure to be found.

So human of her. She didn't take offense. Humans could be cruel, especially when planned. "Forget my face and feast on the rest." She understood his need to see her, because she loved looking at his face, but not to be a cliché, her mask was a matter of life and death.

"Take me, Darkwyn. Hard and fast, and hard, again. Forgive me for the mask and accept me as I am? You practically promised."

"As you are. The one need I held for centuries was to be accepted as I was, and now I am me, instead. This we can do for each other. It is sensual in its own way being accepted by one person more than any other. I accept. Yes, as you are, mask and all." He kissed the mask, while her overflowing heart prevented her from responding with anything but a wholehearted surrender to tactile pleasure.

She learned his body like there'd be a quiz, and she loved the process, long, tight, sinewy, muscular back and chest, thighs and arms.

A phoenix rising from the ashes. His tat spoke of her sex life, the two of them rising to blessed, orgasmic oblivion.

He learned her body the way she learned his, pooling moisture at her center as he closed his lips over a nipple, raising her to ecstasy by using her slick fluids to ease his way.

His groan became a growl, almost feral, both of them wild with excitement. He came before he entered her, a nod to what they did for each other, and she came again just watching his stream. At this rate they'd never consummate.

After that, his third or fourth preview of bliss, he crushed her to him, a habit she already liked. This time, though, he opened his mouth over hers, eating her up with his embrace, his lips hungry and getting hungrier.

Devoured—she was being devoured by her man.

Before she knew it, he had memorized her center, his concentration more on her pleasure than his.

"You are my first on this plane," he said against her lips. "I will make this good."

She ignored the tiny inner voice that said she wanted to be his first and last. "This has been good many times, already," she admitted. "But I'm up for more. Ah, and so are you."

"This will be as nothing before, since my dragon tail knows a few special tricks."

Like splitting me in half, she thought, a bit fearful of his size. "Yes," she said, anticipating him working inside her. Silky soft on the outside, those small movable disks beneath the silk skin of his penis sliding up and back, back and down, abrading her G-spot, stroking her everywhere, to her deepest recesses—deeper than any man had gone before—like the finest five-battery vibrator bunny, all its twirly whirlies and bunny ears running on high.

Her imagination, as it turned out, paled in comparison to the experience, because when he rose above her and barely slipped inside, she soared to the edge of culmination, again.

"Now we will do that 'hide the mattress' mumbo jumbo you were talking about."

She laughed at his mixed metaphor, but not for long, his determination to bring her lethal pleasure nearly her undoing. He found her clit, without using his hands. *Huh?* Aah, prehensile bullet with a brain. That's what he meant by tricks.

Thank you, thank you, thank you, thank you, universe!

No, no thinking. *Too good to waste*, she thought. *Ride me, ride me higher.*

Bronte clung to Darkwyn as he worked his magick, like he was playing a fiddle and dancing to it at the same time. She'd found herself one of those rare *male* multitaskers.

Each time she came, she fell farther and rose higher, and he growled louder, the muscles in his back and arms became taut, rigid, and . . . *lumpy* along his spine? No time to figure that out. Her whole body stretched, and rose in every way possible.

She'd never had a climax as lethal as death, but she did now, ending up so weak, she could barely keep her legs around him, but he raised himself and her, too, and though she practically stood on her head, nothing, but nothing, had ever brought her to this plane of pleasured existence.

He did split her in half, splintered her to shards, and she'd never be whole again, but who the bloody frickin' heck cared? She could die fulfilled.

He raised her off the bed with each multiple multiple, took her outside herself. Crazy out of her mind with ecstasy.

Wrung out from it, she rotated her hips and pulled him to a place so deep, she didn't know it existed.

They climaxed together, muffling their orgasmic shouts with kisses and hands and lips everywhere, and as she fell over the precipice to perfect bliss, the room glowed, literally, with a streak of light that sizzled to nothingness.

SIXTEEN

Lightning. Killian. "We have to get you to a hospital," Darkwyn said, scared out of his mind for Bronte's safety.

He barely got his jeans up and a blanket over Bronte before Zachary ran in. "Bronte?" He shook her with no luck.

"She's unconscious," Darkwyn said, wanting to heal her, but afraid of revealing his ability to the boy.

"No hospital," Zachary said.

"He's right," Bronte echoed, groaning as she raised a hand to the gash on her temple. "No hospital."

"Bronte, did you get hit by lightning, too?" Zachary asked.

"Did you?" Darkwyn asked the boy, slipping his shirt over his head, confused, because Zachary looked fine. "Who else got hit?"

"Ogden got struck on his balcony," Zachary said. "I called 911. But on my way to tell Bronte, I heard the crash in here."

"As long as help is coming," Darkwyn said, "let's have the medics look you over, too, Bronte."

"Listen," Zachary said. "As long as you work for us, neither of us goes to a hospital or gets examined by a medic. *Ever.* Under any condition. Got that?"

Bronte rolled to her back and pulled a pillow beneath her head, blood dripping from the gash on her temple. "Zachary's right, Darkwyn."

"That makes no sense. Why not?"

Zachary huffed. "Dental records, X-rays. You name it."

Scorch jumped to the window from the balcony and curled up on the sill, her black tail wagging, as if the kitten was happy or proud of herself, or . . . her work was done. Darkwyn didn't like that notion. He might say Scorch gave him a Cheshire cat grin.

Meanwhile, Lila, the lilac point kitten, jumped on the bed, raised a paw that glowed brighter than she did, and held it so her light touched Bronte's wound.

Zachary tried to shoo her away but Lila hissed and snapped at the boy. Weird, when Scorch usually hissed and Lila did not. Meanwhile, Darkwyn was glad Zachary couldn't see how Lila's paw glowed.

"I hear sirens," Darkwyn said. "They must be for Ogden."

"Zachary," Bronte said, petting the sweet ministering kitten. "Let them in downstairs and show them to Ogden's apartment. I'll be there in a minute."

"I'll take care of her," Darkwyn told the boy.

Zachary gave him a hostile look. "Yeah, right." Zachary turned and left.

"Lightning with a forked bolt," Darkwyn said, sitting beside Bronte to look at her cut. *One of Killian's finest*, he thought. "Two for the price of one. Half came through our open window, hit that shelf above your head, and gave you that gash when it and everything on it rained down on us."

He moved Lila aside, surprised to note that Bronte's wound looked better—smaller? *Because of the cat?* Nobody healed better than him, except maybe Andra. He cupped the cut on Bronte's temple. "Relax and let me help. I will never hurt you."

"Ouch. Every man I know has uttered those words, and every one broke his promise."

"I am so far removed from 'every man' as to be laughable," Darkwyn said, "and I am not talking about my super cock, here. Not that I think I am better, but I am different. You will see."

"Sure I will, but, oh, I feel better already. You're taking away my headache. How do you do that? Did you get hit? You were on top of me."

Sated like never before, Darkwyn very nearly glowed, himself, from the inside out. "Pardon me for acting cocky when you're in pain. But sex with a human is not underrated."

"I hate to think of the alternatives."

"Deprivation is the alternative. Now shut your wild imagination, she who plays with vampires, and heal."

"Sex is not what we experienced," she said. "Nirvana is, and I have a terrible feeling we can only get it with each other. I'm psychic that way."

"Sex only with each other is bad?" he asked. "Speaking for myself, my tired man part has never been happier." Sure, it was dormant on the island for centuries, if you didn't count spontaneous combustion, but payback was orgasmic. Speaking of which, he should not be turned on just because the blanket over Bronte's breasts slipped.

Change of mind-set. "What's with not going to the hospital?" he asked, finding a subject to take his mind from sex. As if he could forget.

She sat up, taking the blanket with her.

Well damn. He gave her a "what's this?" look and a wave of the hand, after all they'd seen and done together.

"I have to dress and meet the paramedics," she said.

"Do you need help?" he hoped.

"Stand with Zachary to deal with the medics?" she asked, no longer in the sex zone. The weather, or Killian, had intruded.

He looked out the window. "The ambulance is here. See you at Ogden's."

"Across the hall, back-facing apartment," she said. "Thank you."

Darkwyn closed her bedroom door behind him, aware that he'd found home in her. His heart mate, indeed. Now to make her life quest his, whatever that might be. Her secrets included knowing why neither she nor Zachary would go to a hospital. What did "X-rays" and "dental records" mean? And who was Sanguedolce?

Darkwyn met the boy and the paramedics on the landing.

They treated Ogden on his sofa, barely conscious, but coming around. They "got his vitals" and said he would be okay, as Bronte arrived, a fresh Vampiress, all campy vampy in a red mask and corset over a short black and white striped skirt and slick, bloodred boots.

Zachary gave the spot where her gash should be a double take, then checked the other side of her temple. "Great makeup," the boy said.

Dragon's blood, he'd healed Bronte without thought to what anyone else would think, though he'd confessed his magick to her, but, of course, Zachary would be surprised. The boy knew nothing about him.

Not that Zachary and Bronte didn't have a few secrets of their own to impart. Their aura of mystery was obvious.

Her mask, her shiny red boots, the way she dressed to attract attention—*Always in hiding, yet always on display. Who are you, Bronte McBride?*

SEVENTEEN

"*What the Puck?*" *His missing bird landed on the* round red and blue light of what Darkwyn now knew to be an ambulance. As the medics slid Ogden, flat on a wheeled plank, inside, legs and wheels disappeared, and the bird squawked, "Murder. Murder!"

Weird world.

"Misfortune," Puck said. "The kind of fortune that never misses."

Misfortune, also known as Killian, Darkwyn thought.

Puck flew over and landed on his shoulder, bird-blessing a paramedic on the way.

Darkwyn growled low and lowered the cock to his shoulder. "Naughty bird!"

"Cursers!" Puck clicked his beak. "I didn't poop on the *girl.*"

Darkwyn apologized to the paramedic and watched the ambulance leave. "What did I tell you?"

"What? Don't poop on *anybody*? That's part of a bird's alien rights."

" 'Inalienable,' " Bronte said, her lips quirked up on one side, a sight Darkwyn would like to see more often.

"I'm beginning to understand that bartender snapping his towel," Darkwyn said. Yet he liked the honest, fun-loving, no-words-barred, bird.

"Ride in a coffin, drink some blood. That means you're dead, peckerhead." *Squawk.* "Run for your life. Die in your bed."

"Change your tune or you're a quick-roast. We served bigger birds than you as appetizers where I come from."

"You know you like me." Puck ran his beak through Darkwyn's hair, a sign of affection. "Darkwyn's got a gi-irl. Kiss, kiss, kiss."

"Shut it, bird."

"Miss," Puck squawked. "A title with which we brand unmarried women to indicate that they are in the market."

Bronte crossed her arms. "I am *not* looking for a husband."

"He's got what you want. You're what he wants. Sounds like a deal to me."

Bronte bristled. "Darkwyn, can't you teach this bird manners?"

"I'm trying. No sunflower seeds until you apologize. I'm sending for your cage."

"Scumduggers and whatthepucks, you can't cage an American bird."

Zachary rubbed his chin as if he knew what a *beard* felt like. "Shouldn't Ogden have somebody with him at the hospital?"

Bronte nodded. "I'm calling his brother, at Ogden's request." She slipped her cell phone from her pocket and made the call.

Darkwyn turned to go inside. Zachary caught up with him. "What happened to Bronte's temple?"

"You saw the scorch mark on the wall and the shelf hanging by a hinge. I believe the precise weapon was a bronzed cat bookend."

"It was deep, bloody, and purple around the edges when I left the room."

"Correct." Darkwyn now understood the query.

Zachary got in front of him and walked backward so he could see Darkwyn's face. "You *know* she's healed?"

"Yes."

"How?"

"Dental records, X-rays, that kind of thing."

"I don't understand," Zachary said, smacking the heels of his shoes against the porch steps, so he tripped and landed sitting.

"Neither did I, but since that worked as an excuse for you and your aunt, regarding hospitals and doctors, I'm using it, too. My way, she doesn't *need* to go to a hospital."

The boy narrowed his eyes, as if behind them hid a brain overflowing with wisdom. "A smart guy, hey?" the boy said, speaking like one of Vivica's old black-and-white movies.

Bronte caught up near the living quarters and checked her watch. "The Salem Trolley will bring the first tourists in a few hours. Between our shared nightmare, the lightning, and losing Ogden, if only temporarily, I need a Master Vampire and fast."

Darkwyn cupped the back of his head. "Tell me again what a Master Vampire does."

"He's my bodyguard, hosts Drak's, and keeps the peace, so he's also sometimes a bouncer."

Darkwyn hoped "bouncer" had to do with mattresses and nakedness. "Define 'bouncer.'"

Zachary chuckled. "A bouncer picks up troublemakers by the seats of their pants and throws them out so they bounce on the sidewalk."

Not sex as he hoped. "Can I throw them over the balcony? More fun."

"No!" Bronte snapped. "Not the balcony, not even throw. You would just show them the door."

"The doors are plainly visible, Bronte. That would be a wasted effort."

Zachary chuckled.

"The Master Vampire is the host and generally the peace," Bronte said. "Does that give you any Darkwyn?"

"Yes, it does. I will replace Ogden as handyman."

"No, you'll be my new Master Vampire. That's your apartment, by the way." She pointed to the door opposite hers at the end of the hall. "It faces front like ours."

"Hey," Zachary said. "To hit both apartments, front and back, that bolt of lightning had to be coming straight down from above the Phoenix, almost like a claw with us in its grip."

"How old *are* you?" Darkwyn asked.

"Ninety-nine, my next birthday."

"Always a confusing answer."

"You should talk. What happened to the gash on Bronte's—"

"I don't know enough about vampires to be one, thanks."

"Zachary," Bronte said, herding them toward her apartment. "Break out the Dracula DVDs and let's have a bloody brunch while Darkwyn gets a crash course."

"Which ones?" Zachary asked, sorting DVDs.

"All of them. Darkwyn, I'm Vampiress and I need a Master Vampire today. It's the only way to protect me from the male vamps who'd try to make a play for me, otherwise."

What she needed, he thought, was a bodyguard in the truest sense, to protect her from Killian's evil. "I'd rather take the handyman job, but I could still protect you."

"That job's taken. Ogden will be back. The apartment across from this one is for the Master Vampire I hire."

Darkwyn thought about that. "Fine, then I'll live with you."

"*She* already has a roommate," Zachary said. "Me."

Out of the boy's range, Darkwyn gave Bronte a look filled with promise. They *both* wanted more of what they'd shared last night. He needed to be near her to protect her from Killian, and to take on her life quest, still a mystery. "I will watch the vampire movies," Darkwyn said with a sigh. "But no promises beyond that."

Half an hour into a movie, and two bowls of Count Chocula later, Darkwyn hit pause on the remote. "What made you get into this freaky business? Did somebody curse you?"

Zachary shrugged. "We owned the building, and Bronte needed a job where she could take care of me. This is Salem. Dracula's Castle catered to tourists but not vamp role players or Salem's real vamp community. We saw a need. We had a need. We filled both."

"And," Bronte added, "it seemed a natural choice. We grew up around blood and guts."

So had he, fighting wars, feeding his dragon self, but—"You? Blood and guts?"

Zachary gave Bronte a look, before turning to him. "'*The family*' owned a slaughterhouse."

EIGHTEEN

After the second vampire movie ended, Bronte's heart skipped when Darkwyn got up to stalk her. He grasped the arms of her chair and looked into her eyes. "I vant to drink your blood." He used a corny Transylvanian accent, his attention enough to make her remember the night just passed.

"At Drak's," she said, trying not to be charmed, "we're modern vampires."

"Do you count yourself among them?"

"No, but you'll meet actors, writers, giants of industry, people with clout. It'll be a regular who's who of vampires in Salem."

"So your vampires wear pinstripe suits and ear bugs to talk to invisible friends?"

Zachary scoffed. "Ear *buds*."

"Ignore the boy, Darkwyn. Yes, some of my vampires are businessmen."

"Do they nibble on your neck?"

"Of course not." Though she'd let him nibble and nuzzle, lick and suck—oh the memories.

"What the heck are you two doing?" Zachary snapped. "She's offering you a job, not herself as a meal."

"Zachary, we aren't doing anything," Bronte said. "We're—"

"Drooling in your hearts!"

Darkwyn looked from one of them to the other. "Do you two read minds?"

Zachary slammed the box of cereal into the cupboard. "I know how a man thinks."

Darkwyn approached the boy. "Well, you don't know how I think. Are you a man in a kid suit, or what?"

Zachary whipped his head around.

"Both of you, stop," Bronte said. "Zachary, there's no pretense with Darkwyn. He's real—to a fault. What you see is what you get. You can't blame him for having a gleam in his eye." She stood to approach.

"Don't touch me," Darkwyn said, raising his hands. "The loathing in Zachary's expression scares me."

"Zachary, go watch cartoons," Bronte said, and the boy left the apartment, slamming her door and another and another.

"He'll watch in Ogden's apartment." She grabbed Darkwyn's lapels and slid them between her fingers. "I may be able to read you, a bit, sort of, sense your needs is more like it, but I still don't know whether you'll take the job that I so desperately need you to."

"I'll do it," Darkwyn said, capturing her hands, silently offering pleasure—at least she hoped that's what his shuttered expression and bedroom eyes meant.

"I'll be Master Vampire to your Mistress Vampiress," he said, stepping back, "but don't torture me with those vampire movies. Point me to the nearest stack of vampire books and I'll learn what I must."

"Yay." She'd like to kiss Darkwyn, but with Zachary acting like a watchdog, she'd wait till they were alone. "I have to get you fitted for a tux and cape for *tonight*. You can't spend the day reading. You'll have to wing it."

Wing it! Darkwyn aborted a surprised laugh, grabbed his fire-warm chest, and belched smoke.

"Now that's a neat trick," she said. "Don't do it in public."

"No problem, like nobody's business, I can wing it." They flicked glances at each other, given the fact that Zachary had returned and stood in the apartment doorway, arms crossed.

· An hour later, on the way home from the tux shop, in her hearse with Drak's and Fangs for the Memories advertised on the side, Darkwyn read the bag of vampire books she'd brought.

"Read fast much?" she asked, truly impressed.

"Always," he said. "Little trick that surprised even Vivica."

"I can see why."

"What torture next?" he asked on their return. "I believe I'd take any kind of torture . . . if you wield it. Puck was wrong that first day," he admitted. "If I had run, I believe my soul would have missed yours for eternity."

Feeling bemused, a smile forming in her heart, Bronte sighed. "I'll take you through Fangs for the Memories, our fun/horror house tourist attraction, then I'll show you the fairgrounds before we get you ready for tonight."

"No time for a quickie?"

"You learned that fast. But you couldn't be quick, given the size of your talent, if your life depended on it."

"My life might depend on it. Once you feed a dragon, he needs to eat more regularly."

"Uh-huh. Tell me another."

"This dragon would also like a long, slow look in daylight at the tattoo on your inner thigh. A black sword on scarlet dragon wings; it's a dragon slayer tat. Are you secretly looking to kill me, your very own dragon?"

She slipped her arm through his, wishing she could keep him as her own, but even if she wanted to, life had nothing good in store. She sighed and led him down the sidewalk fronting the Phoenix. "I would gladly slay you, Darkwyn Dragonelli. I'd slay you with pleasure."

He slowed. "So your tattoo is a symbol of riding your magick dragon?"

"Yes, a warrior dragon with a fine sword." She batted her lashes, but she'd be lying to herself if she didn't admit she was troubled by a few aspects of this man, like his dragon references. Yet, she found herself fascinated by him.

"Seriously," Bronte said, "the nuclear sex we had last night, and the fact that you refer to yourself as a dragon—" She cringed inwardly. "They top the list of things we need to talk about, *sooner* rather than later."

"Anytime, dear Bronte. What about the butterfly tat at the base of your spine?"

"Ah, now that symbolizes freedom, to which I aspire."

Darkwyn raised her hand and kissed it. "You must put 'Bronte's need for freedom' on your list of things to talk about. Because if that is your goal, I am here to make it happen."

"Like you can fly me to the stars, you can make it happen."

NINETEEN

Darkwyn tried to stay open-minded while Bronte pressed a number code into a little box and unlocked an outside door at the far left side of the building.

Inside, she turned to him. "This is the entry to Fangs for the Memories. A ticket taker works here when it's open." She unlocked a wide, thick carved inner door with a pointed top, two halves that opened at the center with an old-world creak.

On the other side, after she locked it, he pinned her against it, read the need in her eyes, and used his new knowledge to turn a quickie into an eternity of pleasure. It took no more than a fast rise and a couple of tempestuous, mutual multiples before Bronte slid down the door beside him and placed her head on his shoulder.

Catching their breath and righting their clothes took longer than the act.

"A girl could sure get used to that," she whispered.

As could a dragon, he thought. Their kiss lasted longer than their mating.

"More?" he suggested.

She shook her head and rose on shaky legs. "Tourists are due."

Dragon's blood!

She led him along a dark hall, his arm around her waist.

"We're starting at the left of the building," she said. "We'll cross a basement of Fangs for the Memories exhibits, then exit to the fairgrounds. Tourists leave Fangs and the fairgrounds via the matching hall at the opposite side of the building."

"Makes sense," he said, teasing her beneath a breast.

"In this hall," she said on a thready whisper, "are dioramas of vampire carnage."

"Your bloodsuckers are as fake as your movies. Even the drippy candles are. But you," he said, stroking her higher, "are magnificent and real."

"You sure proved that. *Mmm*," she said. "Fake candles because of Salem's fire laws. Fangs is for tourists. Drak's, on the floor above, now that's as real as the vamps and LARPers, or role players, want it to be."

"How can it be real?" he asked, cupping her breasts. "Vampires are *not*."

"The authors of those books you read earlier, and the vampires you'll meet tonight, believe dragons aren't real. You'll see fake vampires, they'll see a fake dragon. It's a wash. Fake is fake. Though I know you're not a fake man, because—"

"You like my tricky dick?"

She leaned in. "I do like it."

He shrugged. "Well, I grant your point about dragons,

however incorrect." He swooped in to kiss her, but jumped when the cover of a casket popped up beside them, and a campy vamp sat up, hissed, and showed its fangs.

Bronte opened her hands toward the dummy as if she sent that sudden colorful burst of snap, crackle, and light the casket's way.

"If cartoon fireworks are all I can conjure," she said, "might as well make it work for me."

Darkwyn raised a questioning brow. "Conjure?"

"I threw the bit of faulty magick at it to go with the laugh track."

Darkwyn admired her resourcefulness. "It was rather effective and unexpected for entertainment value."

"Maybe I'll incorporate it into all the displays down here. I never thought my backassward witchcraft would be of much use."

"Are you a witch?"

"In training, sort of. Mostly, I'm the class clown, a blow-it-up kind of witch and I usually end up with soot on my face. I have no natural talent for the craft. I tried to learn for self-protection, but no go."

"Well, you have me for protection now." He liked that her eyes went dreamy and she moved closer after he said that.

Meanwhile, Jagidy, his guardian dragon, smoke-tested the dummy and got white smoke from the lifeless thing.

He nearly told Bronte the joke, but he guessed it wasn't time yet. Besides, her expression held a clear invitation, so Darkwyn swooped in for a kiss, wrapping his arms around her and putting his hard desire into it.

Bronte moaned and pulled away. "My paying customers are due any minute."

He walked beside her and ran a hand along her spine.

She halfheartedly pushed him away. "Will you please—"

"Sure I will," he said, enjoying this having someone to play with. A woman of his own.

She stopped in front of a closed casket, standing on end, with a sign that said, STEP INSIDE A SPELL.

"What's this, then?" he asked. "A *dead* end?"

"Do what the sign says. Open the door and stand inside."

"Get in with me?"

"There's only room for one."

"We can become one when the door closes."

"It doesn't stay closed long enough even for the world's fastest and most amazing quickie. But if you're afraid to go in alone, use the ramp for scaredy-cats."

"I am no cat!" Darkwyn stepped in, watched the casket door close him in, and felt the back squeal open, slowly, so he couldn't fall out.

He exited to a large dank room with a people-sized spiderweb. No way out except through the center of the web, as indicated by the large floor arrow, but he waited for Bronte.

When the casket door opened, he turned and swooped in for a kiss—but stopped, fast!

A short, skinny, blue-haired old lady giggled. "I *like* this feature. You're quite the hunky doodle dandy."

"Thank you," Darkwyn said. "All in a day's work. Just follow the arrow through the spiderweb. There you go."

Bronte now stood watching, her eyes dancing in a new and amazing way.

"You enjoyed that," he said.

"You have no idea."

He scooped her in his arms, opened his mouth over hers, and she wrapped her legs around him, still as hungry for him as he for her. "Hint," she whispered against his lips. "When the door squeals from the other side, the next tourist has gotten in."

"And it could be anybody, I learned the hard way." He resumed the kiss and walked them toward the web's center, her legs around his waist, their lips locked.

Halfway, he leaned her against a cobwebby pillar and had his wicked way with her mouth.

"Keep it up and you'll bust out of those jeans," she said, abrading the evidence.

Given the extent of his interest, he should keep his back to the next person out. For sanity's sake, he set Bronte down, then she dragged him running toward the narrowing center of the sticky web, and as they arrived, a giant glowing black spider jumped out at them from the opposite side.

Darkwyn shouted in surprise, and Bronte chuckled, highly entertained. "I put that crackling blush on Spider Joe just now. I like it. Guess my half-baked magick is good for something."

"I was not scared," he said, "My mind was—"

"In your shorts. That's why I knew it'd surprise you. Step through, then we go down those stairs to the catacombs."

"Is there a private room down there?"

"No. But there are private caskets. People occasionally try them out."

"Sick bastards."

In the crypt, blood dripped down walls, a pipe organ played a funeral dirge, while along the way grotesque, clawed skeletons posed here and there, including on top, or inside, ornate sarcophagi. He and Bronte passed a private stock "blood wine" cellar, and a display of famous vamps' wall-mounted fangs. She added a few of her magick-spell touches along the way, quite pleased at the colorful, light-show-type results, her delight endearing her to him more every second.

"Ah," Darkwyn said. "I hear happy music."

"I don't hear it."

"I have keen senses. All dragons do."

"We were going to talk about that."

"Sure. Anytime. This is festive," he said stepping out, embracing the sunshine, and enjoying the sights at the fairgrounds.

"From here," she said, "you can go to Bite Me for vampire food, eat and drink in our cemetery picnic area, or inside Bite Me. Tourists can skip Fangs for the Memories and use their trolley tickets to get in the fairgrounds."

"Excuse me. Vampire food?"

"Blood pudding, blood sausage, blood soup. Ethnic foods prepared different ways. We have steak tartar, hold the tar. Bloody claws are curly fries and catsup. Dead cow's a burger. Bangers and elbows: macaroni and sausage. Pub food."

"Sounds delicious." And he meant it. At the fairgrounds, Bronte, the Vampiress of Drak's, was treated like the Queen of the Dead, and she played to her followers, even signed autographs.

After her fans left, she apologized and pointed to a giant wheel standing on its side with people inside. "That's Zachary's coffin wheel."

Darkwyn covered his eyes from the glare of the sun as he looked up. "Amazing."

"The seats are eco-friendly coffins. And beside the wheel, those mythical carousel figures were carved by Rory MacKenzie, a world-class carver, from Salem and Scotland. His wife, Vickie Cartwright MacKenzie, is one of the most famous high priestesses in Salem and my best friend."

Darkwyn took Bronte's hand. "Let's enjoy the sun, since we work at night." On the carousel, he set her on a mermaid figure, taking the sea dragon beside her. "I recognize some of the figures, Asena, the blue-maned she-wolf carrying a cub in her mouth; Pegasus; a silver unicorn; faeries and dragons. Nice."

"Zachary made the sofas from rocking coffins. My favorite figures are the white tiger, the seahorse, and the phoenix, because of our building—and now your tat. Actually, I love the whole mythical carousel. Our unique rides draw people from all over the world," Bronte said. "Wholesome family fun. I didn't take you into every nook at Fangs. It really is a scary, fun-house thrill for the *unjaded*."

"I love this carousel thing," Darkwyn said. "My cares disappear with this music and these colorful figures. That ride, over there, the twirling one; is that Zachary's, too?"

"Yep. *The Tipsy Blood Vessel*. I get nauseous riding in circles, but Zachary and our customers love it. See the red crosses on each little boat; they symbolize blood. That boy invents more things."

"Did he invent the games?"

"Casket Ball and Sucker Bets, games of chance and skill, yep, both Zachary's. I'm telling you, he's a boy to go into business with."

"Let's have a blood-sticky apple and go back inside. I can't kiss you out here."

"Pull up a grave and have a seat," she said, leading him to the Tucker family's historical cemetery, where stone graves sat, like tables, above the ground, because of the water level.

"Grave," Puck squawked. "A place in which the dead are laid to await the coming of the medical student."

Bronte frowned at the bird. "That's not true."

Darkwyn bit into his apple. "It was true when Ambrose Bierce wrote it."

Bronte tilted her head. "Hey, didn't you want to ride the coffin wheel?"

"Zachary wants to show it to me, so I'll wait. He invented it, after all. He is a good boy, your Zachary."

"He's rather out of this world, is my Zachary."

Darkwyn shrugged. "So am I. He's in good company."

Bronte raised a skeptical brow. "I think the jury's still out on that."

TWENTY

With Darkwyn ready to work that night—looking good enough to strip and jump—Bronte brought him to her front door, again, to orient him. "We close to tourists when we open to vamps, who go up to the second floor using either that elevator or these stairs. Both lead to the Master's Den, where you, the Master Vampire, will reign supreme. In your den you take tickets first, then hand out masks."

"Is that all I do?"

"That's only the beginning. It's an honor for a vamp to receive a mask from you, a sign of your approval. White masks for the VIP—Vampires in Play—room. They get black masks if they're heading for the Music Room, red for the Crimson Room, green for the Green Room. As Master Vamp, you wear a gold mask."

"A mask? Me? Bad enough you make me wear a ring. I think I changed my mind about playing vampire."

"A garnet ring, symbolizing blood. This is not play. It's

work. Besides, you're my bodyguard. Who better to guard me than the man who will sleep in my bed, tonight?" she asked, toying with his ascot, hoping to interest his libido. "Please don't change your mind."

"Is this what you call 'manipulation'?" he asked.

"Yes, how am I doing?" Truth was, she wanted him in her bed as much as he wanted to be there. "Abstinence after last night and at Fangs, earlier, would kill us both," she said, "and you know it."

"Are you saying you would deny me if I quit?"

She sighed. "I'm confessing that I need your help."

He looked to make sure they didn't have an audience before he kissed her, his cool lips torturing her with a hint of lust, a reminder of the night ahead.

She went back for more. "Please wear the mask," she begged against his lips before stepping back. "They're our bloody freaking logo. They define us."

"When you get mad, your breasts rise and get all heavy," Darkwyn said, appreciating the sight. "I like it." He combed his hand through the curls along her spine. "I am in lust with a violet-haired seductress," he admitted, indicating that he was on to her turn-him-on tactics.

"I will wear the mask," he said after focusing so much on her breasts, her nipples stood to attention. "Thank you for asking so sweetly," he whispered in her ear.

She stepped away, to regain her composure. "I'm sorry I'm throwing you into the deep end tonight with little to no training."

"The deep end of what?"

"Drak's." She started up the stairs, sensually aware of Darkwyn behind her. At the top, she turned to look down at him, almost. "You look 'take me to bed' sexy in your tux."

He raised his chin uncomfortably. "I hate the stand-up collar on this cape. Did you say bed? Now?"

She rolled her eyes and led him to his station. "The v-shaped counter is for you to stand behind. It's made from the toothy grill of a junkyard car Zachary cut up and converted into your glitzy-gold station, and a vamp's first stop."

Darkwyn approved with a stroking hand. "The gold and black magnificence of my den calls to me."

"That's a man/car thing." Bronte shook her head as she took a fresh gold mask from behind the counter. "Turn. You're the handsomest vamp mate I've ever had." She slipped the mask on and hooked it behind his ears. "Good fit."

He faced her. "Mate?"

"Yes, mate, as far as anyone who comes to Drak's is concerned."

He brought her close. "As far as *I'm* concerned—" Mid embrace, Darkwyn was ripped from her arms.

"Boris!" Bronte shouted. "No!"

Quickly getting the upper hand, Darkwyn raised the man in the air by his collar, and whipped him back as if to throw him across the room.

"Darkwyn, don't. Boris was trying to protect me."

"Sire," Boris said, voice trembling. "I had not seen your Master's mask, the sign of your station. I humbly beg pardon."

Darkwyn set him down and pulled her aside, making Boris nervous. "Sire?" he asked her.

Bronte straightened Darkwyn's ascot and smoothed his tux lapels. " 'Sire' is a term of respect for you."

"Is he for real?" Darkwyn eyed Boris.

"Tell him I'm yours," she whispered. "Vamps take their lifestyles seriously."

"The Vampiress is mine," Darkwyn announced, and pulled her against his side. "I would protect her with my life. If she had not intervened, I would have broken your neck."

"Way to sneak in a threat." *Hopefully, Boris will pass the word*, Bronte thought, *and that will be the first and last threat Darkwyn receives.*

Boris bowed, first to Darkwyn and then to her. "You have done well for yourself, mistress. He is taller and broader than the others, wider of shoulder. His strength is unparalleled in our vampire community."

"She knows my qualities," Darkwyn said. "As I know hers. In the physical sense."

She pinched him.

"Do it again," he whispered, as Boris watched.

Boris cleared his throat and set a ticket on the counter. "I'll look over the selection of blood drinks," Boris said, turning and steering clear of Darkwyn, who actually *wanted* to kick some vampire butt, or so it seemed to her.

"Darkwyn," Bronte said. "You have the key to the private stock of blood drinks. They're stored on the opposite wall," she said, dragging him toward the Music Room. "Customers run a tab or use a credit card. Zachary will take payments tonight. Watch and learn."

"Have you ever slept with Boris? Because he looks like he *wants* to sleep with you."

"Of course not. Pay attention so you can do your job."

"Your wish is my command, in and out of bed," Darkwyn proclaimed, a little too loud.

"I know this is a weird world, and Boris got possessive," she said, "so I forgive you, but stop trying to stake your claim."

Speaking of stakes. "Why do silver stakes and knives of all kinds decorate these walls?"

"Silver and stakes are fictional ways to kill vampires. Call it symbolic artwork."

"Right, forgot. Learned that today. Did you ever have to stake a customer?" he asked, running his hands up her purple corset.

"I'm gonna stake you if you don't get your stroking thumbs from beneath my breasts."

TWENTY-ONE

Jaydun and Bastian crashed Drak's as they delivered Puck's aviary-style floor cage from Vivica's. Darkwyn had them put it in the corner of the Master's Den.

Puck flew in behind them. "Watch the bloodsuckers. Eat some garlic. Can't drink my blood!"

Darkwyn put Puck in his cage, and leaned in to whisper. "One more comment about Bronte's customers and there's a black cage cover between you and them. Just sit here, watch the nice, ordinary freaks, and keep your bird mouth shut."

"Ordinary?" Puck ruffled his feathers. "Faith: Belief without evidence in what is told by one who speaks without knowledge, of things without parallel." Feathers flew. "Weirdos!"

Bronte had to smile at the way Darkwyn attempted to keep Puck in line. "Nice ordinary freaks, indeed," she whispered in Darkwyn's ear. "Weirdos?"

Darkwyn grabbed the cage cover.

"No. No freaks, no weirdos. Just sweet, kind vampires. Puck'll be good. Nice Puck. Smile for the vamps." He *click, click, clicked* his beak,

Darkwyn put the cover away. "For now," he said, and returned to work. "Bronte, I understand the private stock of blood drinks, but what if someone wants a mixed drink?"

"For cocktails, call Bite Me, downstairs, to have them delivered. Food, however, is not allowed in Drak's."

Darkwyn made the call and told the customer he'd bring it to the Crimson Room. "Bronte, are people going to take bites out of each other? You said they live like vamps."

"Read the sign."

"No bloodletting, blood bonds, blood-play, or fangbanging on the premises. *Violators* will be prosecuted."

"I don't want to know what that means," he said, "or maybe I should loosen up and try it. Fangbanging, hey?"

"Try and you're dragon toast. The police will come if I call. People going to the Music Room can rent iPods, disposable headsets, bedrolls, or they bring their own. I've already set up the light show and it'll run all night. Sleep masks are available to rent to vamps who don't like the light."

"Seriously? Vamps come here to sleep?"

"The Music Room is for the 'I vant to be alone but vith my own kind' vampire. It has black walls, bunk-bed style coffin slabs where they lie down and wear earphones, listen to music, enjoy a light show, or not. They might stay for a while and then move into the Crimson Room when they unwind."

Darkwyn squeezed her hand. "Where will you be all night?"

"Everywhere. Pretty much everybody wants to talk to me. Some guys try to put their hands on me. That's when you turn into a bouncer. I'll let you know when. Kick the bastards out. No, don't kick. Order them to go. And if a woman tries to touch you, I'll be on her like blood on a silver stake."

"Nice," Darkwyn said. "A woman as ready to fight as me. We're made for each other."

"You'll excuse me if I need a discussion or three, dragon man, and a bit of time with you, before I respond to that."

Darkwyn bowed, which she loved. "Yes, mistress."

"We close at 1 AM because that's the law for Salem bars, and some of our private stock blood drinks have alcohol in them. Those belong to the people who use the Crimson Room. It's like a higher class club. Be friendly at all times, but stern at closing time, and get them out by one o'clock."

By nine PM, Drak's was hopping, and Bronte wished she hadn't had to start Darkwyn on such a busy night. Still, he held his own.

Unfortunately that ended when Raven Shadow arrived. Raven, with her spare-cut spiderweb outfit, stockings, and fingerless gloves, latched onto Darkwyn, despite the adoring male entourage she brought with her.

Instead of accepting her mask, Raven Shadow went around the counter and practically stuck her tongue down Darkwyn's throat.

He initiated their separation, and Bronte liked that he didn't know what to do with her.

Fortunately, Bronte knew, though her immediate inclination was illegal. Nevertheless, she grabbed a red mask, handed it to Raven Shadow, and led her into the Crimson Room, where she handed her off to Boris, who was only too glad to take the seductress in hand.

Back in the Master's Den, she checked on her "mate." "You okay, Darkwyn?"

"Kissing that woman was repulsive, bitter to the taste, and not a little alarming." Where was Jagidy when a freaky she-vamp needed a smoke test? Dragon's blood, I must have shut him in my apartment, again. "We're not used to doors."

"*We* who?"

"Oh, sorry, I'm talking more to myself than you. That woman stunned me."

Bronte patted his cheek. "I'll calm you, later."

He caught her hand. "Promise?"

Back in the Crimson Room, Bronte got chatted up by a couple of her finest and most frequent patrons, with no choice but to be polite, until Raven Shadow disappeared.

As Bronte noticed, Zachary rushed in and pulled her into the Master's Den, where Darkwyn stood, the center of attention.

"It's not quite Darkwyn's fault," Zachary whispered. "A role player, the reality-show psychologist who makes people confess their darkest secrets, he goaded Darkwyn by challenging his manhood."

"I'll give him his manhood," Bronte whispered, "on a skewer."

"He's alpha," Zachary said. "Cut him a break. Defending his manhood is instinct."

"After the Sorceress of Chaos transformed my legion into dragons," Darkwyn said, "she banished us to the Island of Stars. That's the farthest life plane from here, right before the nearest death plane."

"Suddenly you're defending him?" Bronte asked Zachary.

"He's following his instincts. It's the way he's survived."

"What's it like there?" a vamp asked Darkwyn.

"It's a death trap now, with the lava sea overtaking the island, but it was beautiful, once. Our four moons change color with the seasons, a green sky, beach sand made of raw diamonds."

"Diamonds?"

"Some the size of your fists."

Greed, Bronte saw in some eyes, and not only for the diamonds. Grist for the sensation mill, a gossipmonger's or a slimy journalist's dream.

"What's it like being a dragon?" Raven Shadow asked, clutching Darkwyn's arm. "Did you have a lady dragon?"

"We were a Roman legion of *male* dragons, claws, big teeth, chase your food and eat it kicking."

The crowd laughed. But Bronte felt sick, for more than the usual reasons. She tried to get Darkwyn's attention by waving from the back of the crowd, but failed, and if she made a fuss, his words would rise in importance. *Stay cool*, she told herself.

"What did you like best about being a dragon?"

"Flying, just for the fun of it."

"So do you still have a little dragon in you?"

"I still have a big dragon in me." Darkwyn spread his hands wide, big-fish-story style. "You don't wanna make *me* mad."

Bronte wove her calm way through the crowd. It made her nervous that a role player took notes. Some snapped cell phone pictures or recorded him.

"Everyone, back to the room you came from," she suggested, playing Vampiress.

Darkwyn's audience groaned as they cleared his Den, all but Raven Shadow, her body wrapped around him. "There you go, Raven, back to play with your vamps. This one's mine." *To kill.* "Zachary, go on up to bed."

Alone with Darkwyn for a minute, Bronte turned on him. "What the hell were you thinking? Some idiot's bound to think you were telling the truth."

"Truth," Puck said. "An ingenious compound of desirability and appearance."

"Shut up, bird," Darkwyn snapped. "Bronte, Raven Shadow has fangs with blood on them?"

"You really don't focus well, do you? Dentists create fangs. Raven's have lipstick on them. They stick out too far. She got a lousy fang job."

"You mean they're fake?"

"As fake as her boobs *and* your dragon stories."

"I should be insulted." He stepped away from her. "Bronte, do you still have a three-inch gash on your right temple?"

"No."

"Roar."

TWENTY-TWO

"So now I know," Darkwyn *said at one that morning as* he followed Bronte to her apartment, getting his hand slapped away from her furiously silent person.

"I understand now," he said to draw her out. "I dole out masks, classical music, private label blood drinks, and I bounce fangbangers, but not so they really bounce. I'm friendly, meaning I don't beat up the customers, even if they attack me, and I don't talk about who I *really* am."

"Too late. The barn door's open, Dragula."

"Do we have a barn?"

"Up yours!" she said.

"Up my what?"

She turned on him, again, at the top of the stairs.

A step below her, he fought to keep from falling, he was so surprised. "I don't understand why you're so mad," he said. "I told you I was a dragon and you didn't tell me to shut up about it."

"I thought you were delusional."

"You did not. Well, maybe you did. Let me look up 'delusional' and that word Vivica used before I left, though I can't remember what it was. It had to do with my situation. Be . . . something . . . about my situation."

"I'll bet it wasn't 'indiscreet.' "

"No," Darkwyn said. "Not that word." He started to follow Bronte into her apartment, but she shut her door in his face, and her lock clicked. "I could break this down if I wanted to," he shouted.

"Do and I'll call the dragon police."

He could push the door in with a finger, but he wouldn't, out of respect for his heart mate.

Smart-mouthed heart mate. Too bad he wanted her so bloody much. *Blood, all vamps drink is blood.* He supposed being a blood-thirsty dragon had been good preparation for vampirism. *Though dragons are nicer and more polite than vamps.*

Darkwyn turned to the apartment door opposite Bronte's, and for the first time, he stepped into the "home" she assigned him. The minute he did, he found himself whisked into some kind of rope trap, trussed up to hang by his wrists and ankles in his own doorway.

Zachary appeared in his living room and laughed like a boy should. Darkwyn almost didn't mind being made the fool to hear it.

Bronte appeared in her doorway, crossed her arms, and tapped a foot at the two of them.

"Head rush, here," Darkwyn said. He could be down in a blink on his own, but he liked Bronte's attention.

"Cut him down," Bronte said, shutting herself back in her apartment.

Zachary came at him with a knife.

Darkwyn sighed. "You mean for me to land on my head, don't you?"

"Anybody ever say you're a brilliant man?" Zachary asked. "I didn't think so."

"I'm paying a high price to make you laugh," Darkwyn admitted.

The boy cut the rope, and Darkwyn hit the floor with a manly *thud*.

"That's for last night," Zachary snapped, then he, too, went into Bronte's apartment and shut him out.

Darkwyn flexed his hands and ankles to get feeling back in them. Hardly any pain, hardly a blink from his inner dragon. He looked around. His apartment mirrored Bronte's in almost every way, black and white, except that he had zebra stripes, an animal he'd read about. She'd thrown in some color with royal blue pillows.

Pleasant, if tepid, after the color on the Island of Stars. Now he understood why Bastian and McKenna's Dragon's Lair bed-and-breakfast seemed so appealing. Bastian had recreated Island color in his wall murals.

Darkwyn stepped to his balcony to gauge its proximity to Bronte's. *Perfect.* Only two windows separated them. He'd retained his dragon leap, though he hadn't used it the night he arrived so as not to frighten Bronte.

Having Bastian and Jaydun come to earth before him kept him from committing the same mistakes they did. So far, he'd committed an entirely new set.

He'd tested his leap on the second day, getting to and from Bastian's roof with his brothers. Test two, coming up, or down.

Yes, he could still leap, but farther than expected. He overshot Bronte's balcony and hit the ground beyond it. *Scumduggers.*

She rushed out to her balcony, still fastening her mask. "Anybody there?" she called, the room's light showing through her nightgown. He fisted his hands at her clear silhouette, surprised at his soul-deep yearning.

He wanted Bronte for more than sex, which had been incredible, and would be again. But he also wanted Bronte to walk beside, to sit beside in daily life, to kiss after breakfast and before work, to turn to in sleep, to hold and cherish.

He watched her go inside, understood why she enjoyed the vampire movies, the underlying love stories, and wondered if he was good enough for her.

As her light went out, he leapt to her balcony.

She screamed and he switched on the light.

A beauty sitting in bed, scrambling to fasten her mask, angry enough to beat him senseless.

Zachary barged in and came right to the French doors where Darkwyn waited for an invite. "Dragonelli, again. You gonna make a habit of breaking into Bronte's room?"

"I was invited the first time."

Bronte slapped the covers. "Thanks, but I wouldn't exactly call it an invite."

"Maybe not with *words*."

"Whatever," she said, the fighting light in her eyes making him edgy on several levels. "Did you scale the building this time, too?"

"I didn't need to. I've retained my dragon leap, which I did not use the first night, so as not to frighten you."

"Zachary," Bronte said, "take Mr. Dragonelli to his apartment, without tricks, if you please. There will be no more *leaping* between us."

"Sad," Darkwyn said. "I could leap my heart out with you."

Bronte's eyes got all big and needy, but she still let him go.

Back in his apartment, he figured if he couldn't have Bronte, for now, he would indulge in another earth vice, a bubble bath, the secret enjoyment of which he would take to his grave. Not even the bird knew how much he loved bubble baths.

A short while later, settled in his bath, Darkwyn wished more than anything that Bronte could join him. He missed her. Not a week's acquaintance, and his every heartbeat sought hers. Being heart mates must yield its own high-powered magick. Look at Bastian and McKenna, deep in love, and Jaydun and Vivica, deep in denial, but still.

Darkwyn fell near to sleep in the bath, until he heard a scurrying in the wall. He remembered few things of earth, but rodents were one of them. Roman armies slept in mud and dirt and if they were lucky, hay, with rodents.

As he put more hot water in his tub, the scurrying became a scrape, a groan, making him hope this rodent stood as tall as him.

Then it happened. His shelves of towels and bath supplies moved. At first, he wasn't sure he'd seen it, until they moved another inch more.

"Hello?" He hoped his invader would answer.

A hand slid through the opening and waved with a five-finger wiggle and purple fingernails. "Are you decent?"

"Bronte, are you breaking into my apartment after you threw me out of yours?"

"Yes, please. I'm rather fond of leaping . . . with you. Are you decent?"

"Decent enough to leap."

She squeezed into his bathroom from behind his shelves, certainly hiding a connecting door. He covered himself in suds and tried not to gasp, the way she stood there, uncertain, in a pink mask and floaty pink night wisp, through which he glimpsed her beauty, except, of course, her face.

"I will never tell another living soul that I am a former Roman warrior and dragon, if you promise, my leaping playmate, to keep my weakness for bubble baths a secret."

"Who are you really, Darkwyn Dragonelli?" she asked, standing there, tantalizing him.

"Outwardly, I'm an alpha male, no matter my current species, wearing unseen scales and spikes like armor. Inside, I'm a dragon who naps in flower beds, likes bubble baths, and is looking for a lady dragon of my own. Deep down, despite the centuries, I'm a man, still, looking for a woman . . . to have sex with."

"In flower beds?"

"I'd like that."

"Let's do. Soon." She dropped the pink gown and stepped into the tub with him, a delightful surprise, though he'd be twice as excited if she'd removed her mask.

He made room, reached for her, and pulled her against him, so she could use his chest as a pillow. "Now, you will feel some festive gymnastics in the region of your lower back," he warned. "Ignore it. It has good memories of last night and wants more."

"Your man brain has a memory?"

"I fear so. Tell me why you were so upset about the truth of my past, tonight."

"The truth? It's science fiction."

"Define—?"

"Hold that question, because I'm freaked. Darkwyn?"

"Yes."

"I know we talked about dragons, so maybe it's the power of suggestion or I'm hallucinating, but I think I see a little green dragon, his knees on my midriff and his face between my breasts, one little hand plumping the right one like a pillow."

"Jagidy!" Darkwyn snapped, moving Bronte forward as he sat up, sliding Jagidy down her belly and into the water.

The guardian dragon came up sputtering rainbow smoke, coughing, and spitting water at them, then he hung in the air, furious and insulted, arms crossed.

"Jagidy, you do not invade a lady's bath."

"No, you don't," Bronte said, "you let the lady invade yours, where . . . she *imagines* sex-starved mini dragons?"

"Bronte, let me introduce you to Jagidy, my guardian dragon, also from the Island of Stars. Jagidy, this is Bronte, never again to be touched by *you*."

Jagidy's jaw dropped and he whistled as he shot from the bathroom into Darkwyn's apartment, emitting a cloudy gray blue smoke.

Darkwyn reached, from the comfort of the water, to slam the bathroom door beside the tub, and bar the pocket dragon's reentry. "Don't mind him. He's having a tantrum."

Bronte turned in his arms. "You *are* from another world?"

"Another plane, sweet. But a man, again."

"Oh, *that* I can tell. Do your sex parts never sleep?"

"Not when you're around."

TWENTY-THREE

*Bronte turned in his arms so she could read his expres-*sion. "Darkwyn, if you really do have the power of a dragon, what did you mean by promising to make my goal of freedom your own?" Her heart raced awaiting his response.

He settled her in his embrace so she could see his every expression.

Meanwhile, his growing sex managed to slide between her legs and settle there. She liked it, all of it, including his dragon boner, an organ already proven for hours of . . . otherworldly? . . . pleasure. Which made a certain sense. She didn't think a man could normally come as often as Darkwyn had.

"Let me explain why you can trust me," Darkwyn said. "One of my goals here on earth is to make your life quest my own. The other is to best an evil sorceress named Killian, Crone of Chaos. She's the one who turned the

Roman legion I belonged to into dragons. Following me so far?"

"More or less. Suspending disbelief is the problem."

"What, guardian dragons are normal for you? Here," he said, presenting his left hand, palm up. "What do you think of this?"

Bronte traced a tattoo that looked like two Rs back to back with a line between. "It looks like the symbol of a fraternal organization."

"It does. It means I belonged to the Roman army. Killian, who uses lightning like confetti, turned us into dragons because we were trying to break her hold over a poor Scottish village."

"When did you get this tattoo?"

"Centuries ago. This on my hand, and this phoenix rising from the ashes on my chest survived both transformations—from man to dragon, and back again."

"The palm tattoo is unusual, but it doesn't prove anything."

"You suspend disbelief about me, and I will suspend it where Zachary is concerned."

She let her relief, despite his keen observation, calm her. "Deal."

"I am a Roman turned into a dragon, and now I am a man, again. Not a myth. I am here to stay, I think you should know. Both my tasks will help me reclaim the magick Andra expended sending me here."

"Makes a magick sort of sense," Bronte said. "But who is Andra?"

"The Sorceress of Hope. She kept us safe and took care of us after Killian banished us to the Island of Stars."

"Why did Andra send you *here*?"

"The veil between the planes in Salem has been made thin by human magick, I have been told. It is easiest to come through the veil here. Coming was necessary because Killian made the volcano on the island erupt. The heat from it evaporated our endless deep blue sea. Lava replaced water, and now the island shrinks in a sea of boiling lava. Andra is getting us off the island, one by one, to save us."

"Why one by one?"

"You ask a lot of questions."

"If I'm going to trust you, I need answers."

"Trust does not come easy to you."

"I trust only Zachary. For good reason."

"Killian makes it difficult for Andra to move us back to earth. But Andra found that when one moon covers another—you call that an eclipse—Andra's white magick is shaded from Killian's black."

"That's good."

"Yes and no. 'Shaded' does not mean hidden. Killian caught Andra's first spell, when she sent Bastian back. Killian tossed out a dark counterspell at a point where she was able to cause our 'man lances' to resemble our tails. Earth doctors have assured me and my brothers that this is an anomaly that belongs to us alone and will not affect our offspring." Darkwyn paled. "Not that offspring is the point."

"Of course." In another life, a safe life, she could have cared for this man.

"Why doesn't Andra change her spell, so you don't suffer that blip? Though being the recipient of its attention, I wouldn't want it any other way. Forget I suggested it."

Darkwyn rumbled deep in his chest, almost a chuckle, though no smile marred the perfection of his focused expression.

"Andra dared not change the words for fear the spell would no longer work. It turns us back into men and gets us here, so every word stays the same, and every one of us will be, ah—"

"Gifted?"

"Why thank you. Yes, endowed, in that way. Now, where were we? Your questions distracted me, and your love of my, er, spell blip, turned my thoughts to, well, leaping."

"You were explaining *why* I can trust you, something to do with Andra's magick."

"Ah." He took to lathering her breasts, indicating that his turned thoughts remained, while his dancing dragon tail prodded her hip with sexual intent.

He had to work harder now to focus on his story, and she, to ignore his tricky dick.

"I remember where I was," he said, not quite coming out of his sexual haze. "If I don't get Andra's magick back by helping you overcome your problems—"

"Why me?"

"Karma? Fate? Destiny? For Bastian, it was McKenna. For Jaydun, it is Vivica. For me, it is you. Why question the mandates of the universe? You need help, do you not?"

"I need help like you wouldn't believe, and not just for me."

"For Zachary, as well, I expect."

With a nod, Bronte swallowed her fear and refused to give in to the sob stuck in her throat.

Darkwyn took her by her chin and raised her face to his for a kiss, deep and hungry, but sincere, his soul stripped, his vulnerability bared, even to her disdain, or worse, if she wished. "Bronte, you can trust me, because if Andra doesn't get her magick back, she won't be able to send the rest of our legion to earth the way she sent me, Bastian, and Jaydun. Now you see why I am to be trusted? I have the welfare of my brother dragons at heart. If I fail you, they will die."

"Your brothers would drown in hot lava, if you failed *me*?" She wrapped her arms around his neck. "I don't want them to die, Darkwyn. My sense that you were someone I could get involved with that first day at the bar; it frightened me. Made me doubt my instincts. Life has been too dangerous for trust. I haven't allowed myself to believe in anyone. I ran because I thought you were someone I selfishly wanted, for myself. And I must put Zachary first."

"What is at risk for Zachary?"

"They'll kill him, if we're found."

"They, who?"

"Bronte?" Zachary called. "Are you here?"

"I'm in the bathroom. What is it?"

"News trucks from as far away as Boston and Providence are lining up outside."

TWENTY-FOUR

Darkwyn held Bronte tighter, saying without words he was there for her.

"Bronte," Zachary said. "This is serious. We have two hours until dawn to figure out what to tell them about dragon boy."

Zachary probably stood in Bronte's bathroom, given the timbre of his voice.

"Don't come in here," she warned.

"I'm twelve. I'm not stupid."

Darkwyn kissed Bronte's temple. "The news crews are here because I talked about myself? That is not good for staying hidden, is it?"

"Zachary's in more danger than I am."

"I'll never forgive myself," Darkwyn muttered. "Zachary, we will meet you in the living room in a few minutes."

Bronte rose from the tub, allowing him to admire the

butterfly at the base of her spine, a reminder of freedom, her goal.

"Zachary," Bronte called. "Don't go outside or crack a blind."

"Sure. And Auntie dearest?"

"Yes."

"Your bathroom door was open. I can see that it's empty."

"Because you're standing in it. I'm wise to you."

"Whatever." The sound of the boy's voice receded on the word.

"He caught us together, again," Darkwyn said. "I'm sorry."

"Who broke into whose place?"

"But he is only a boy."

"He's an old soul, is my Zachary."

Darkwyn sat forward. "What do you mean by that, exactly?"

She wrapped a towel around herself. "I think Zachary should be the one to tell you."

"I looked up the 'barn door' thing," Darkwyn said, following her from the tub, unembarrassed by his obvious physical interest. "I can tell you right now that it is entirely too late for you to shut that door." He stroked her from her nose to her chin, along her swanlike neck, between her breasts, to the towel, which he grasped, yanked, and let fall. "Now that's what I'm talking about."

A cat mewed, and they looked up to see Scorch curled atop the towel cupboard.

"When did she get here?" Bronte asked.

"I'm afraid she might have been here the whole time." *Very afraid.* Killian should not know the details of their relationship or trust. She would use it against them. Then again, he might be wrong about Killian using the cat as a host. Right now, he could not see the cat's wings. They must tuck back when the cat's at rest.

He reached up to scratch the kitten behind its ears as Bronte returned to her own bathroom.

Scorch hissed and clawed his hand.

He healed it with the other, then saluted. "Killian."

A few minutes later, he and Bronte met Zachary in the kitchen. The boy had cooked ham and eggs and French toast. "I thought we needed nourishment. It's going to be a long day." He gave Darkwyn a look. "Also, you two need to keep up your strength."

The double meaning hit Darkwyn as if Zachary were holding a gun. "Are you sure you're only twelve?"

"About that," Zachary said. "After breakfast, care to ride the coffin wheel with me?"

"We have another problem for after breakfast," Bronte said, devouring her meal. "Or have you forgotten?"

"Right," Zachary said. "Memory's going. I'm getting old."

Darkwyn raised a brow but said nothing. "Bronte, you don't have to face the news crews. I will. Just tell me if I should wear jeans or my Master Vampire disguise. And do tell me what I can and cannot say."

Bronte nodded as she sipped her coffee. "I'll write you a script."

"Even better." Darkwyn tucked into his breakfast, and went back for seconds.

Zachary rubbed his chin in that having-a-beard way of his. "I think Darkwyn should wear the Master Vampire outfit, mask and all, get Drak's some free publicity. We might as well profit from his ridiculously tall tales."

"My only tall tail belonged to the black ice dragon on the Island of Stars. And it was long not tall, and lethal."

"Black ice? You had ice on a tropical island?"

Scumduggers, that boy can be flip. "No, but Andra *knew* about it. I was a huge, black dragon. She named me Black Ice, because she said I was less playful than most dragons, and deceptively dangerous. Evidently, one cannot see the potential danger in black ice or know it is there until one is on top of it and out of control."

Bronte raised her orange juice his way. "I can attest to that."

"Stick around a couple of months," Zachary said, not looking up from his eggs. "We'll find some black ice and I'll throw you at it."

A sensation lightened Darkwyn's chest and erupted without notice. Laughter from deep down, a release of sorts, heralding his optimism at finding these two people who mattered so much to him. "If you saw me in dragon form, you, too, would see the humor in your statement."

"Satire," Puck said from the open window, "an obsolete kind of literary composition in which the vices and follies of the author's enemies are expounded with imperfect tenderness."

Darkwyn ignored the bird he'd released after Drak's closed and worried about Bronte's fear. "What will happen if the people who are looking for you find you?"

Zachary slammed a fist on the table. "Bronte, you told him?"

She ignored the boy's outburst. "They'll start by taking us back."

"Back where?"

"Canada."

"As I understand it, Canada has a border. Wouldn't kidnappers be stopped there?"

"At the border, they'd force us through. We're Canadian citizens, not American. We don't have green cards. Being legal would help protect us from going back, but we're illegal."

Darkwyn sat forward. "Vivica can make you legal."

"Not fast enough. The quickest and easiest way to get legal is to marry somebody who is."

"I'm legal."

Zachary stopped clearing the table. "A legal dragon?"

Darkwyn ignored him. "Marry me and you're legal. But wait," Darkwyn added, fork halfway to his mouth. "What about Zachary? Would they take him back?"

"As my ward, wouldn't he have to stay with me?"

"Bronte," Zachary said. "If Sanguedolce couldn't take us back, he'd have his goons kill us here. Or kill me, I should say. But then you, too, 'cause you'd know *who* killed me. And I'm not sure you've got a handle on that green card business. I should have stopped building coffin wheels and carousels long enough to do the research."

"That settles it," Darkwyn said, leaving the table. "First I'll read our statement to the news crews; then, Bronte, you and I will get married; then Zachary, you are going to tell me why you have this non-age-appropriate wisdom, and are nearly as weird as I am."

Bronte stood. "You want me to marry a dragon?"

Darkwyn tilted his head. "You would rather die?"

TWENTY-FIVE

Inside Bite Me, before it opened, Bronte stood beside Zachary in the pub's dark recesses to watch Darkwyn approach Roger Rudder and the psycho sidekick who'd goaded Darkwyn into talking last night.

Lila and Scorch followed Darkwyn down the Phoenix porch steps to the sidewalk. They were her cats, yes, but they adored Darkwyn. She could relate, though if he screwed this up . . .

She spelled a silent plea to Darkwyn and the universe for positive results:

"Stand strong, back straight.
Questions are to bait;
Count to ten and wait.

Ruffle not a hair.
Show not a care.
Truth bends; be aware.

Twist Rudder's tongue,
So mote it be done.
This, I will, harm it none."

The press held mikes out to Darkwyn as he arrived, but the minute she finished her spell, *fizzle* and *hiss!* Cartoon-like fireworks popped at Roger Rudder's feet, sounding like cereal on steroids. Or microphone interference. Good, he looked like an idiot, jumping around like he needed a men's room.

Darkwyn raised his chin and waited while the journalist danced to her tune, an idiot doing a fast tiptoe through the tulips. Could only Rudder see her wonky spell? If so, it half worked.

"Well," Zachary said. "Whatever spell you cast, you put a little fear of magick into the loser. Rudder, I mean, not Darkwyn."

She squeezed the boy's shoulders. "Shush."

After Darkwyn read the statement and put her script in his pocket, he picked up the cats and continued to shake his head as if refusing to answer questions. "Good man," Bronte said. "Now get out of there."

"Did you ever hear of a cat that glowed in the dark?" Zachary asked as he opened a bottle of whiskey and held it beneath his nose, his sigh filled with regret.

Bronte took the bottle and put a stopper in it. "There is no breed of cat that glows in the dark."

"I didn't think so."

"Why hasn't Darkwyn walked away yet?" Bronte asked no one in particular.

"You really like him don't you?"

"Yes, I do."

"Are you going to marry him?"

"Probably."

"He's that good?"

"Will you at least try and act like a twelve-year-old? We're not alone anymore. You're not very good at hiding that old soul around the house, in case I never mentioned it."

"Why start now?"

"Darkwyn's not as simple as Ogden. And if I marry him, it's because he can protect us."

"I'm glad Ogden's recovering. I especially like that he kept to himself. I wish Darkwyn would. Can he be trusted?"

"Not if he just answered a question, which is what it looks like."

"Are you evading my question?"

"No. No, I'm not. Yes, Darkwyn can be trusted. He came highly recommended by Vivica, trouble free, healthy as a . . . dragon . . . and he's got a story as astonishing as yours, and, well, I have good instincts. I'd stake my life on the fact that he can be trusted."

"You *are* staking your life on it."

"Darkwyn Dragonelli may be the best break we've ever had."

"That's not hard. He would be our *first* break. My mother was the lucky one, dying young."

Bronte's eyes filled. "She was my sister. Do you mind?" Bronte said. "I'm selfish enough to wish she had survived your birth."

"Look," Zachary said, "your dragon's coming back and the press vans are leaving."

"Goddess, he's gorgeous," she said. "He takes my breath away."

"You *love* him."

"Of course not. In lust with, maybe. It's only been a few days. But seriously, when's the last time I ever stumbled across a gentle man?"

"A dragon nicknamed Black Ice? Does he breathe fire? And if he does, wouldn't that melt his ice?"

"You know, he does have the hottest breath." Bronte tapped the bar. "You're right. I'm such a loser."

Darkwyn stepped into the dark pub and locked the door behind him. "Paperboy just came." He placed the newspaper on the bar beside them. "I'm sorry," he said.

Bronte picked it up. "What are you sorry for?"

Zachary ignored them, took the rolled paper from her hand, and unfolded it. "Front damned page. Nice headline: 'Drak's features Vampire Dragon.'"

"Oh no," Bronte said. "That's a picture of me last night on my balcony."

Darkwyn slipped an arm around her. "I like you in that pink nightgown."

She squeaked. "You can practically see through it."

"That's what I like best."

She leaned into him. "So what are you sorry for? Can I just say, on the plus side, that at least they didn't get a picture of us *leaping.*"

Darkwyn flipped the page over. The bottom half featured two pictures of him, one in midleap, between his balcony and hers, one between the ground and her balcony, the caption: "Vampire Dragon flies, but does he breath fire?"

"They did get a picture of you leap—oh, never mind," Zachary added. "Euphemism. Got it. *Can* you breathe fire? Seriously."

"Yes. Yes, I can."

"Cut it out, both of you," Bronte snapped. "This is a disaster, or it will be, if these pictures go viral."

Zachary scoffed. "You don't for one minute think they won't?"

"Bronte," Darkwyn said. "Don't cry. Do you think *they* will come from Canada, if they see this?"

Zachary groaned. "Exactly how much have you told him?"

"He doesn't know who or why or anything. He knows exactly what you heard during the green card talk at breakfast."

"I am not invisible," Darkwyn muttered. "Now I know how Jagidy must feel."

Jagidy raised a clenched fist in thanks.

"Who the heck is Jagidy?" Zachary asked.

"He's my guardian dragon. Small, green, invisible, and in love with your aunt."

Zachary hit his ear with the heel of his hand like he had water in it and couldn't have heard correctly. "Nothing much magickal matters at this point, I suppose," the boy said. "Darkwyn, would you breath fire for Bronte if she needed saving?"

"Absolutely."

Bronte rounded on her nephew. "Honestly, Zach!"

"Please call me Zachary. My dignity is at stake. Listen, if dragon man here breathes fire, I'm all for you marrying him. I'd *like* to see him to turn Sanguedolce and his henchmen into crispy critters."

Bronte gasped. "I've never known you to be so bloodthirsty."

"Yeah, well, maybe I've had enough of running. Truth is, they might as well have taken a gun to my mother's head, and to both of us, as well."

"Don't put it past them. But that's the jaded old man in you talking."

"So it is."

TWENTY-SIX

Tired of being the one with all the answers, Bronte turned to Darkwyn. "What's our next step?"

"First we watch the news," Darkwyn said, "I am on in fifteen minutes. Then we plan our wedding. Then, Zachary, you and I are going to have a talk."

"About the birds and bees?"

"No, *old man*—which I've heard one time too many to be a mistake."

Zachary got his guard up. "You can't believe—"

"I was a Roman warrior turned into a dragon. I *can* believe. I do believe."

They sat on the sofa and turned on the TV to wait for the news.

"Darkwyn, what did you say to them?" Bronte asked. "They wouldn't be saying 'stay tuned for a word with Salem's own Vampire Dragon' if all you did was read the statement."

"I might have attempted to discredit myself."

"That's bad." She punched him in the arm. "Bad dragon!"

"*Shh*," Zachary said. "Here's the segment."

"You look good on camera," Bronte said, and Zachary rolled his eyes.

"So," the reporter asked him. "Are you a Vampire Dragon?"

"Yes, I am. And my cats have wings and glow in the dark with a sort of prehistoric phosphorescence."

Zachary sat forward. "I knew it!"

"The wings are invisible to you, but they're here," Darkwyn told the reporter. "This one is Lila, because of her lilac points. And this little kitty just might be Killian the evil Sorceress of Chaos. Hers are black leather wings. Since lightning is Killian's specialty, and this little kitty looks a bit charred, we call her Scorch." He waved their paws. "Wave hello to all the witches out there."

"So, ladies and gentlemen," the reporter said, once again dancing to her silly fake fireworks like a puppet on an invisible string. "Decide for yourself." He wiped his brow. "This is Salem, after all, and I've been reporting on supernaturals coming through the veil for months. The evidence is overwhelming. Is this man one of them? Is he a man at all? Ask yourself this: Is Salem's Vampire Dragon, Darkwyn Dragonelli, telling us the mystical truth while making it sound unbelievable to throw us off the scent? This is Roger Rudder, your eye on the veil."

"Good going, Bronte," Zachary said. "Your backfiring spells worked, more or less."

"So did my brilliance. I'll take a kiss, Bronte," Darkwyn said. "For doing so well. Then I'll kiss you for your spells."

Bronte crossed the room to evade him. "Mind your manners."

"I can't take it," Zachary said, jumping off the sofa. "If you two get married, I'm moving to the fourth floor. I'll eat here, maybe, if I'm invited, but I'll call ahead."

Darkwyn gave her a look. "He really doesn't sound like a twelve-year-old."

"Look at him," she said. "He's a cranky kid."

"Maybe, but as for watching what I say, heck, last week I was a dragon. How do I know what manners to watch?"

"Or how to keep your mouth shut," Bronte mumbled.

"Or that. Nevertheless, I know a lot about protecting the people I love, so we *are* getting married."

"You sound happy about that." Bronte felt a little glow inside. "I'm scared." She wasn't kidding. "And I want a proposal."

"I *am* happy, but I have to look up 'proposal.' I'm not even sure I can afford one?"

"*Ask* her, you freakadelic dragosapien. Propose marriage."

Darkwyn shrugged, Zachary's insults rolling off his back, charming the hex out of her.

"There's a three-day waiting period in Salem," Darkwyn said. "But the county clerk can waive that without a court order, with the proper paperwork, so it's possible we could get the license *and* get married today. Vivica's taking care of the paperwork for us. So will you . . . marry me?"

"I'm underwhelmed. How does Vivica know?"

"I called her between breakfast and meeting the press. She already has a Wiccan priestess, licensed to perform the ceremony, on standby."

"Scorch!" Bronte said of the cat taking a tightrope walk across the top of the flat screen, wings balanced upward. "Darkwyn . . . she *does* have black leather wings. Lila, where are you?" Bronte called. "Come to mommy."

Here came Lila, lilac lace wings bouncing as she ran.

Bronte felt like she'd entered another dimension. "Why didn't I see their wings before?"

"For the same reason you didn't see Jagidy. You didn't have any dragon magick."

"Now I do?"

"I made a tactical error when I let you into my bath this morning."

Bronte gave him a pout sure to make him horny. "Now, you're hurting my feelings."

"No, I liked having you there, but dragon magick passes through water. The smaller the body of water, the more intact the magick."

"You know," Zachary said, "I didn't need to know that you two shared a bath this morning, especially not how much you enjoyed it, perv."

Bronte raised a hand to her hip. "Zachary, you know my bathroom connects to his; you know I was in there. You're hardly innocent. Spare me the dramatics."

"Fine. Now tell me these cats do *not* have wings."

"They do. And there's a tiny green guardian dragon flying around you who blows colored smoke."

Darkwyn nodded. "That's how he tests people to see if they're safe."

"What color is unsafe?" Bronte asked. "Now that I can see him, I'll be able to tell if any of our guests are Sanguedolce's men."

"Black smoke means evil intent."

"Jagidy's smoke isn't black around Scorch right now. It's green. So Scorch isn't Killian?"

"I'm not quite sure. But Scorch is scary. Watch what you say around her. And green smoke means neither good nor bad, like for people who don't give a bustard's ear about us, or in this case, I'm guessing it means that Killian is, at this minute, doing her evil deeds elsewhere."

Zachary waved his hands back and forth over the cats' backs. "So Roger Rudder is right about supernaturals coming through the veil?"

"He is, but he sounds like a jerk when he says it, doesn't he? He's been stalking Vivica, but my brother Jaydun is protecting her. She helps all of us who come through. She's like the gatekeeper and the best judge of character I know."

"What other color smoke should I look for?" Bronte asked.

"Red smoke is celebratory. Purple is for love, which is why Jagidy blows purple your way. Yellow means good intentions or good people."

"What was with the rainbow after he fell in the tub?"

"The water he swallowed probably screwed up his 'fire to smoke' proportions for a bit."

"I know I'm out of my twelve-year-old mind for asking, but is Jagidy a real dragon?"

"Are you a real boy?" Darkwyn raised a questioning brow. "Yes, Jagidy's real. He's an elder, a lech of a dragon, the way he chases Bronte, but he's real."

"He's not the only chaser where Bronte's concerned," Zachary mumbled as Jagidy flew invisibly around him blowing yellow smoke.

"Andra, our sorceress," Darkwyn told Zachary, "shrinks the elders to get them here, one with each of us. It's like repurposing them. Preserves their strength and ability to travel, and extends their lives. Otherwise they wouldn't survive the trip or they'd die on the island. We learned about the possibility when Whyzind got caught up in the spell with Bastian."

Darkwyn turned on a dime. "Bastian's place! That's where we can have our wedding, in the apple orchard at the Dragon's Lair. You can meet my family. I'll call my brother Bastian right now."

"I can't wait to bounce dragon babies on my knee," Zachary mumbled facetiously. "Hey, do you hear that noise?" Zachary followed the sound to her balcony. "You're not going to get away for a wedding today," he shouted from the bedroom. "Fangs for the Memories hasn't opened yet but there are like a hundred tourists blocking the sidewalk and road to get in. Roger Rudder is out there interviewing customers, and he doesn't seem to be working alone. That psychologist who goaded Darkwyn is filming Rudder's interviews."

"Guess I didn't do such a good job of making Roger look like an idiot," Darkwyn said, standing back while looking out at the crowd.

"Roger makes Roger look like an idiot," Zachary said. "If we try to leave here today, to go to Bastian's, those hounds of hell will follow. Think how the public would like attending your wedding. Vampiress marries Vampire Dragon. Story at eleven."

TWENTY-SEVEN

"Last night, a Master Vampire," Darkwyn said hours later. "Today, a waiter."

"I've never seen Bite Me overflow like this," one of the waitresses said as they stood waiting for their customers' orders to be filled. "I guess it's a good thing?"

"I am not sure." Darkwyn looked around. "I assumed that waiting tables would be easy. But breakfast has run into lunch, and lunch into dinner, with no breaks in the crowd."

"Even our Vampiress is waiting tables."

"I am forming a great respect for waitpersons," Darkwyn said. "Thank you for working overtime today."

The waitress grabbed her plates and went to distribute them.

He and Bronte had been working beside the regular staff all day, to keep customer flow at a bearable pace.

Customers loved meeting the Vampire Dragon in per-

ANNETTE BLAIR

son. He shook more hands than he took orders, but he tried to help.

"Are you eating blood pudding?" Bronte asked when she found him taking a break in the supply room.

"It is also called blood sausage. Yes, I am starving."

"That's made with real blood, you know."

"I know," he said. "Oddly enough, this one is called Boudin and is made in Canada. And this soup is blood soup. Hey, don't blame me. It's your menu. Try some, it's delicious."

"No, thanks. Eat, before your soup clots." She turned from his offer of a spoonful. "I ate it as a kid, before I knew what it was." She shivered and he put down his fork to rub her arms, and pull her close.

"Want a sip of my decoffinated coffee?" He practiced his wink on her. "When I was a dragon, I chased supper and ate it when and where I caught it. Get the picture?"

"Yuck. Yes, I get it."

"Do not worry, I will brush my teeth before I kiss you."

"And I'll find a spell to erase my memory of your former eating habits. *Yeesh!* Oh, look at the time. I have to go and change my clothes, turn into the real Vampiress, so I'll be ready to open Drak's for the vamps. I'll be right back."

The pub had a line of its own with a door spotter who let two people in when two left, or three or five, whatever. Darkwyn had learned to respect and appreciate maximum capacity laws. It saved on havoc and bar brawls. Not to mention its original purpose, the safety of customers in case of fire.

Given this turn of events, Darkwyn wished he had landed on earth in a closet with the door shut, or his mouth stapled, at the least. If he knew then what he knew now, he would probably still be there, so no one could learn where he came from.

Then again, the universe meant him for Bronte. Smart universe. He would be less than whole without her. He guessed he landed in the right place. Though, with his misplaced honesty, he might have given Killian more power than he would like her to have. Worse, he had promised to take on Bronte's enemies but didn't yet know who they were.

He supposed things could be worse, but he wasn't certain how.

A few minutes, or hours, later, as he grabbed napkins and condiments, Zachary came running into the supply room. "After the morning news," the boy said, out of breath, "Roger Rudder got an anonymous tip about the day you got here. Now he's asking everyone in line if they were in the pub when you rolled in behind the bar. Your news video did go viral, by the way, and he's asking for witnesses online, too. Darkwyn, do you hear what I'm saying? People are answering him and telling him all about it." The boy frowned. "Naked? You stood in public, naked?"

"I had just been turned from a dragon into a man. Dragons don't wear clothes. They wear scales, which fell off. Go back outside, Zachary, and walk the tourist line, pay attention to what people tell Rudder, but try to stay out of his sight. I'm calling Vivica."

"No need," said Vivica, the owner of Works Like Magick coming in behind him, slamming down her purse. "I left my boat in Cat Cove and snuck in the back door."

Darkwyn took a deep breath. "I suppose that means you can't help?"

"It means I was right. You left Works Like Magick before you learned enough. I said before you left to be circumspect about your situation. Why didn't you listen?"

"Circumspect! That's the word I was supposed to look up. So being circumspect means shutting your mouth about your background?"

Vivica's sigh contained a bit of a growl. "Pretty much. Next time I get a problem student, he or she is staying longer. Not that I'm saying *I told you so*."

"But you *are*."

"Well, this is serious. And I did warn you that someone could get hurt, someone other than you, and there were a million things in my head I needed to say. If you had stayed and let us take it lesson by lesson, maybe—"

"I get it," Darkwyn said. "This is my fault and I will make it better."

"Let's say we're both at fault and move on. Is everybody okay?"

"Yes, so far. More or less." Other than Zachary and Bronte being sick with worry about being found, heaven knew why.

"So far so good, then. I had to come in through the back because Roger Rudder's been stalking me, again. I don't want him to know that I'm anywhere near you."

"No inviting him to the wedding, then?"

"Wedding. Right. Here's your paperwork, by the way. You and Bronte are getting married tonight, in the small window of time between closing to tourists and opening for vampires. I went to see Ogden and he needs an evening away from his brother. He's going to come and fill in as Master Vampire for the night. After the wedding, if you and Bronte want to take a short honeymoon, I'll play Vampiress."

"You think of everything," Darkwyn said. "So in which closet will we marry?"

Vivica chuckled. "It won't be quite that covert. I think you'd be okay in Bronte's apartment or out by the water. The fairgrounds, along Cat Cove, are fenced off from the road and get shut down between shifts at that time, right? They're out of camera range and away from Rudder's stalking soul."

Vivica eyed Darkwyn. "You made the decision to marry as fast as you left Works Like Magick. Be careful your actions don't come back to bite you in your fine dragon butt."

"Does that refer to his marrying *me*? And that butt is mine, thanks." Bronte hugged Vivica and made an exaggerated sad face at him over her shoulder. "I'd like to run away for a honeymoon," she said. "But we can't with this mess. Whimper."

Darkwyn fell deeper in love. *Love?* When had lust turned to love? "We could take Zachary with us to keep him safe," he said to cool his thoughts, despite the brilliance of the idea.

Vivica rolled her eyes. "Congrats, by the way. Darkwyn's a bit ADD—doesn't finish his homework—but he's a good man."

Darkwyn ogled his future wife, her evening's corset and mask violet, like her hair and eyes. *Nice.*

She saw his regard and looked down at herself. "Does this dress make me look dead?" She chuckled.

He did not.

A premonition hit, followed by shock, denial, then a wash of fear. He pulled Bronte against him, so his shudder became hers. "Don't joke, Bronte, not even about your vampire persona."

"Okay, husband-to-be, if you feel that strongly. But this slut dress, purple patent leather boots, fishnets, violet mask, and corset—not exactly my dream wedding dress."

"You're gorgeous," Darkwyn whispered against her ear, kissing her velvet lobe.

"Earth to Darkwyn," Vivica said.

Warmth rose up his neck. "Vivica, I don't suppose you have a plan to get rid of the vultures out there?"

"You suppose wrong. I have a plan to confuse and disillusion them. A plan I've already put into action."

Bronte caught up slowly, her eyes widening from dreamy bride to stark reality. "What plan?"

"Bastian and Jaydun are out front, dressed like vampires, claiming to be your dragon brothers."

Darkwyn gave his acclimator a double take. "Which they are."

"The crowd doesn't know that. Jay and Bastian are doing fakey magick and passing out leaflets for some of the other Salem tourist attractions where my clients work."

Bronte pursed her lips. "What's the point?"

Distracted again by Bronte, Darkwyn had to force himself to pay attention to Vivica and not his future wife's perfect mouth.

"They're turning the scene into a circus, like you tried to do with the cats on the news this morning, Darkwyn. Making it look as bogus as a well-orchestrated publicity stunt."

"I guess, when you come right down to it," Bronte said, "the harder we attempt to agree with the truth, the less true it sounds."

"Right." Darkwyn nodded. "It's like protesting too much in reverse."

"Exactly. Oh, and Bastian's wife, McKenna, is here. She's quite the actress, hawking her dragon kites and Frisbees like a pie seller on the streets of London. She keeps a good stock of both on hand at the Dragon's Lair for her B and B customers' children. She had this idea, and I went for it. The look of 'cashing in' just adds to the general air of tactical publicity, raising it another notch toward the ultimate faketastic rip-off."

"One of the bigger news crews pulled away just after she set up her booth. I think it's working."

"It makes me, as the owner of the Phoenix, look greedy, though, doesn't it?"

"Bronte, always remember that even negative publicity is good publicity. Pay attention, because soon you'll see other tourist spots trying to cash in, or tout their own supernatural being. Call it advanced marketing, Salem style."

"I suppose you're right," Bronte said, frowning and chewing the lip that Darkwyn wanted so badly to kiss.

TWENTY-EIGHT

Because they needed to close Fangs for the Memories to tourists on time, tonight especially, Bronte sent Zachary to tell Bastian and Jaydun not to let anybody else off the trolley and to put the END OF LINE sign behind the customers already in line.

Finally, at dusk, with a half hour window before Ogden and Vivica planned to open Drak's to the vamps, and while the fairgrounds staff prepped for the evening shift, a small group of wedding guests took their places on the beach by the fairgrounds.

Bronte looked forward to meeting Darkwyn's family: Jaydun, his best man, Bastian and his wife, McKenna. But from inside, she saw Rory MacKenzie, friend and carousel carver, alone among the guests, which made no sense.

She guessed she'd find out why Rory came *without* Vickie after the wedding, though she'd much rather have her friend beside her. Meanwhile, she flipped the switch to light the fairgrounds with thousands of colored bulbs.

Vivica came in carrying a box.

"I don't know if I'm doing the right thing," Bronte said.

Vivica opened the package and set a lovely vintage fingertip veil on her head. "This is from Vickie, especially for you from The Immortal Classic."

"It's beautiful, but—is Vickie stuck there at her vintage dress shop, and unable to come? Because I saw Rory outside."

"One question at a time," Vivica said. "You don't know if you're doing the right thing? Do you love Darkwyn?"

Bronte shivered, worried about what she was getting him into. "I'm afraid to. Loving him could kill him."

"But you can't help yourself?"

"What if I'm just bringing him into danger and he dies because he wanted to marry me? Why, Vivica, does he want to marry me? It can't be just to give me a green card?"

Vivica looked up from the veil. "What green card?"

"The one you gave him that made him legal, of course, to make me legal when I marry him."

"Sit," Vivica said, and she sat, as well. "Bronte, the only green card I gave Darkwyn was my business card. I'd need to do some research, but I'm not sure the holder of a green card can make a spouse legal."

"We're marrying for nothing?"

"I wouldn't say that." Vivica took her hands. "You've never confided in me, but I'm a good judge of character, yours and Darkwyn's. Darkwyn is marrying you because he wants to be here for you. Because he wants *you*. He's no dummy. You're a prize, Bronte McBride. A real catch."

"A catch!" When she so desperately wanted *not* to be

caught. "I'd laugh at the horrid pun, if I didn't want so badly to cry."

"I'll have to ignore that. Biting my tongue on my curiosity comes with the job description."

"Zachary and I are running from the mob," Bronte admitted. "So if anything happens to one of us, you do what you have to do to take care of the other, please? And keep this between us."

"I hear you, and I'll keep your confidence. But if you're trying to protect Darkwyn, he's a grown man. He knows what he's doing. Haven't you heard? He's a famous and powerful Vampire Dragon. And he's yours."

Nausea rose in Bronte. "What does that mean?"

"It means this is the best life he's ever had, because of you, despite any potential danger from either direction, yours or his. You're his other half. His heart mate, and that means a lot where he comes from. He cares deeply for you, Bronte."

"I wish I could believe that, though he's so . . . special. But I'm not lovable. I'm not."

"He watches you all the time, winces if you bump your knee, melts if you glance his way. He'd give his life for yours."

"*That's* what I'm afraid of."

Vivica stood and went back to arranging her veil. "Your groom is hero material. What we all want in a husband. He knows the real you and he wants you, anyway."

"But he *doesn't* know the real me. I need to tell him before he marries me—a full disclosure—so he knows how dangerous saying 'I do' could be for him. Vivica, will you send him inside for a minute?" So he'd know, before taking a wrong step, that winning her was a battle lost before it started.

Vivica went to get Darkwyn while Bronte paced. "I'm a fake!" she said as he walked in.

He cupped her shoulders, brought her a hairsbreadth closer. "I know you are not a *real* vampire."

"No, it's worse than that. My name is fake. So is Zachary's. We're running from the mob."

"I can protect you from a mob."

"Not a mob. *The mob.* One of the Canadian families."

"A mob is like an army, no? I've fought armies with skill, and I wasn't half so strong back then."

"No. No, you don't understand. Mafia? Mafioso? Mob. *The family.* The godfather?" She huffed at Darkwyn's blank look. "My stepfather, Zachary's stepgrandfather, is the head of a mob family. He lends people money, and when they don't pay him back, he murders them for kicks. Zachary and I, we know too much. We have to be eliminated."

" 'Eliminated.' "

"Listen, Darkwyn, let me put it this way. My tattoo, the sword in dragon wings, it's a symbol of my need to slay my past, mine and Zachary's."

"That explains why you got a dragon slayer tat before you knew I existed. Now as for your stepfather wanting to eliminate you. That means push you aside, right? Why not just leave you here, then?"

Darkwyn so didn't get it, but why would a gentle dragon who ate his food "still kicking" understand the feral brutality of the mob? "No, listen, Darkwyn, Enrico Sanguedolce, my stepfather, married my mother, Zachary's grandmother, and he murdered her, too, among so many others. You're not safe, Darkwyn, if you stay with us. Go be a dragon man somewhere else. I'm letting you off the hook."

"Hook?" He looked above them. "I see no hook."

"Do you know what *sangue* means? Blood. And *dolce* means sweet. That's my stepmonster's motto. Blood is sweet."

Darkwyn brightened. "So that's why you opened a vampire haunt, to go with your name?"

"Wha—No! That is so *not* meant to be my name."

His eyes twinkled.

Was he about to tease her at a time like this?

"What care I for blood? I told you, Bronte, blood doesn't make me faint." Darkwyn took her in his arms like he . . . cherished her. "I was told that I would find my heart mate here on earth. That she would not be easy to find, or keep. And I found her—you—within minutes of arriving, then I feared I'd see a heart mate in every female, but no. No one else, that day or since, has a heart that speaks to mine, only the woman who mocked me and then ran from the power of our connection. You knew right away, too, Bronte, did you not, that we were heart mates?"

"No." She turned her back on him to give herself strength. "No, you're wrong. Go now, before you get killed for that naïve, if generous and open, heart of yours."

He embraced her from behind, pulled her firm against him, her back to his front, his hands poised oh so carefully, almost *beneath* her breasts. "Away from you I will wither and die," he whispered, warming her ear with his hot breath, her dear dragon, "and I do not just mean that my physical need will wither. The rest of me will, too. My heart especially. And my soul."

"At the moment," she said, her voice cracking, "I rather doubt your ability to wither." Bronte half sobbed, half laughed. "There's another problem, and this is the worst of it: Darkwyn, I can never really love you."

"I do not ask you to. I do not know the meaning of love. We are alike, you and I, bruised hearts encased in stone. Love? What is that? How can you miss what you never had? I accept the lack. You should, too."

"No, I'm dangerous. Seriously. Everyone I love dies. Dad. Mom. My sister, Brianna, even Gina, who was like a grandmother to me when I was little."

Darkwyn cupped her face. "You still have Zachary."

"And sometimes I'm *afraid* to love him, too, but I do love that boy, and, Darkwyn, Zachary comes first always, before you I mean, even if you and I marry. Do you understand?"

He tilted his head, even his mouth tilted, his eyes bright and all for her. Eating her up with his gaze, she would say, and liking it, the dolt. She huffed. "Why are you still standing there? Most men would have run by now."

"I understand you better than you think. I see no problem. And there is the leaping, which is very fine, indeed. Can we get married now?"

"Dumb damned dragon!" She stepped into his arms, and he brought her high so he could bury his face between her breasts. She wrapped her legs around his waist to hold on and revel in the touch of his tongue against the tender skin of her breasts. "My best feature, my breasts," she said. "I call them Sugar and Spice, because they're everything nice."

"Mmm." He came away with glazed eyes. "You are everything nice. *You* are your best feature. Wedding now, please?" His eyes opened wide. "And Bastian has been telling me about something called a honeymoon. I cannot wait."

"You looked that word up, didn't you?" Did he ever look like an old-world rake right now. If she were a Regency virgin, she'd swoon at the sight.

He slid her down his body until their lips were inches apart, and he kissed her with ravenous hunger, almost as hungry as she was for him. His gentling of her, so tender and sweet, made her forget why they weren't outside getting married already.

He set her down. "May I have the honor of escorting you to the high priestess who will perform our wedding ceremony?"

"I don't want to put your life at risk, and I don't need you, I don't." She fisted her hands against his chest.

"Yes, you do, and what's more, you want me. You need me and you want me. I am grateful."

"More importantly, Zachary needs you. I am marrying you for Zachary's safety, and for no other reason. Just remember that."

"Whatever you choose to believe, and choose to deny, especially to yourself, is fine with me, as long as your answer is yes." His kiss calmed all her doubts, disappeared them in a magick more powerful than she'd known, more powerful than Jagidy and flying cats, until only they existed, and they *must* be together . . . for Zachary.

She toyed with a button on his vest. "In a physical way, I guess I do *want* you," she admitted, "but, Goddess help me, I shouldn't be so weak."

"Are you finished fighting with yourself now, my Bronte?"

"You should know that I can be weak *and* stubborn."

"I think I knew that." He offered her his arm. "Wedding anyone?"

"Don't say you haven't been warned."

"I never will."

They stepped outside, arm in arm, and the carousel music began. "Smile, Smile, Smile," came the Wurlitzer organ recording. "Pack up your troubles . . . and smile . . ."

If only she were certain this wedding wouldn't make all their troubles that much worse.

TWENTY-NINE

Bronte screamed when they got outside, and Darkwyn went on alert, until his bride threw herself into the arms of the woman waiting to marry them.

"Vickie, you're our high priestess?"

"Surprise!" Vickie said, embracing his bride a second time.

"Darkwyn." Bronte took his hand. "Vickie is one of my dearest friends. This is her husband, Rory MacKenzie. He carved our mythical carousel figures."

Darkwyn shook hands with the husband of the high priestess, not pretending to understand the rules of this place, this Salem, where he landed, just happy to have Bronte in it.

"My sisters," Vickie said, "insist on giving you a wedding reception at Paxton Castle on a date to be determined, with Melody, Kira, Vivica, all their families, and Darkwyn's."

Bronte bit her lip, her eyes bright.

Lots of emotion at a wedding, Darkwyn thought.

"How kind," Bronte said, her voice wobbly.

Vickie arranged him and his bride to stand side by side facing the water while lightning played over the cove—a reminder of Killian's power, of her hold on him—maybe on Bronte, too, with them married.

As Vickie prepared to begin the wedding ceremony, Darkwyn held up a hand. "A minute," he said, pulling Bronte from the center of their guests and toward the carousel. "Killian, my enemy, I just realized, will likely become yours, now, too, if we marry. You have to know that before we take another step."

Bronte cupped his cheek. "An even playing field, both of us with dangerous baggage. I suppose we could join forces and fight our enemies side by side."

"As it is meant to be," Darkwyn said.

"Destiny," she agreed. "I have never been surer."

They returned to stand before Victoria Cartwright MacKenzie, high priestess.

Enhanced winds brought a swirl of autumn leaves that appeared to bless them with a wash of color like confetti.

Scorch sat in a tree not too far distant and hissed when Darkwyn glanced her way.

Lila, on the other hand, stood between them wearing a collar of glistening flowers. And why they glistened, Darkwyn had no idea. Unless . . . Andra, Sorceress of Hope, chose to inhabit the lilac point for her stay on earth, as Andra had come as the faery Dewcup to Bastian. It followed that she could have chosen a cat because Killian did. He might never know for certain, but, in this case, Lila's, or Andra's, location and stance at this crucial time could be a matter of seeing them through the ceremony and protecting them from Killian's tricks.

Almost on cue, as if the kitten read his thoughts—which Andra could—she meowed and licked a paw. Well, if his white magick sorceress guardian was using that cat as a guise, she was not giving herself away.

Victoria straightened, her full-length gold robe reminding him of Roman royalty. In his honor, Darkwyn imagined, she wore ancient gold dragon jewelry, and in Bronte's, she donned a gold mask before opening her book. "Let us begin."

Puck, on a branch well above Scorch, fluffed his feathers. "Marriage," the bird squawked. "The state or condition of a community consisting of a master, a mistress, and two slaves, making in all, two."

Vickie raised her head toward the bird, and blinked. After that, Puck's beak worked but no sound emerged.

"Darkwyn," the high priestess said, "please raise Bronte's veil."

Darkwyn did, wishing he could remove her mask as well, but he pushed negativity aside. If a mask added to her comfort and security, so be it. "Wait," he said, requesting his gold mask from Zachary and putting it on. "A mask for the Master Vampire to show his bride that he accepts her in every way."

Bronte grabbed his hand and squeezed.

What did she really mean by the "mob," the "mafia," and so forth? he wondered, planning to look on the computer, later. After the honeymoon.

At Vivica's suggestion, he wore his tux, without the cape, while his bride looked gorgeous, as always, and lovable and kissable and—

Later. He would think about that later.

He took Zachary's hand and brought the boy to stand beside them. "You belong here. We're family now."

Zachary's nod revealed a vulnerability Darkwyn had

never seen, as if a true twelve-year-old peeked through. After the ceremony, he would talk to the boy and clarify his plan to make life better for all of them.

Colored lights behind them, and lightning claws before them, almost dancing above Cat Cove, made the ceremony memorable and blessed, despite the threat, which Killian the evil sorceress must despise.

As Vickie spoke about the depth of their commitment, a short-lived spray of rain brought the moon from behind the clouds to reveal an evening rainbow, brighter with lightning—odd that—while the mist glistened like stars and dissipated so fast, they stayed dry. Magick, no doubt— enough magick to make a grown dragon shiver in his man shoes. Enchantment all around, from Andra or Lila, or even Bronte, or Victoria the high priestess.

The lightning danced closer, until Lila the kitten stood on two feet, turned in a circle between them, and the bright threat dropped back, far into the distance.

Scorch hissed and circled their legs, but Lila hissed, too, showed her claws, and Scorch howled and ran.

Darkwyn turned his attention to the ceremony.

Every interruption, whether white magick or black, or somewhere in between, made him fear this wedding would never take place.

Worry not, my Darkwyn, came a telepathic comment. Andra!

You will have your heart mate. It lies only with you as to how long you can keep her.

THIRTY

*How long he could keep her. The words echoed in Dark-*wyn's head and put an ache in his heart as, with a trembling hand, he slipped a ring swirled with diamonds on Bronte's finger.

A ring bought with part of the proceeds from the raw diamond he'd brought from the Island of Stars. For the necessities, according to Vivica. He would have picked a plainer ring but he appreciated her purchase on his behalf. "The ring is nearly as beautiful as its wearer," he whispered, knuckling Bronte's cheek.

What mattered was their marriage, not their possessions. He did not want to become a human collector of objects. He would rather collect people. Friends. Family. Like his brothers and their heart mates, and most important, Bronte and Zachary. Perhaps even children of their own . . . if he could manage to keep her.

He would move heaven and earth, do everything and anything in his power to keep her, he vowed.

No longer trembling, but comforted by the prospect of their future together, he looked into Bronte's violet eyes before he spoke the words that would unite them, husband and wife for eternity. He meant each from the bottom of his heart. But Bronte's eyes overflowed.

"This cannot be good. Do not cry," Darkwyn whispered, bending to kiss his bride's tears away.

"I'm crying from happiness," she responded, a chuckle rattling through her raspy words.

He kissed her ear. "Is that not human contrariness? 'Crying from happiness?'"

"Yes," she said, letting him dab at her tears with a tissue from Vivica.

"Still, give me the honor of claiming your happy tears," he said. "There. All dry. Now, say the words that will make you mine."

She spoke them, and beautifully, her eyes bright with joy. He said nothing because his throat seemed clogged with *her* tears. How odd.

"By the power vested in me by the State of Massachusetts and the Life Wisdom Circle of Salem, Massachusetts, and Caperglen, Scotland, I now pronounce you husband and wife."

Guests and fairgrounds workers applauded, and the Bite Me chef produced a wedding cake, as people surrounded them with congratulations. They accepted thanks, shook hands, hugged, and Darkwyn made new friends.

"I never imagined you could make it so special, Vivica," Bronte said, "and to have Vickie officiate when I didn't know she was home from Scotland. Well, it was perfect."

"And so will your Paxton Castle reception be as soon as

you're ready," Vickie said. "Harmony, Destiny, and Storm forced my promise to make you agree."

Bronte slipped her hand in his, Darkwyn noticed. "We agree," she said. "Don't we, Darkwyn?"

Bastian laughed. "She's already speaking for you, brother." His McKenna, smiling, too, shoved his arm.

"We agree with thanks," Darkwyn said, planning to look up the meaning of "reception."

Zachary whispered something in Bronte's ear, and she nodded. "Absolutely." She removed her hand from Darkwyn's as easily as she'd placed it there. "This is a celebration after all. I'd love to see the two of you go up together."

Zachary slipped his hands in his pockets and toed the dirt like a real kid. "Darkwyn, do you want to come for a ride on the coffin wheel with me? I always personally escort VIPs."

"Is that another word for vampire?"

Zachary chuckled. "It means: very important people."

Ah, a gesture of welcome and acceptance from Zachary without the proud boy having to speak the words. "I'd be honored to ride your invention with you."

They got on the coffin wheel with Zachary explaining that he'd turned twenty eco-caskets into seats for up to four people each, to conform to amusement ride codes. "Real caskets would have been too heavy and we couldn't have fit them properly with crash bars."

"I see." Darkwyn did not miss a word, because he had the sense that the boy had something of great import to impart and not only about this modified amusement ride.

"When Bronte called you back to the house right before the service, I figure she told you about Sanguedolce and the mob, right? I knew she couldn't bring you into the circle of fear—by that I mean, we have targets on our backs—

without giving you a chance to run. She's worried about you. She warned you away, didn't she?"

"She did. For my own safety, she wanted to let me go."

"She wasn't kidding. They're killers, you know."

"Why are they after you? You and Bronte are family, are you not?"

Zachary chuckled. "Everybody is family to the mob except, maybe, relatives. I became one of them, twice, both times as a child."

Darkwyn tilted his head, and Zachary held up a staying hand, so Darkwyn held the many questions tumbling around in his head.

"My father," Zachary said, "worked for them, so I got the job by default when I became a man—"

"But you are only a—"

"Ever heard of reincarnation?"

Zachary was born an old soul.

THIRTY-ONE

Zachary watched him closely, Darkwyn noted, so he tried not to show his reactions.

"Do you understand the concept of reincarnation?" the boy repeated.

"Yes. I find it fascinating." *Shocking but fascinating.* "Tell me more." Darkwyn waited, glad for a chance to listen and fit the pieces together.

"I had a hard time stomaching my position working for the mob. I knew about every kill, and I don't mean for food."

"What job did you do?"

"Little bit of everything. I became the record-keeper, like my father before me, but soon they caught on to my inventive talents and I fabricated, well, torture devices, for lack of a better word, and for me, things got worse. Sanguedolce is ruthless. He's got an insatiable taste for blood, and not to drink like vamps. He needs to spill it to get high. I started taking pictures of my inventions, and when I could, I took pictures of the bodies, to keep with my personal set of records, and I hid them away."

"Sounds like a dangerous game you were playing."

"When I got approached by the RCMP—those are the good guys, the Royal Canadian Mounted Police—I agreed to spy on the family."

"That must have put you in grave danger." Darkwyn wondered how Bronte and this twelve-year-old boy fit into a story being told as if by an adult, and someone other than the boy before him, but he could wait.

"One night everything came to a head," Zachary said. "The family, also known as the mob—the killers to be precise—were on to me. That was the night I had planned to turn everything over to the RCMP. Bronte's sister, Brianna, had walked in on me pulling the evidence from the attic rafters. She was nine months pregnant with, well, me—the twelve-year-old you're looking at."

Darkwyn sat forward, feeling a frightening tension radiate through him. "What happened?"

"They didn't care that Brianna, soon to be my mother, was in the room. I was a traitor, they said, and though they never saw the evidence, which I'd slipped back into the rafters, they slaughtered me right there. Brianna witnessed my death and was so traumatized, she went into labor.

"I died a slow death, but I passed a split second before Bronte delivered Brianna's baby. One minute I was looking down at my dead body, the next, I was in Brianna's weak arms, being told how much she loved me. People who study reincarnation call the process from which a soul leaves one earth suit to enter another 'ensoulment.' Before long, Bronte took me from Brianna and held me while she cradled us both, and watched her sister die."

Darkwyn swallowed hard. Here was a boy talking about witnessing his mother's death at his birth.

Darkwyn had never known Brianna, but he hurt for what Bronte—his wife—must have gone through at losing her sister. "How and when did you and Bronte get away from them?"

"Oh, not for years. Bronte raised me as her own, but before long, she figured out that I knew things a kid shouldn't. She told me to keep quiet, but toddlers ramble. After I wised up to the reactions I was getting from Sanguedolce and his men, I shut up. Most people don't keep the memories of the people they once were, but I did, big-time. I built this coffin wheel with *his* knowledge, not my own."

Darkwyn squeezed the boy's shoulder. "How does it work? Do you have two people in your head?"

"No, we're one, but sometimes I act more like an old man than a boy, like after you and Bronte shared a bath. I wanted to punch out your lights."

"Punch out—I have no lights. Explain."

"Beat the crap out of you."

"Oh, well, I can see why you would have the need to hurt anyone who hurt Bronte, but I would protect you both with my life. This I promise. Or you can punch out my lights, if you wish. I would let you. How long have you two been running from Sanguedolce?"

"When I was ten, I went digging around in the attic for the evidence my old soul hid. I knew it was there somewhere, and I got caught by Sanguedolce, though once again the evidence stayed hidden. For all I know, it's still there."

"You would be dead, if he saw it, yes?"

"Yes. At some point, he started asking dangerous questions, and once he started, Sanguedolce was always full of curiosity about me. Meanwhile, a rival family planned to take over the Sanguedolce family, and Bronte caught wind of it. I told her who to call in the RCMP—I remembered old Zachary's contact—and a group of special agents whipped us out of there and got us across the border to the U.S., then they washed their hands of us."

"What did you do?"

"Whatever Bronte told me to. She took it from there. She got us here on her wits and the money she stole from Sanguedolce."

THIRTY-TWO

Bronte stole money. Darkwyn smiled. She stole from killers to save her nephew. Bless the resourceful Vampiress; he adored his gutsy bride. "Tell me more about the old man inside you."

"He's an ancient soul, I suspect, a mystical traveler, through no fault of my own, and I mean that literally. Despite the fact he and I share this body, I'm comfortable in my skin, and tend to mock my double-minded self. Because of him, I'm well aware that I'm a fly speck in a universe too vast to imagine. I have clear priorities, specific intentions, and strong motives—staying alive, and keeping Bronte alive as well. Oddly enough, I seem to be growing older and younger at the same time, which can be confusing as well as exhilarating."

"You handle it well. I'm not sure I could."

"If you're telling the truth, dragon man, I should think that you'd understand me better than anyone."

"You're right. I could and I do handle pretty much the same. I went from being a centuries-old dragon to being a man in his, I don't know, late twenties/early thirties?"

Zachary examined him and then raised both shoulders. "Beats me. I'm only a kid, but speaking for the old man in me, life is a roller coaster. I feel happy and guilty to be alive, but horrendously sorry that my memories got Bronte in this kind of trouble. I wish I'd shut up as a kid, like she told me, but hey, I didn't know better."

"I can relate."

"Earlier I was especially sorry because my actions forced her into marrying you to save us, but I'm rethinking that. Don't get cocky, now. I haven't decided yet whether to be glad or sad about this turn of events."

"Just know, I'll do my best to keep you both alive, so you can be glad we got married."

One nod. "Appreciate it."

"It occurs to me," Darkwyn said, "that both our memories got Bronte in trouble."

Zachary seemed taken aback. "Ah, you're right. So they did. Are we somehow karmically related, do you think?"

Darkwyn ruffled the boy's hair. "Not unless I reincarnated from your centuries-old, hundred-or-more-great-grandfather."

"Not bloody likely. Though, the Sanguedolce family is basically from Rome, way back, I wasn't related to them." Zachary looked down at the view. "I love seeing the world change from up here. If it weren't for my quizzical nature and thirst for knowledge, I'd probably have lost my mind by now. I'm incurably nosy, philosophically inclined, and I value intelligence more than most."

Zachary gave him a bold eye to eye. "Which is one of

the reasons I grudgingly like you, by the way. I haven't had such a great sparring partner in years."

"Your irreverence amuses me," Darkwyn said. "And it is new for me, sparring with words. In my first life as a human, when I sparred, I used weapons."

"Well, I prefer words over weapons, wisdom with wit, and constancy above all. If I didn't think you intended to give Bronte your fidelity, you'd have the stepgrandson of a mobster to answer to. And I mean in every *bloody brutal implication* you can imagine."

"You have a cynical streak that I find admirable, and frightening," Darkwyn admitted. "I may be ancient but my mind is fertile, and my love for Bronte is genuine and deep."

"Hurt her, and I know a guy," Zachary said with brutal honesty. "Vile, but I was brought up to think that way. Is it my choice? No. Is Bronte my life? Yes."

"Was that a threat? My earth vocabulary covers only about two-thirds of everything you said."

"I think you underestimate yourself. But you'll look it all up tonight. Well, maybe not tonight, because you have a honeymoon to look forward to."

Darkwyn's elation over the prospect was short-lived. He suddenly sat forward, unease washing over him. "Is that Raven Shadow talking to Bronte?"

"Yeah, looks like she's congratulating her."

"Black smoke!" Darkwyn tried to stand in the moving coffin wheel, but he was locked down. "Bronte," he shouted. "Bronte!"

She waved and so did Raven Shadow.

"What's wrong?" Zachary asked.

"Raven Shadow is dangerous. Jagidy is smoke testing her and the smoke is black. See the way Bronte is edging away? She sees the smoke and knows its meaning: danger."

"Raven Shadow could be one of Sanguedolce's mobsters."

Darkwyn pushed back the crash bar, their coffin seat swaying precariously.

"Are you going to jump? I mean, I hear you have a leap, but we're ninety feet above the ground."

In his anger and panic, Darkwyn began to morph into a dragon faster than he anticipated, and if he didn't get off this ride soon, he would crush it beneath his weight.

He lifted Zachary like a babe in arms and leapt to the roof of the Phoenix. That distracted the people down below, even Raven Shadow. "Zachary," Darkwyn said, setting the boy down. "I'm about to lose my ability to speak, so watch me for signals. As soon as I'm a dragon, I want you to get on my neck and latch on to a horn, or whatever you can, even if it's a hunk of skin or a handful of scales. I won't talk, but I will fly, so keep your head down and stay close to my body. You won't hurt me and I won't hurt you. I'm going to get you and your aunt out of here."

"No news vans out front for the first time today," Zachary said. "Luck might be on our side, because you'd make a hell of a news item."

Darkwyn nodded. His voice was going, but Jagidy's smoke had paled, which meant that Raven was no longer focused on evil. Good, that would buy him time. He leapt, again, carrying Zachary to the far end of the roof, away from the watching crowd. He crouched low as his final transformation was about to take place.

Pain shot through him, his wings stabbing through their muscle sacs, his hands growing nubby and clawlike.

"Whoa," Zachary said, backing up almost too far.

Darkwyn swiped the teetering boy off the edge of the roof and gave him a little shake for his carelessness.

"R-ride you, right," Zachary said. "Boy, I'm glad I got to see this." He scrambled around to try and climb on.

Darkwyn laid down a wing like a ramp, his scales steps for Zachary to climb to his neck. When he felt the boy grab hold, Darkwyn swooped from the roof, down in Bronte's direction, and just as he did, Raven buried a knife to the hilt in Bronte's chest.

THIRTY-THREE

Bronte's pain seared Darkwyn like a fire in his chest, the shock to her system a shock to his, and her need to call out to him like an emotional hit with a double-barreled shotgun.

Jagidy had already taken to healing Bronte, a ray of hope, however small.

The width and breadth of Darkwyn's wings made everyone duck, except for Bronte, who understood his purpose. He performed a perfect dip so his wing claw slashed Raven Shadow from navel to neck.

"Long live Sanguedolce," Raven Shadow said, as her knees folded beneath her, the last words she would ever speak.

Zachary's triumphant shout was lost as Bronte, herself, began to crumple. Without a thought, Darkwyn scooped her into his dragon arms and flew up and over Cat Cove and beyond until, high above the clouds, he leveled off.

Jagidy, still in Bronte's arms, continued trying to heal her, but his small hands were no match for the width and depth of the gash in her chest, nor the blood spiraling and spreading down her violet corset.

Had the knife pierced her heart?

His heart said *yes* with the pain of a thousand knives.

Darkwyn put down on a small island, so small it could disappear in a wave, similar, but smaller than the Island of Stars, except that he could leave here and not die from flying over an endless lava sea until he dropped and burned to a crisp. This, however, was more a matter of life and death than ever. This was about saving Bronte, please! Every moment counted.

Her gash was so deep, he saw her heart, its beat slow, slower, becoming irregular . . . beat, stop, beat, stop longer, beat, full stop . . .

He retracted the claws on his right hand, fired it free of germs, and reached for Bronte's heart.

"No, Darkwyn, don't," Zachary shouted.

With the back of a wing, Darkwyn swept the boy softly aside to give him an opportunity to heal Bronte, sorry he ever studied biology and germs. Saving her only to have her die of an infection worried him as much as the possibility of not saving her at all.

Agony met ecstasy. He willed her to live. He roared to the heavens his dragon demand that she survive. Her blood bathed his burn, warm and pulsing, and exacerbated his own chest pain as he hand-pumped her heart while he worked his finest dragon magick, healing, as he attempted, beyond rational hope, to bring her back to life.

A healer's mind played as much a role in the process as did his hands, so killing the germs from the knife or any foreign object, including his dragon hand, was as important as healing the bloody cut he finally noticed in her heart.

As long as it beat on its own, he carried hope of healing that specific cut. He would have time, later, he believed, to heal the slice in her chest, so wide it bled more profusely now that he separated it to reach her heart.

When the organ beneath his hand seemed to take over, he continued to hold and heal, to catch a beat if she dropped it, and while he waited, and healed her, the organ became bolder in its pulsing, more steady.

How long to wait for steady? How steady was steady enough?

After what seemed an eternity, at the point where Killian's lightning claw teased and electrified the water around them, one zap after another, and as the charged water got closer, Darkwyn removed his hand from Bronte's chest.

She sighed and went limp.

Darkwyn roared his fury to the universe.

THIRTY-FOUR

"It's beating," Zachary said. *"Darkwyn!"* he shouted. "Bronte's heart is beating."

Darkwyn caught himself midroar and burned his tongue with the aborted back draft, but that did not matter. In his arms, his wife breathed on her own. Her heart, nestled in her chest, *beat* on its own. Blood no longer trickled from that organ, though she was losing plenty via the gash in her chest.

They were not out of harm's way yet.

He repositioned Bronte in his arms so as to close the gash.

Zachary stood firm and quiet beside him, the boy's tight white fists relaxing at the sight of Bronte's even breathing.

Darkwyn lowered his wing for the boy to use as a ramp, once again.

Jagidy, Darkwyn said telepathically, *while I fly us to safety, lay your body over the wound, hold tight to keep it*

*closed, and put everything you have into healing Bronte.
I'll finish when we find safe haven.*

Again, Darkwyn rose to the heavens, thanking every
blessed god or goddess known to dragon and man for
strengthening Bronte's heartbeat, and asking for her well-
being, please, to last.

He cursed the lightning that caught up with them, like-
wise the hailstones that followed as the claw of light faded.
A wink of hope, Killian had given him, then, *snuff.* The
evil goddess kept up with them, pelting them with the
knowledge of her presence as certainly as she pelted them
with hail.

For a few minutes, Puck flew beside him, but then the
bird hung back and joined Zachary. Darkwyn felt exactly where Puck's claws dug into him. "Meander," Puck
squawked, and Darkwyn with his dragon hearing missed
not a word despite the hail. "To proceed sinuously and
aimlessly."

Smart-ass bird was right. He did not know where he was
going, and the hailstones blinded him. Killian kept them
small to form a curtain. Larger stones, while more painful,
would have allowed areas of better vision.

Meanwhile, the pain in his burned hand barely compared to Bronte's chest pain, which stabbed at his chest
mercilessly even as her blood loss weakened him.

Zachary must have surmised the navigation problem,
because the boy began shouting directions, and in the event
the brilliant inventor knew where they should go, Darkwyn
followed, until he circled a mountain capped with snow.

He had flown north, away from the ocean, above the
clouds whenever he could, to keep from being seen. One
piece of luck: the moon stayed mostly hidden behind the
clouds. He might attribute that to Andra.

At Zachary's urging, Darkwyn flew downward into the

cloaking tree line, but Killian's lightning followed, splitting trees beside them, forcing him to dodge falling trunks.

"Well, shiver me timbers," Puck squawked. "*Ack*! Look out below."

Darkwyn spotted a hostelry. Dark. Deserted. He went in for a landing, and after he stopped, he looked back at Zachary.

"In late October, nothing's open on Mount Washington," the boy shouted.

This could work in their favor.

With his dragon strength, Darkwyn removed the hotel's main door to get them in, then from the inside, he fired it so the metal of the doorway, and the door itself, melted together and remained in place.

"*Hmm*," Zachary muttered. "Door must be made of steel."

Whatever, Darkwyn thought. In the high-ceilinged foyer, he set Bronte down beside a fireplace large enough for five humans to stand in. Zachary filled it with the wood and kindling stored in a cupboard beside it. Then Darkwyn fired the raw tinder until an inferno filled the hearth and warmth filled the room.

Darkwyn lay beside Bronte and wrapped his wings around her, to further warm her while he cupped her wound to heal her. His scorched hand could wait. Bronte's heart, according to the weakness in his, could not.

Raven Shadow had been sent by Sanguedolce to kill his wife. The world blurred for Darkwyn, then he felt a warmth on his cheeks.

How that happened, he did not know, but, dragon tears, he vaguely remembered hearing, carried a powerful magick, so he removed his hand from Bronte's heart, tucked his head beneath his wings, and let his tears fall on the death slice in her chest.

By all that is good and holy in the universe, let my tears do their magick.

If Bronte died, he would never forgive himself for speaking of his past. He should cut out his tongue, but losing her would wither his heart, anyway. He wouldn't care to have either without her.

Jagidy, Darkwyn silently told the worried pocket dragon, *help Zachary find something to eat, and get him to fix Bronte warm tea or broth.*

As the two left the foyer, Darkwyn willed all his healing powers into Bronte, his hands, his tears, his own life beat. Take mine, he thought. *Stop my beat, but not hers.*

Throughout the ordeal, he tried to keep from shifting back into a man so as to keep his wings around her still wet and shivering body. He would send Zachary for blankets when the boy got back.

All electricity in the building had been turned off, so Zachary put a bowl of broth near the fire to warm; then he let tomato juice trickle down Bronte's throat after capturing it in a straw.

She remained unconscious.

That worried Darkwyn.

Zachary stood. "There are enough canned goods to stay the winter, and I'm going to see if I can turn on the electricity."

Blankets first, Darkwyn thought, using his wing to mime covering Bronte for the brilliant young inventor.

"Right, blankets," Zachary said. "Right back."

Darkwyn watched Zachary leave the room and turned back to Bronte. While her gash healed on the outside, he worried about the depth of it and whether it healed as well on the inside. He tucked his head beneath his wings, and against her chest, again, and he prayed.

Darkwyn woke, still trying to heal her, and realized

he must have fallen asleep, because he had become a man once more. He regretted it; his dragon hands were bigger and covered more of her wound, and his wings had been taken away from warming her, and now she was shivering beneath her blankets.

He tried to shift back into a dragon, but his heart was too weak, after her blood loss. *This has taken a dangerous turn*, he thought.

He had assumed he could shape-shift at will. When Bronte got better, he needed to fly her out of here. But ah, her chest moved more forcefully, just then, did it not? One would think she breathed easier, slept deeper, though her breathing had become shallow.

That could not be good, unless she did it unconsciously to ease the pain in her chest.

He listened to his own breathing, tried breathing deeper, and understood he was right. But he felt a slightly renewed vigor in himself, as well, an improvement since their arrival.

By turns, he tended Bronte and dozed.

The lights came on about an hour later.

Zachary took the bowl of broth to the microwave, then they dribbled the warm soup down Bronte's throat.

"You undressed her," Zachary said, seeing Bronte wrapped in the blanket he'd fetched, Darkwyn's hand beneath the blanket, still on her heart.

"I removed my wife's wet clothes to keep her from catching a chill. Yes."

"Right. Your wife." Zachary shoved a hand through his hair, and then his fist through the fire screen.

Darkwyn understood. "Give me your hand. One minute only."

Zachary did, and Darkwyn covered it, until the bleeding stopped and the cut disappeared.

"Thank you. I'm in control, again. I see that your pain is crippling, I know, because it's Bronte's pain, yes? Sorry I doubted you. I understand now that you're putting your life force into healing her. Thank you."

"Zachary, you're as psychic as Bronte is."

"A curse I inherited from my mother, her sister."

"Not always a curse," Darkwyn said. "Thank you for understanding."

Zachary shrugged. "Now that we have electricity and heat, I'm going to find a hot shower and then a bed. I promise, though, it'll be within roaring distance. Oh, and there's quite a storm whipping up outside. Looks like there are even a couple of twisters brewing. Just thought you should know. Night."

The brewing storm had a name: Killian.

Everyone else eventually slept, or appeared to, Jagidy tucked against Bronte's left side, adding his elder healing power to his, while Darkwyn healed his hand to heal Bronte better, and he stayed awake thinking of ways to deal with the people who did this to his wife. Her people, more or less.

When he finished with Sanguedolce, Zachary and Bronte would never have to run again.

THIRTY-FIVE

Bronte's sweaty back hurt something fierce, as if she'd awakened on a marble slab inside an oven. She threw off her blanket and turned on her side to let a wash of cool air bathe her.

Despite the need, it hurt to move, the mattress didn't give, and Jagidy's squeal became amplified by his panic as he struggled for release. She rolled back to free him from beneath her left breast, both of them sticky with blood.

Now her eyes were open.

Leaving a trail of purple smoke behind, Jagidy gained his freedom, his escape bringing Bronte a jumble of unwanted fears and a jarring sense of shock. She sat up, memories coming to her in hazy bits—pain, anger, darkness, doubt, loss, and . . . defying death.

No, she had not defied death, not entirely. For one equalizing moment of respite, she had wanted death, welcomed it. But Darkwyn, her savior and lover, would not let her go.

Beside her now, his arms an anchor, his hands on her bloody breast, he did not sleep. He kept watch. The relief in his violet eyes eased her panic, almost made her feel foolish for her instant fear. How long had they been here? How long ago had she died?

When did she come back to life?

She no longer needed to fear the worst. It had happened. One of Sanguedolce's finest had killed her. What would happen if she let her stepfather think that was true?

"I died," she said, "but I'm here."

Darkwyn released a shuddering breath. "Well, Vampiress. Isn't that the way it's supposed to work?"

His joke did not lessen the tension in his arms and neck. She stroked each taut rope of muscle, hoping to soothe him, but he wouldn't be comforted. She'd try another tack. "We're naked. Darkwyn Dragonelli, did you have our honeymoon without me?"

He pulled her gently toward him and buried his face against her, his silence speaking volumes, louder than any avowal she could crave. She kissed his dark wavy hair and finger combed it away from his temple, over and over again, giving him time to let go of his fear while she tried to come to terms with this business of rebirth.

"How do you feel?" he asked without lifting his head, his hand absently tracing a trail across what appeared to be an angry scar.

Ah, yes, she remembered now. Raven Shadow with a knife. But where, if anywhere, did Sanguedolce connect to Raven Shadow's actions?

Darkwyn had asked how she felt. Like she'd won over darkness, yet the light was not as bright as it should be. "I feel like . . . Persephone, ready to leave the underworld—the mob—as it applies to the fears I've been harboring for years and running from forever."

"Do you compare yourself to the Queen of the Underworld? Even dragons know that tale."

"I was a happy kid," Bronte said. "Brianna and I both were, and then our mother married Sanguedolce. He's the King of the Underworld who pulled us down to Hades with him. How about you, Darkwyn? Were you sent by Zeus to help me?"

"No." He wiped her sweaty brow and neck with the corner of a blanket. "I was sent by Andra, Goddess of Hope. Though making your goal my own is part of my mandate."

"Close enough. My mother's marriage kept us in the underworld, where we collected our own personal demons and lived the dark side of life."

"Life is not a fairy tale, Bronte."

"I'm talking about hell on earth, Darkwyn. I *know* it's not a fairy tale. I've simply seen the parallels in the myth—lived them—and I'm thinking about using the myth as a road map."

"How so?"

"I have to stop running and ignoring my mistakes, like running in the first place. I need to rescue Zachary and myself. I can't let *you* rescue me. I have to stop being a victim and take a stand."

"I ran tonight, and I took you with me," he said. "We're on Mount Washington in the state of New Hampshire, home to the world's worst weather, according to Zachary."

"Fancy that. A New Hampshire honeymoon."

"Let me help you take a stand against Sanguedolce," Darkwyn begged. "In doing that, you would help me save my brother dragons."

"In that case, yes. As long as *I* am helping *you*."

"I may be a magick dragon, but that doesn't mean I can't be rescued by a damsel, no longer in distress, thank the stars."

"Now who's treating this like a fairy tale?" she asked, tracing his lips and getting her fingertips kissed.

"This wound"—he indicated the angry scar—"is not child's play. It is madness, ordered by the madman Sanguedolce, and unacceptable everywhere *but* in the underworld."

"Granted," she said. "Absolutely. We have to take a stand. We strike, but how?"

He shivered and pulled her blanket up to her neck. "As I see it, we have several steps to take, but first, you have to recover a bit more."

"And," she said, allowing her hand to wander toward that sleepy but amazing part of him, "we have a honeymoon to enjoy."

"Not until you're well."

"I died last night."

"Yes, you did."

"Thank you for bringing me back."

"My greatest moment; my greatest honor."

"I think we should celebrate life. My recovery is progressing by leaps and bounds. What I prescribe for the bride of Darkwyn," she said, "is a *gentle* honeymoon, like a rejuvenation of sorts, *before* I go back to face my demons."

Darkwyn looked doubtful. "You will face your demons *only* with me by your side."

"Don't sound so stern. Yes, from honeymoon to demon moon, we will go. Hey that could be a nursery rhyme."

"I think not," he said. "Let us discuss this honeymoon."

"Let us *have* this honeymoon, you straitlaced man dragon. Who knew? A dragon draggin' his tail."

"I protest."

"Say it with fire and I'll believe you. I want to talk honeymoon in a bed," she suggested, "after a bath. Wash off this blood."

"Speaking of blood," Zachary snapped, sloshing into the vestibule wrapped in a towel, feet bare and wet. "Small green bloody thing? Whistles and shivers the air with yellow smoke? Resembles a dragon the size of Darkwyn's fist?"

Darkwyn gave Bronte a wink. She loved being flirted with by her husband. She also loved Zachary's old-fashioned indignation. "Don't tell me," she said. "You took a bath and our Jagidy got into the tub with you? Dragon magick travels through water, didn't you hear? Now you'll see the wings on our cats and the warning smoke made by the pocket dragon sitting on your shoulder."

"What the puck?" The bird snapped, coming in for a landing and tilting his pretty bird head. "There's a dragon on his shoulder?"

THIRTY-SIX

"By the way," Zachary said. "My room's near the foyer on this floor, if you need me." Her nephew went mumbling back in that direction, dragging the blanket and leaving a wet trail.

Jagidy seemed torn as to which of them he should spend the night with.

"Let's get a room upstairs, so I can scream all I want," Bronte said as Darkwyn picked her up to carry her.

"A *gentle* honeymoon," Darkwyn said. "You're not up to screaming, and I won't do anything to make you."

She laid her head on his chest. "But what if *I* plan to make *you* scream?" She walked her fingers up the phoenix on his chest. "You can frown all you want but part of you is doing a happy dance whether you want it to or not. Get my drift?"

"Cut out the verbal foreplay," Darkwyn said, "until we're out of earshot of the children. And there they go."

Slam. He shut the door before Jagidy and Puck made it inside.

A *thump* and a *whack* followed, and Bronte winced.

"Romance," Puck squawked from the other side of the door. "Fiction that owes no allegiance to the 'God of Things as They Are.'" Puck's running commentary faded as both magick creatures changed direction.

"Rude bird," Darkwyn said. "Zachary is going to have company."

"Poor boy. Jagidy is a major cuddler."

"With you, maybe. And Puck swears in his sleep." Darkwyn carried her right into the bathroom. "Let's get you in a warm, but not hot, bath, to wash off the blood."

"Yes, yuck, out, out damn blood."

"Works for me." He lowered her in his arms while he turned on the faucet to fill the Jacuzzi type tub. Then he lifted her higher in his arms, and took her into the shower to rinse the major blood away, with a handheld shower on a very soft spray.

"Watch the mask," she said.

"I'd like to rip it off you."

"You could have removed it at any time since we left Salem. Thank you for respecting my wishes. If I could explain the mask without sounding certifiable, I'd try. Really I would. I can only promise that it's not about you but about me, and sometimes I'm not certain I understand the depth of my need for it, not entirely, not beyond my obvious need to hide, that is. When I know the time is right to remove it, you'll know, too. I promise."

"I can't ask for more than that," he said, kissing the mask near her mouth, then finding her mouth and losing track of the spray, so they got rained on.

"You wilted my mask!" she said, not minding at all after that kiss.

"Almost by accident," he said, his wink filled with promise.

She shivered, from more than the chill in the air.

"Hold on. You'll be warm in a second. I pronounce you clean enough for a bath. And after your bath, you'll eat."

She opened her mouth to argue but he crossed her lips with a finger. "Food will bolster your strength, or no honeymoon."

"In that case, I'll eat a little something." She stuck her tongue out at him.

He shook his head. "No foreplay until after dinner."

"I hate to protest," she said, "but it's three in the morning."

"You missed dinner, you were so busy dying. God, that makes my knees weak," he admitted, setting her in the warm water.

"Why is the water not hotter?"

"I'm trying to take it easy on your system. Too hot and it'll raise your blood pressure."

"With all you have to learn, you've taken up studying medicine?"

"Zachary warned me not to make your bathwater too hot after your—"

"Stabbing? Anyway," she said. "I thought *you* would raise my blood pressure."

"We'll see, if you're up to it, but I don't want any competition." He knelt beside the tub and gently swished a soapy washcloth around her scar. "It looks like it happened last year," he said, the tension in his shoulders easing.

"*Mmm.* Feels that way." Loving her husband's ministrations, Bronte leaned against the back of the tub and closed her eyes to savor his touch and fantasize about the night to come.

Darkwyn cleared his throat. "Watching you makes me think you're too exhausted for a honeymoon."

She opened her eyes. "*Not*. I'm imagining it. And whether you want this to be foreplay or not, it's workin' for me."

"It's working for me, too."

She reached over and shoved his shoulder. "Go get us a snack, then get in here with me so we can soak and nibble vitamin-rich food and each other. I'm a sucker for my multitasking dragon man."

Darkwyn grabbed one of their blankets off the bed to use as a robe and covered himself, in the event Zachary got hungry and went looking for food, too.

When he got back to Bronte, he set down a small table beside the tub, dropped his blanket, and got in with her. "You're having corned beef hash or Spam for breakfast, my lady's choice, but for now, a light snack."

"Cream-filled chocolate cupcakes? Yes! Where did you get these?"

"From a robot that didn't give them up easily, but I won the fight."

"You beat up a vending machine?"

"When I finished with it, it did look quite defeated. A machine, heh?"

"You're supposed to put money in them."

"Ah. I did not know that."

She opened the package and took a bite, letting her new husband see how much she enjoyed the treat he brought. "Now, this is what I call a feast." She made a sound that visibly affected him, then tested the sound twice more before giving in to a fit of the giggles. "This coming back to life," she said, licking the frosting off the cupcake, "is quite exhilarating."

"You won't get anywhere near as much pleasure from

eating me up with your eyes as you will from chocolate icing," he warned.

"Hah," she said. "I beg to differ. You don't care about my body, do you?" she asked, sitting forward, his answer and expression especially important to her.

"I care a great deal about your body, every delectable inch. I just haven't had enough time to show you."

"No, I mean the fact that I have a pretty full figure."

"You have a pretty *perfect* figure. Were I still a dragon, and I caught you, *after* skipping lunch and dinner, I would not eat you, just so I could look at your amazing curves any time I wanted."

"That's serious."

"I love your height—it is a match to mine—I adore your shape, every arc and bend, and you are so graceful that I feel like a clumsy oaf beside you. You, Bronte Dragonelli, are magickally, seriously, delicious."

"I'm not a breakfast cereal."

"Good, because I want to eat you up all day long. Man or beast, I worship your figure. If my hands were not occupied with healing right now, they would be testing the artistic flow of each and every dip and hollow, until you screamed your delight, or you shouted, 'Enough already.' You make other women look like their bones will poke through their skin. Not for me, baby."

She experienced a moment of perfect joy, rare for her, halved the second cupcake, and shoved one piece into Darkwyn's mouth while his gaze was otherwise occupied with her nipples bobbing in the water.

His mouth overflowing, he raised his brows with dire inquiry.

"Hey, I got screwed out of shoving wedding cake down your throat after the ceremony. Indulge me. Eat cake on our wedding day. Chew for Goddess's sake."

Darkwyn obeyed, his eyes still on the prize: wet nipple a la chill.

Bronte rose on her knees, smeared cupcake filling on her undamaged breast, and aimed the creamy thing at her new husband's mouth.

"No fair," he said, pupils dilating, irises brightening to all the violet shades in a perfect seaside sunset.

While he was otherwise mesmerized by her offering, she took him by surprise and impaled herself on his firm interest, so slick and ready herself, she swallowed his perfect beast with ease.

Darkwyn's eyes widened.

Her sex pulsed. His did, too.

"*No* freaking fair," he rasped. "No f-fairrrrrr."

Darkwyn controlled his hips with every muscle, even the ones in his neck, arms, chest, and back. She felt every taut cord beneath her wandering palms. She moved, and he released a groan, and came for her mouth. He took it hostage, brutalizing her lips with his kiss, and she couldn't get enough. He used his lips and tongue the way he wanted to use his sex, and she welcomed the invasion, his rough hunger a contrast to the gentle pleasure he brought her.

Eventually, his head came up, both of them breathing heavy, and while she read a certain resentment in his expression, probably at her taking charge, she saw enlightenment, as well, before he came for her cream-covered breast. He licked the cream and woke every nerve ending, nipped at her, laved her with enthusiasm, then he tugged and suckled her, pulling nourishment and pleasure from her at one and the same time.

When she moaned, he let go. "I got carried away and you're hurt. I'm sorry, damn it. I did not want you to exert yourself."

"Hey, I'm not moving. Your mouth is doing all the work,

thanks, and tricky dick's pretty frisky, too. I've come several times. You?"

Darkwyn swore, pulled her close, and went back to ravaging her mouth while adoring her with his touch. His right hand did wondrous things, nearly as amazing as his acrobatic tongue. Even his left hand performed a kind of magick as he cupped the side of her scarred breast, radiating warmth and a soothing—

She pulled back. "Are you healing me while you have your beastly way with me?"

"I'm not a beast, you see, because I am not moving or making you move."

She kept her inner smile from her expression. She could not afford to care for this man. "Between the two of us," she said, "throbbing and pulsing against each other, you hung like a bull, my horn sucking your plenty, we're going to have a fi—a fine—honey . . ."

Somehow Darkwyn knew how to make the unexpected cliffhanger last, so she rode the crest evenly, no sharp edges or fast falls, just the slow blossoming wonder of a perpetual orgasm, pleasure roiling through her, no muscles to stretch, just ecstasy everlasting.

And into the silent bliss . . .

A tree fell through the window, starry shards of glass raining down on them, the prickly, pointy top of a Christmas pine like a knife at Darkwyn's throat.

THIRTY-SEVEN

Bronte froze, in more ways than one, but her scream carried no sound while a blizzard rushed in at them through a broken window, sprinkling them with snow as well as glass.

"Gee, you think Killian is trying to tell me something?" Darkwyn got out of the tub, icy air curling around them, but she couldn't seem to move on her own. He lifted her again, like a babe, dusted glass and snow off her, wrapped her in a body towel, and carried her out through the cozy blue striped bedroom she'd been looking forward to sharing with her sexy dragon man.

Silly detail. "*Brr,*" she said, shivering in his arms, hers as bare as his.

He nixed a corner suite because it had "too many windows." But he grabbed blankets from every room he rejected. They settled in a cozy purple room, so lush the walls looked velvet, with a homey quilt to match, and only one narrow casement window near the far wall, opposite side of the room from their king-sized bed.

He sat her in a chair, toweled her completely dry, then wrapped her in a blanket and placed her between the sheets, covering her to her neck with the quilt.

"I should set you free," she said. "I put your life in danger and I swore—"

"I put my life in danger by stealing you and flying away with you. This is not your enemy stalking us, but mine. No setting me free."

"You make a confused kind of sense."

"Warm the bed," he said. "I'll be back to wrap myself around you as soon as I'm sure Zachary is okay."

Moments, or hours, later, he slipped into bed beside her. "Zachary?" she asked, groggy and ashamed of herself for falling asleep, though his relaxed body told her all was well.

"Is fine. You were right about Jagidy. He's a cuddler. When I tiptoed in, Puck the bird started rattling off dragon jokes but Zachary and Jagidy slept through the monologue."

Feeling frisky after her rest, she snuggled into him. "What dragon joke was he telling?"

"What happens when a dragon gets mad?"

"I don't know. What?"

"He gets all fired up."

"Fire when ready," she said, curling his chest hair around a finger. "Darkwyn, were you—you know—as *satisfied* in the tub as I was?"

"How could I help myself watching you?"

"But was it as good for you as for me? Because, 'incredible' hardly explains it."

He kissed her temple and covered her hand to stop its southbound wanderlust. "I got all fired up. Lay on your back."

"Oh, goodie. Time to play?"

He placed his healing hand on her chest, above her wound, and tucked his face into her neck. "Time to heal."

Before she worked up a good pout, he fell swiftly into a deep sleep, his snore rather growly—perfect for a dragon. He must be tired after flying so far, carrying her in hellacious weather, dodging trees, expending healing energy, worrying about her, Zachary, Jagidy, *and* Puck. What a honeymoon. "Rest," she whispered. "We have the mob and an evil sorceress to fight. Together."

Her poor husband.

Husband—shocking word. Forever. Till death do us part.

Death made her think of Sanguedolce. She shivered, and when she did, Darkwyn spoke her name and pulled her close, utterly aware of her. No other woman's name tripped off his tongue with his guard down, his mind sleep fogged. Only hers.

Her turn to stay alert and filter night sounds, hoping none resembled the stealth of an underworld assassin.

Someone knocked on their door. Her eyes opened wide, guilt her first instinct. Some night guard she turned out to be, falling asleep.

"It's me, Zachary. Bronte, you in there?"

"We're here," she said.

"Breakfast is ready. Canned surprise. Wake up the flying machine, will you?"

"I'm awake. I'm awake." Darkwyn sat up and scrubbed at his face with both hands.

She chuckled. "Trying to rough yourself up?"

"I needed a brutal wake-up call."

"I'll remember that."

"No, I was really out, and I'm annoyed with myself for that."

Bronte rose to sit on the side of the bed, aware she breathed easier and felt nearly as bossy as her old self.

Darkwyn got up and tossed something toward the bed. "I found coveralls last night when I checked on Zachary, and you get the only down quilted vest in the place. Wear it against your skin, to protect your scar from the coveralls' rough fabric. Need help getting dressed?"

"Nope, if we ever want to leave this room, I'd better do it myself." She wiggled her brows and he looked stricken by his reaction. "You don't mind my scar, do you?" she asked.

"Me? I'm a regular five-scar production, and I have not heard you complain."

"I like your scars," she said. "They give you character."

"I feel the same. You'd better dress before I have to show you how much you matter to me."

She disappeared into the bathroom, high on the power of her effect on him.

Darkwyn had left the room by the time she came out. The "coveralls" was actually a jumpsuit, but English wasn't his first language. It had been brilliant, and thoughtful, of him to suggest the vest to protect her wound. A gentle man, in and out of bed. Not a bad catch for a woman who swore she'd never marry.

Whoa. What had she done marrying a dragon man?

Bronte stopped before rounding the corner from the hallway into the foyer, to regain her composure and check on Darkwyn and Zachary in the hostelry's self-serve, common, cooktop dining area. Make sure they were really okay, with the situation and each other.

"Really," Darkwyn said, sipping his coffee. "Was the old Zachary Tucker married?"

Bronte was surprised Zachary had told Darkwyn about old Zachary. This made three living people who knew.

"Yes, old man Tucker's wife died young. Left him free to be married to the mob." Zachary hesitated, groaned, and held his head with both hands. "Why didn't I ever suspect?"

"Suspect what?"

"Gina's car accident. The mob wanted all the old man's time and attention, and after he lost Gina, he was so broken, he gave them everything."

That jarred Bronte. She hadn't considered the mob in Gina's death, either. How stupid was she?

"I'm sorry," Darkwyn said.

Zachary smacked the table with the side of his fist. "I could kill th—no, see, that's what they do to you. They turn you to vengeance at any cost, like them. Gina's probably been waiting to scold the old man for years. I hope this reincarnation thing isn't an unending cycle."

"If it is," Darkwyn said, "you might find Gina in this life, in college, maybe, and hey, maybe she'll remember you like you remember her."

Zachary chuckled. "I think I hear the old man snorting. Thanks for pulling me out of the funk I was about to fall into, though."

"Which are *you*, exactly?" Darkwyn asked. "The old Zachary or the young?"

"Funny thing happened on the way to running from the mob. The old guy's name was Zachary Tucker. He had inherited the Phoenix Hotel building—a secret he guarded well, but, then, I know what he knew—so we grabbed the hidden deed before we ran. I took the old man's name as my alias so I could claim the last Zachary Tucker as my great-grandfather, and inherit his building.

"After your reincarnated ramblings as a child, you don't think you gave Sanguedolce a reason to search for Zachary Tucker after you left?" Darkwyn asked.

Zachary flipped the Spam in the pan. "Believe me, my

killer grand-monster was afraid I was repeating something I overheard from one of his men. He watched me only because he wanted to know who to kill. Sanguedolce believed only in himself, his ultimate power and control. In a million years, he wouldn't believe in reincarnation or anything smacking of the supernatural. Ever. Besides, there are like a million Zachary Tuckers on the Internet. Bronte and I hid, literally, in plain sight."

"No problem inheriting the Phoenix."

"Nope. Vivica gave us the right papers and put the building in a trust for me. You know that woman can do anything. Anyway, my signature actually resembles the old man's. Must be a by-product of reincarnation."

Darkwyn sipped his tomato juice and nodded. "How is the old guy with all this?"

"His earth suit may be worm food, but his memories are as sharp as when I lay in my crib counting the tiles in the ceiling."

"Do you ever feel *stuck* in a twelve-year-old body?"

"What better place for a centenarian than inside a fresh, agile body? What twelve-year-old wouldn't want the mind of a brilliant inventor?"

"Invent us an escape," Darkwyn said. "From Mount Washington—in a blizzard that could last for days—to Salem, Massachusetts, *with* an ingeniously stunning preemptive strike on the mob ready to launch."

"I said I was brilliant, not God."

THIRTY-EIGHT

"Speaking of deities," Darkwyn *said, "all of whom I* thank profusely for saving my wife, I need to go see if she needs help. She's taking longer than I—"

"I'm fine," Bronte said, turning the corner. And she was, except for the reminder of the enemies they must soon confront.

Zachary got up and went to the cooktop. "If I had been telling the truth about your breakfast, it'd be cold or burnt by now."

"You know me well," Bronte said, planting a kiss on Zachary's head and one on Darkwyn's lips.

Puck flew in and perched on a brass rail. "Sunflower seeds, over easy."

"A handful of mixed nuts for you," Zachary said, placing them in the middle of a table. "Sass me and I'll give you another shower."

"No sass for badass," Puck said, grooming his feathers. "Do dragons breathe fire?" *Squawk*.

"No," Darkwyn said, pouring himself another can of tomato juice. "They breathe air. Spam all around, Zachary. Need some help? We have to fly out of here as soon as we finish breakfast."

"There's a whiteout blizzard out there," Bronte warned.

"Fortunately, this place rents ski mobile suits. You and Zachary will be warm as toast."

"And our pilot?" she asked.

"Feathers and scales," Puck squawked. "Feathers and scales. *Brr*. Makes you wanna ride in a coffin."

Darkwyn shook his head. "Hopefully I can shift back into a dragon and use my fire to melt the snow for maybe ten to fifteen feet around us, enough to get us above the clouds."

"That's nearly as bad as flying blind," Zachary said.

Puck tilted his head. "I fly blind. Follow me."

Zachary nodded, a half smile on his face. "Puck's right. He may not return to Capistrano every year, but birds have a flawless sense of direction. They have a genetic predisposition to migrate with the ability to sense the magnetic field of the earth. Puck made the trip here. It's in his memory banks to make the trip back. No sight needed."

"I would have that ability if not for Bronte's loss of blood."

"What?" she asked.

"I suffer what you suffer. My brother Bastian says it is normal to feel a heart mate's pain."

"You never told me. I'm sorry."

"It is a blessing. I will always know when you need to rest, or anything."

"Anything?" *Like when I want to make love*, she thought.

"Yes, that," he said.

"What? You can read my mind, too?"

"The closer we get the easier I can read you, but that can be a good thing. When I am a dragon, I cannot talk, but I can communicate telepathically. It would help on the trip home if you could, too. Try opening your psychic mind to mine. Close your eyes and listen. Everybody else in the room, close your minds, please."

"Yeah, right," Zachary said, walking away, his hands over his ears, singing one of the old man's favorite songs: "Fools Rush In." Probably as a warning to them.

Bronte tried to listen for Darkwyn's inner voice. She really did. "I can't hear you, Darkwyn," she said after a few minutes, her emotions mixed about reading him so closely.

"Listen again," he said. "No, do not crumple your face like that. You are trying too hard. Relax and let my words in. Listen with that big beautiful heart of yours."

Why did you run when first our eyes met? That easy, his question came to her mind. She couldn't have made that up, couldn't have anticipated him asking.

She formed an answer in thought: *I knew you would change my life if I let you. I was afraid, and my instant attraction to you scared me.*

I was awed by you. You are perfect and psychic.

Psychic when I least want to be. Like now. Never perfect.

"Yes, you are," he said, speaking out loud and leaning charmingly near. "We communicate well without words." He gave her a look that promised: more to come.

I love you, she thought she heard, an unacceptable sentiment. *Scary words.* Words she refused to acknowledge. An emotion she resisted, love. A non truth. A non possibility. Especially for her.

"You missed something," he said out loud.

"I ignored it," she responded. "Don't think it again. Not that."

How about: I want to see your face, he communicated. *No mask.*

No doubt about it, she "heard" that perfectly.

I promise, she thought in reply, *when I take off my mask, you will be the first to see my face.*

He took her hand and squeezed. "Good enough," he said so Zachary and the pests could hear. "You are psychic, or you would never have picked up on the telepathy."

"I admit, I've thought I read you a few times before this, but not specific words, just intentions. My psychic abilities have always been sketchy."

"Believe in yourself," he said. "We will talk about this, again, when we are home in Salem. Time now to dress for the snow."

"This trip feels crazy," she said. "Flying over clouds in a dragon's arms. Seriously? Fairy tale much?"

"It is crazy, I have no doubt, especially with Killian waiting for us. One thing we have to do midflight is communicate fast. Listen to every word. Mine will be few and filled with meaning."

"I understand." She cared more for this man by the minute and wished she regretted it.

"Leave a note from me for the owner of this place," he said, "care of Works Like Magick, with Vivica's phone number, and tell them we'll pay for goods and damages."

"Fair enough," Bronte said.

"I'd prefer you didn't watch my transformation," Darkwyn said. "The in-between feels ugly, so it must look so. Do this for me. Wait fifteen minutes, then come out."

"You transformed faster at the house," Zachary said.

"Because I was under duress, fearful, and furious. It

takes longer to force a shift, especially in this instance with Bronte's injuries weakening me and my awareness that I'll be putting her in danger again with the trip."

"We don't have a choice." Bronte met Darkwyn's troubled gaze. "Sanguedolce has forced our hand."

"I am well aware of that." He removed the door, causing a general gasp, and left them.

THIRTY-NINE

Outside, Killian appeared to him as a young woman, hiding her malevolent inner crone, but he could still see her black heart. Something of a soulless specter, but with more substance than a ghost, she projected an eerie confidence. Toyed with him to keep him from shifting, her smile enough to make him, a grown dragon, shiver.

He ignored her but she lingered as he took forever to shift, and she screamed her fury when she faced a dragon once more, strong and bold.

In her rage, she aimed bolts of lightning his way, shots of concentrated destruction straight from her fingertips.

Focusing on the force of his connection to Bronte, Darkwyn raised his dragon hands, and bounced ten glowing streaks of live energy back the evil one's way.

With the thermogenic cocktail made by blending her negative energy with his magick and defensive aggression, ultra potent given his heart connection to Bronte, Killian went up like a power plant on steroids.

She disappeared in a black funnel cloud that exploded, a reaction that would make the weather service trying to name and track this particular electrical storm short-circuit.

Yes, he'd slowed Killian down, but he hadn't stopped her. He'd delayed their journey as well. At this rate, it would be dusk before they left, which might be best, flying under cover of darkness.

The sooner they took wing, the safer for all of them. Darkwyn roared to call his family and lowered a wing so Zachary could get on his back. Bronte, Darkwyn would cradle in his arms, the way he brought her here. At least he could limit his fear this trip to Killian.

Not a small worry.

With any luck, he would get Bronte safely home before Killian could strengthen her energy source. Her power fed on her hate for Andra and her determination for revenge against the Sorceress of Hope. Why? Because Andra dared care for the legion of dragons Killian struck down.

Andra, their guardian not only kept their legion alive as dragons, she'd poured acid on Killian's oozing hate-wounds by sending him and his brothers back to earth as men.

That sin, Killian the Crone of Chaos would hold against Andra for longer than his legion could live as men or dragons.

He took Bronte in his arms, close against his body, to protect her from the elements, and turned his thoughts to the positive and enticing, rather than the vengeful and negative.

Comfortable? he asked her, using telepathy. *You don't hurt anywhere, especially your chest?*

"I told you. The wound seems ancient." She stroked several of his scales. "Beautiful sheen, but Darkwyn, you look scary as a dragon."

I am deadly, make no mistake. But, you *are safe.*

"If it weren't for the violet of your eyes, I wouldn't know you," she added, examining his face thoroughly, making him feel like his big ugly lumbering self. "Your lids turn your eyes into slits," she said. "Did you know?"

Limit your words, he snapped. *We fly.*

"Guess that means shut up?"

He did fly, roaring and shooting his fire upward to keep Bronte warm, but not too warm. The clouds were nearer than he expected and before long they rose above and cleared the blinding sheet of snow.

Puck could not take the altitude for long, nor could Bronte, so as soon as they escaped the Mount Washington blizzard, Darkwyn regularly dipped below the clouds.

The world is dark but beautiful from here, Bronte communicated.

He looked straight at her. *It is, this trip.*

Sooner than he expected, following Puck, they approached the fairgrounds, which meant he had taken a terribly circuitous route getting there.

Drak's is dark hours too early, Bronte said.

Wait for me to shift back before you go in. I do not like this dark.

He set her and Zachary down near the carousel where Bronte could sit, rest, and wait for him.

Zachary headed for the water's edge while Darkwyn ambled into the trees beside the cemetery to shift.

It took becoming a man again to realize . . . "Bronte," he called.

"Yes, naked man?"

"You knew."

"I'm surprised you didn't anticipate the problem. Want a utility crew jumpsuit?"

"You have a jumpsuit?"

"Zachary stuffed several into his backpack, in case of a naked dragon."

"I love that brilliant boy."

"Don't tell him. He'll punch out your lights. Here it comes." She tossed the backpack and got him square in the gut. He wondered if she'd slugged him on purpose, but no way could she see him in here.

When he met her, she chuckled. "I would have liked you better without the jumpsuit."

"I *wouldn't* have," Zachary said, falling into step beside them on their way to the Phoenix. "Watch what you say, will ya? I'm an *impressionable* kid."

"Right, and I'm a big lizard."

Bronte elbowed him, and Zachary actually cracked a smile.

"Seriously," Darkwyn told Zachary. "I did not see you over there. Thank you for the jumpsuit, by the way."

"In case of customers, I thought you should arrive dressed," Zachary said.

"Ya think?" Bronte mocked them both, but in moonlight, Darkwyn saw concern replace her playful expression.

"Maybe Vivica and Ogden only kept Drak's open the night we left?" Bronte speculated. "And couldn't come back today. I mean, the place is utterly deserted. Then again, why would the manager close Bite Me early, even if Ogden and Vivica didn't show?"

"Stay behind me," Darkwyn said, going up the porch steps.

The creak of every door echoed in the empty building, or it seemed empty to him. They heard a yowl, likely Lila or Scorch, and followed the sound.

Darkwyn almost wished he still had claws as he climbed upward, except he'd crush the stairs with his dragon weight.

The yowl led them to the Crimson Room where tapestries hung crooked from dislodged rods on red damask walls, and copies of *Vampire Daily* and the *New York Times* had been left scattered about. Casket sofas sat near casket coffee tables, several on their sides.

Lila scratched at the top of a salmon coffee table, her claws bloody. Yowling when she saw them, she jumped down, stood on her hind legs, and pawed at a coffin latch.

Darkwyn unhooked it, and raised the cover.

Vivica lay inside, gagged and bound, hands and legs, eyes closed, body still as death.

Darkwyn lifted her from the coffin, her skin cold and clammy, and disliked her gasp of pain. He laid her on a sofa to take off her gag.

"I know CPR," Bronte said, pushing him aside. "You call 911. My cell phone works here."

Bronte feared she was too late, but Vivica finally began to sputter and cough, at which point Darkwyn tried, without Vivica's cooperation, to sit her up.

"Leave her the way she's most comfortable until the paramedics arrive," Bronte said. "At this rate, they're gonna program the Phoenix into their GPS." She got Vivica a glass of water. "Drink," she said, "though I can get whiskey, if you'd prefer?"

"Water," Vivica said, unable to grasp the glass with her stiff fingers, so Bronte held it to her lips.

"Ogden?" Darkwyn asked.

"Home. He hadn't fully recovered. I asked Jaydun to come tonight."

"Where's Jay, then?"

Vivica's eyes filled. "They shot him, and you know, Darkwyn, what happens when a shape-shifter is wounded."

"He shifts."

Vivica nodded, tears slipping down her face. "The more dragonlike he became, the more he towered over them, the more rounds they fired into him. From the air, he kept looking back but I screamed for him to save himself."

"Don't worry about him. He's probably hiding in some cave healing himself. I'd know if something happened to him. For that matter, I think you would, too."

She bit her lip with a half nod. "I guess I would."

She'd as much as admitted with those words that Jaydun was her heart mate, but he'd leave it alone until she said it outright. "How about you, Vivica? What happened to you?"

"Two thugs dragged me up here and gagged me. As they put me in the coffin, Bronte, they said if I lived, I should give you a message: 'Sanguedolce says your time is up.'"

FORTY

Darkwyn kept an arm around Bronte as they stood on
the sidewalk watching another ambulance leave the Phoenix, this one with the owner of Works Like Magick inside.
Since his acclimator had no visible wounds, he thought it
best for her to see a doctor.

Vivica insisted Bronte stay with her building and talk to
the police, who were now doing a room-to-room, floor-by-
floor search, from basement to attic.

He and Bronte made their way toward the fairgrounds.

Zachary, his hands in his pockets, stood waiting, miffed
at them both for making him stay near the carousel and out
of harm's way.

"He hates being treated like a twelve-year-old, the more
so because of his unique wisdom. He figures he could out-
smart Sanguedolce, if I let him. Let him get killed, more
like. I promised my sister I'd raise him, vowed I'd get him

to adulthood, hale and whole. And despite Zachary fighting me all the way, I intend to keep that promise."

Darkwyn agreed, head and heart. "You're right. He's where he should be."

Before the three of them went back inside, Darkwyn walked the grounds. First the porch, to peek into Bite Me, but the pub and café was empty. When he turned to speak to Bronte, she was gone. Damn, they should have coordinated their search. She must have taken a different direction, but not outside. Darkwyn made Zachary stay by the woods near the cemetery on the opposite side of the fairgrounds until he declared the building safe and free of Sanguedolce's thugs.

He took the tourist route through Fangs for the Memories, fanning out to the storage area for Bite Me. Also empty.

Time to head for Drak's second-floor rooms, but before Darkwyn got halfway up the stairs, he heard several consecutive pops. *Gunshots?*

He ran toward the sounds, fully aware that the cops had guns, too, so either good or evil could be wielding them.

He found a wounded officer in the Green Room, dialed 911, and fielded the usual questions. While he talked, he recognized Bastian's art on the walls. Skinny Christmas pines, tall and pointy, hiding colorful mushrooms, and faeries beneath. An eco-friendly background for the "green" room . . . and death.

With help on the way, he bent to the cop. "Who did this to you?"

"Big bruisers," the cop said, and passed out.

Sanguedolce's men were still here? "Bronte!" Darkwyn shouted. "Bronte?"

In the Crimson Room, two men aimed big guns his way

while night air blew in through a gaping hole in the back wall. A dragon-sized hole. Jaydun's escape route, perhaps?

Darkwyn did as he was told and tried to stay positive. Jaydun could have healed, come back, and taken Bronte to safety. If so, he hoped they picked up the boy as well.

Darkwyn wanted to peek out the side window to see if Zachary was still beside the cemetery, but he dared not. The mobsters, if that's who they were, should not suspect anyone could be out there.

He sent a telepathic warning in hopes that Bronte or Zachary would at the least *sense* danger. *Hide. The mob is here.*

"What happened to . . . the girl?" Darkwyn asked the gunmen as he inched toward the opening in the back wall.

"Dead," one spat, the words a literal knife to Darkwyn's chest. And though he knew logically, as a dragon man, that he would have felt Bronte's pain and the snuffing of her life force, his inner dragon was less easy to control. He fought rage, but his beast became stronger, grew claws, scales, and it fed on fury.

"Another one!" a gunman said.

"Don't shoot," the other warned. "Shooting makes them *mad*."

As the two backed away, Darkwyn gave them a fiery roar before he jumped out the gaping hole.

Gunshots followed, but he hit the ground leaping and reached the carousel without the ability to shout for Zachary and Bronte.

Zachary was gone.

Darkwyn roared, turned full circle, and saw fire shooting from the windows of Drak's. The roof, itself, smoked. Had *he* set fire to the second floor while trying to frighten the gunmen?

But why the roof? There were two floors between Drak's and the roof.

Scumduggers, the wounded cop was still inside—the place hadn't been on fire when he left him—and he couldn't be sure where Bronte, Zachary, or the animals were.

Darkwyn wanted to get everyone out. He had time; it was only a small blaze, well, two, but his heavy, lumbering dragon body would get in his way, not to mention breaking the building, though he could use a bit of dragon strength, now more than ever. Nevertheless, he ran as he transformed again. No matter how uncomfortable, he appreciated the ability, as he stumbled through the shift. His claws became hands. He tripped and went sprawling when his feet transformed beneath him.

He stood and did the safest maneuver in a transformation if you needed to keep moving: he tucked and rolled, and came up a man, naked again, but who cared? "Rain, damn it!" he shouted to the heavens. "Andra, send rain! Please!"

He got hail instead, as if that would stop him. Oh, but wet, mushy hail. Good.

He imagined Andra and Killian working against each other, circling, neither as strong as she'd like. Wet fire-snuffing slush was good enough for him. He'd take what he could get.

He raced up the stairs, and when he hit the second floor, fire licked at his man skin, and he roared more with an agony of soul than body. Where was his family? He jumped through a wall of flames, healing his burns even as he scanned empty rooms.

More flames, more pain, which motivated a dragon, made him madder and stronger—made him turn into a snarling beast, impossible to control.

FORTY-ONE

~

Staying sane over not finding Bronte and Zachary caused the kind of suffering Darkwyn had no power to heal.

While trying to keep his inner dragon from reappearing, he found the wounded policeman, coughing and bleeding, picked him up as if he weighed no more than a kitten, and carried him down and out to the curb.

"I wish you had a big S on your chest," the cop said. "It would be easier to tell the guys at the precinct I was saved by *Super* Naked Guy."

"Tell them you were saved by the Vampire Dragon."

"That you? Okay. I'll leave out the part about you being naked."

"Appreciate it." Darkwyn sat the cop on the curb, turned, and blessed be, Bronte shouted his name. Prickles of relief attacked his limbs as if he might pass out; he'd been that scared.

He turned to the sound, and a jumpsuit flew from the

bushes. He slipped into it as Bronte came running, and a huge weight slipped from his shoulders. He grabbed her and kissed her, and kissed her again. "You're safe," he said. "Thank the Goddess. Isn't that one of Zachary's backpacks? Where is he?"

"I wish I knew."

She grabbed his sleeve in a tight fist. "Darkwyn, find Zachary for me."

"My next order of business. Ambulance is on the way."

"Good," she said. "You find Zachary and I'll stay with our friend here until help comes."

The cop nodded. "Thanks, both of you."

Darkwyn glanced at the Phoenix roof where slush balls the size of his fist landed and smoked the place up. He squeezed Bronte's hand on his sleeve, kissed her quick, and went back inside. Meanwhile, the room where the slush got in through the hole in the wall smoked.

If only the slush could reach the fire inside as well as the gaping hole on the back side.

Darkwyn pushed out the front window, eliminating a bit of wall with it, his dragon strength immense on the cusp of transformation. Now the room gaped open on both sides.

Slush reached the edge of the fire, melted and dribbled toward more flames. It would take a change in the wind's direction to get the fire completely out. "Andra," he shouted. "Help!"

Whoosh, the wind changed, picked up strength, and blew the slush right in. Sizzle turned to smoke.

Darkwyn saluted, and ran up the stairs.

Killian must be tired after his besting her earlier, then the trip home, with all that bad weather. Andra wouldn't usually get this much help to him without Killian stopping her.

He found the family floor empty. Upper-floor apartments, also empty. Zachary was nowhere to be found. Darkwyn shivered at the implications, and let his roar shake the rafters, though he held his fire.

Yes, even as a man, he could use his fire to fight, to warm his family, but he could destroy with it, too. The evidence, a throat-burning reminder of his horrific blunder, a blunder that curled around him in the tendrils of smoke rising from the ashes.

More transformations would be called for. More nakedness, more clothes. He grabbed his things and tossed them off his balcony, cursing his own weakness.

Strengths could turn on you to become curses. Worse than the destruction of the Phoenix, was that the fire might have given Sanguedolce's henchmen the opportunity to abduct Zachary.

"Zachary!" Darkwyn shouted, heart pumping, guilt eating at him, his hope as sturdy and dependable as the air in a balloon.

How could Zachary let himself be caught? Zachary knew things. As a child, he'd fearlessly searched for evidence. He would be an asset in any situation, especially to a man like Sanguedolce, who would want a brilliant enemy nearby, where he could keep an eye on him, boy or not.

Zachary knew that and he would use the knowledge.

That boy had better not have hitched a ride back to Canada.

Who was he kidding, trying to talk himself into believing Zachary was all right, albeit in the wrong company?

The boy had not been tied up and left in the burning building. Darkwyn made sure of that. Right now, he should think about getting Bronte to safety, but she wouldn't go without Zachary.

He'd take another run through Fangs and make sure nobody had been bound and left behind after his earlier check, then he could concentrate on getting Bronte out of here.

The cop and his gun should be enough protection for Bronte, until the ambulance left when she would be alone out there.

"Zachary?" he called as he fast-forwarded through the flames that made their way inside the walls to the first floor. "Zachary?"

Near the spiderweb, he heard shouting. "I'm too young to die. Save me, and these rodents, too."

"Puck!" Darkwyn found the hysterical bird caged in a diorama with Scorch and Lila.

Scorch licked his face, which meant Killian had outgrown her host. The evil sorceress would need her own form to exert full power as their struggle grew. Lila patted his face and stroked his cheek. Oddly, he appreciated the vote of confidence, real or accidental.

Cats in his arms, clothes singed, skin burning, with a parrot who wouldn't get off his head, Darkwyn walked through Fangs and opened every casket, but no Zachary.

Damn, he wished he'd opened the caskets upstairs.

He took the critters out via the front door, and noted that firemen were taking charge. He sent the animals to Bronte, still waiting near the curb. "I need one more look upstairs for Zachary."

She shivered and rubbed her arms. "Darkwyn, I'm scared. Scared they got him."

"Either way, we'll get him back."

"Oh, good. I thought I'd have to talk you into taking me to Canada."

"To Canada and the man who would kill you? I said *I'd* get Zachary back. We'll address your role in the rescue, if you have a role, after I look upstairs. In case Sanguedolce's men are still around, hide in the woods by the fairgrounds, and take the animals?"

"Who's an animal?" Puck snapped. "I'm a bird, a long-tailed parrot of the genus Ara, a Catalina macaw, and I'm bea-u-tee-ful."

"Puck, in any other situation, you'd be entertaining as hell."

"Ex-cuuse me."

"The woods," he said to Bronte, and she blew him a kiss and ran, the parrot flying beside telling dragon jokes.

On the way upstairs, his mind raced. That boy had a spare generation of wisdom on his side. He was too smart to get caught by the mob . . . unless he wanted to be.

FORTY-TWO

Darkwyn opened every casket in Drak's, and destroyed every sofa in his growing panic that the mobsters had stuffed Zachary beneath the seat of one.

He evaded firemen giving the smoking carcass of the Phoenix a final hose down and slipped out the Fangs exit to the fairgrounds, from concession stand to amusement park ride, and on, until he ended up in the cemetery, an ironic place to seek respite.

Darkwyn turned toward a scrabble in the woods behind him, broken twigs, a clumsy step, unsure of what to expect, and his survival instincts kicked in. More than anything, he wanted Zachary and Bronte to step out of those trees, but he prepared himself to face the worst, his heart beating with both high-rising hope and deadly purpose.

A figure appeared, and his heart jumped with joy and disappointment that she was alone. "Bronte, thank God you're safe."

She walked straight into his arms.

One loved one safe, one to go.

Bronte's chin came up as she pulled from the embrace. "We have a problem."

"I know," Darkwyn said. "Zachary is still missing."

"Worse. I found a note pinned to his superhero backpack, here."

Darkwyn stepped away from the possibilities. "What? A ransom note? A mob threat? Did those somebitches threaten Zachary's life?"

"They're son-of-a-bitches. Never learn vocab from a thug. It's a note from Zachary. I recognize his handwriting."

"Read it."

"'Bronte,' it says. 'No matter what, go to Montreal, and DO it. For Mom. You promised.' He capitalized DO, and the stinker's trying to guilt me into it, the same way I guilt him into cleaning his room."

"*Do* what?"

"Get the evidence out of hiding and hand it to the police up there."

"How risky is that?"

"I know Castello Sanguedolce like the back of my hand, or the front of your—"

Darkwyn kissed her. "I'm afraid for you, not me, sasspot."

"Face it: you can't do it without me. Zachary signed 'Zachary times two.' He's reminding me that he's had two lives." Her breath shuddered. "He's ready to let go of this life, if he has to, but he wants Sanguedolce out of business."

"Or," Darkwyn said. "'Zachary times two' could mean that both young and old Zachary want you to do this. Our boy is smarter than the average genius, Bronte. He can take care of himself."

"Sure he can. Until he can't."

"I don't know," Darkwyn said. "I'm still thinking he's around here somewhere."

"He is resourceful. If he's here, and playing us like puppets, and if we go to Montreal, he'll probably go to Vickie and Rory's, or to Jaydun, or Bastian. Even Vivica when she gets home from the hospital would take him."

Darkwyn lowered himself to sit on a cement burial vault and pulled her against him. "If the mob took Zachary, Montreal is the place for us to go."

"Right, and I promised to do it for my sister, Brianna, Zachary's mom, and for countless others. Don't look at me like that. You're not going without me. Besides, you couldn't find Sanguedolce or Montreal, and you sure wouldn't recognize Castello Sanguedolce, itself, because the mansion/castle, whatever, doesn't look anything like a slaughterhouse."

"Bronte," Darkwyn said. "Going seems destined to me, but how does it feel to you?"

"I'd rest easier if we knew where Zachary was."

"Which goes without saying, but while you were out here hiding, did you see anything, or anyone?"

"Oh good grief, yes. I almost forgot in my panic over the note. I think one of your brothers tried to help. A dragon leapt from Drak's and took off over Cat Cove—I can't believe I can say that so easily—then a claw of lightning grabbed the roof until it smoked. That happened right before you jumped from the second floor, also before you rescued the cop."

"Calamity," Puck said. "A more than commonly plain and unmistakable reminder that the affairs of this life are not of our own ordering."

"Bronte, I think you saw Killian strike the building."

"I saw a rather determined bolt of lightning strike, and

not let go, until a fire started up there. Did you think you had?"

"Yep, I sure did," Darkwyn said. "Puck's quote holds true. I may not have started the fire alone, but I am partly to blame. I talked about my past, which turned the world's attention, including the mob, to Drak's. And now, Zachary is—hey, maybe Jaydun has Zachary. Bronte, do you still have your cell phone? Call him. Ask him if Zachary is with Vivica. Or if he knows where the boy is."

Bronte called, asked the question, listened, and hung up.

"That was fast," Darkwyn said.

"Your brother is all healed and at the hospital waiting for a minute alone with Vivica so he can heal her."

"I didn't know she needed healing, or I would have done it."

"Broken ribs. She didn't let on."

Darkwyn growled low. "That's why she had trouble sitting up. Damn. Any sign of Zachary?"

"Jaydun hasn't seen him but he'll join the search as soon as Vivica's set. Bronte swiped at her eyes. "Zachary, damn it, where are you?"

FORTY-THREE

"Bronte," Darkwyn said, "you and Zachary have a soul connection. You'd know if the worst happened. You might be worried right now—all right, scared to death—but he's okay. You know that, do you not?"

"I suppose I'd know if something happened to him."

"Good, so, Montreal? In case he's there, and because you promised?"

"We don't have passports."

"Sweetie, no formalities, which I assume a passport is. You're taking the Vampire Dragon express, but you have to ride up back this time; it's hell on my balance flying with you in my arms, though I love looking at you."

"I'll ride you, dragon boy."

"Don't go getting saucy while I'm in the air. And you have to speak telepathically after this."

"Will do. Darkwyn?"

He stopped in his tracks. "Yes?" He turned for a spontaneous embrace, both of them seeking comfort, holding tight for a long minute. He rested his head on hers, a comforting gesture. "We'll find him."

"Thank you for being here."

He kissed her before he went into the woods to shift. Too soon, he returned as a dragon, determined to let hope sustain him. He lowered his wing for Bronte to climb on, Puck, too, it turned out, and roared his way up into the air headed toward Canada and the man who threatened Bronte's and Zachary's lives.

Bronte, I need directions.

Montreal, Canada, the Mount Royal section. Big mansions. Rich people. Fly over Cat Cove and hook a left. Stay north until I say west. She repeated the directions in English for the bird's sake. "That sound right, Puck?"

"Bien, oui, mon cherie."

Darkwyn looked back. Puck the cock made Bronte laugh. Normalcy amid chaos, like the eye of the storm, deceptively calm, death and destruction pulsing just out of sight.

"I'm glad we don't need to worry about a passport, Bronte said telepathically.

No, but keep an eye out for Killian.

Don't think of her. It's probably like calling her.

Wise woman.

I don't feel the least bit wise. I misplaced my nephew, don't forget. Darkwyn, suppose Zachary's on his way to look for the evidence, himself?

He can't be, unless he found a dragon of his own to ride.

Right, because he doesn't have a passport, either.

"Passport." He really did have to look up that word. But right now, he had to concentrate on not letting himself get blinded by the city lights. Flying by night could be a challenge when approaching a place like Montreal. They would be too visible, so Darkwyn found himself seeking cloud cover.

The mansions in the Mount Royal section, castles nearly, surrounded by well-groomed grounds in highbrow walking distance of Montreal proper, screamed money.

At the Sanguedolce mansion, where the roof would make for a perfect dragon landing, Darkwyn had to dodge a series of moving security cameras. He needed an eye-of-the-storm type moment, now, when all cameras pointed toward gates, walls, driveways, doors, anywhere but at the roof.

It happened, not magickally, but for a natural second. He moved toward the roof fast, landed, and crouched low so Bronte could slide off.

"Here," she said, dropping Zachary's backpack beside him. "I stuffed a couple pairs of jeans and shirts inside that I found below your balcony, but shape-shift twice without thinking, and you're nothing but naked in Canada."

He waved her away so he could turn back into a man without creeping her out.

She stood with her back to him near a small rooftop dwelling. His wife. He couldn't quite believe that.

It took him only a few minutes to shift and dress. He felt almost normal in a shirt and jeans. If only he'd thought of tossing out a pair of shoes.

"Listen, Darkwyn, I'm suddenly sure that Zachary can't be dead. I sense his living spirit with a whole heart, as surely as I sensed his worry that night you climbed my building, and you and I got to know each other, in the biblical sense. Zachary thought you were using me. He couldn't accept that I was using you."

"You were?"

"Best sex ever. I'm not stupid."

"Fine time for you to tell me. Now I want to demonstrate, and I can't."

"You bet you can't, not here. Think of something else."

He looked around. Something else, something— "What is painted on the roof, there?"

"It's a helipad. To land a helicopter? Flying machine," she added when he didn't seem to understand. "Big whirlybird. No wings, or sarcasm, like a certain dragon I know, just a motor and twirly blades?"

"If you say so."

"What's big and black and flies straight up?" Puck squawked. "A dragoncopter! What do you get when you tickle a dragon?"

"Eaten!" Darkwyn snapped. "The bird stays out here!"

"I agree." Darkwyn followed his wife to the small rooftop dwelling, which opened to a stairway used presumably by the family to get to the copter thingy.

"You grew up *here*?" Darkwyn asked, pulling her up short at the top, before they took the stairs, and he kissed her because he needed to, really kissed her, and she returned his kiss with the same desperation, like it might be their last.

No, he thought. That wasn't a last kiss, it was a kiss to hold them until they found Zachary and could take him home. They couldn't give up, especially not in spirit.

"Nice," she said, when their lips parted.

"I want you to understand," he said, "that my life is better, now, with you. I care a whole hell of a lot. You can put your trust in me, though you might not believe it, and Bronte?"

"What?"

"I'd give my life for you and Zachary."

"I think I knew. It's just so hard to believe that anyone would do that for us."

"Believe it. Learn to trust."

She looked over at the lawns sprawling for miles, the indoor pool beneath a glass dome, the outdoor pool, tennis courts, the greenhouses, and crossed her arms in front of her. "Trust comes hard. I know this looks like privilege, Darkwyn, but with a murderous stepfather and the RCMP breathing down our necks—with good reason—it was hell. You've heard of pop quizzes; we had pop searches, not that Sanguedolce didn't leave the police some prime evidence now and again, to throw them off the trail."

Darkwyn took her hand and squeezed. "Doesn't sound pleasant."

"Rival mobsters often tried to show the world they were better than Sanguedolce by trying to kill him, though they usually died themselves. This house has bulletproof windows, a tunnel that leads to a garden shed on the next property, and one to a municipal building in the city. Yeah, Sanguedolce has highly placed friends.

"This is where my sister died at Zachary's birth while the body that previously housed his soul bled out on the floor beside her. That, Darkwyn, was life here at Castello Sanguedolce."

FORTY-FOUR

❦

Darkwyn started to shut the bird out of the stairwell.

"Fair warning," Puck squawked. "'Alone,' means 'In *bad* company.'"

"One of these days," Darkwyn said, "I'm gonna get one bird with two stones."

Bronte smiled. "That's two birds with one stone."

"Yikes!" Puck squawked. "I resent that."

Darkwyn shut the bird out. *Annoying cock*. "Where to?"

"To the attic and back out again," Bronte said. "Three minutes, if we're really lucky."

Inside, they heard a muted voice talking nonstop and identified the sound in a small but large-windowed room, facing the stairs, off a landing six steps down. A guardroom.

Inside, the guard, with his back to them, nodded off in front of a television, an empty gallon bottle of cheap whiskey beside him. "This, out of Salem, Massachusetts," the newscaster on the TV screen said. "A follow-up to the viral newscast where journalist Roger Rudder claims to be interviewing a Vampire Dragon. There he is on your screen— the reporter, not the Vampire Dragon.

The Vampire Dragon is clearly in disguise, and we won't insult your intelligence by showing the interview."

Darkwyn kissed Bronte's ear and communicated the only way they could in here, telepathically. *They think I'm a fake.*

You are. She nuzzled his neck. *Well, half fake. True dragon, fake vampire. And do you really want the world to know it?*

Darkwyn sighed. He didn't like being a fake. It occurred to him that none of them were who they said they were— not him, Bronte, Zachary, his brothers, the vamps, the role players. *It's a fake world after all.* He could practically hear the words put to music. Where had he heard that tune?

"Behind me," the reporter continued after a commercial, "is the Salem vampire spot known as the Phoenix, which houses an eatery and pub appropriately called Bite Me, and a vampire nightspot known as Drak's. After the national attention started by Rudder yesterday, the Phoenix was set ablaze last night, under suspicious circumstances. An investigation reveals bullets embedded in walls, inside and outside, everything scorched around the edges. On the roof, the popular tourist spot seems to have been struck by lightning—talk about the wrath of the gods. The sad turn is that the owners, Bronte McBride and her twelve-year-old nephew, Zachary Tucker, were found in the rubble. They did not survive."

Darkwyn's legs gave, and without choice, he sat on the stairs.

Bronte sat beside him. *I always aspired to be found in rubble. But, of course, I'm not dead.* She rubbed her cheek against his sleeve. *Darkwyn, what about Zachary?*

He smoothed the lines of panic from her face with a finger, one by one, to soothe and reassure her. *Zachary is no more dead than you are. Get with the television show.*

I think you mean program. You believe it can't be him, right? she asked, seeking reassurance. *I mean, like you said, Zachary and I have a soul connection. A living bond,* she repeated for her own sake. *I believe that . . . when I'm not scared to death. Bit of a pun that.*

Look, Darkwyn said. Cameras panned bodies being wheeled out of Drak's on stretchers to the coroner's wagon.

Dumbfounded beside him, Bronte raised her hand to touch her face. *Yep, I'm alive.*

You look damned good for a dead woman. He kissed her, quick, given their location. *Shouldn't we get out of here before the guard snaps out of it?*

He only gets sober on Tuesdays and Thursdays. But yes, let's get out of here so I can collect the evidence and slay our past for Zachary, and everyone else I cared about who suffered or died here.

You cannot admit you loved any of them, Darkwyn said. *Are you hiding shame behind that mask? No, don't answer. I'm trying to figure this out. At first I thought hiding was a gimmick to promote Fangs and Drak's. Then you told me about your past, and I realized it was a device to avoid being recognized by the mob. Later, I thought maybe you wore a mask to hide your guilt for not saving Zachary's mother, or you couldn't look at yourself in the mirror because you didn't save her.*

Bronte huffed. *Your point?*

You're hiding from yourself. You've got to take off the

mask and give yourself permission to be you. To love yourself.

She stood, spine straight. *Too* straight. *Not today, thanks. Today, I have to avenge my sister and find her son, or die trying.*

FORTY-FIVE

Bronte left him reeling with that jarring thought and went to the landing at the turn in the stairs, a landing as wide as the huge Gothic door beside it.

Shaken by her readiness to die in this attempt, he followed and saw her press a series of numbers on a keypad by the door. The tiny light on the keypad turned green. She scoffed. "Sanguedolce is so sure of his invulnerability, he didn't even think to change the code after we left." The door clicked, and Bronte went in.

Darkwyn could now safely assume that attic was a vast expanse where unwanted furniture and ugly statues went to die.

Cameras, she communicated, and covered her lips with a finger. One by one, she clicked switches, and covered each camera lens with flat paper caps well-hidden around each camera. "All done," she said out loud. "The sound's off and the cameras are covered with the exact photos of the angle in the room each camera would view. Whoever's watching the security screens will see and hear an empty, quiet attic, as usual."

"Zachary's idea, I presume?"

"Of course. He was ten; the year before we left. He played up here for hours. Nobody ever comes up, though we forced it once. For the longest time, we let them see us playing with some old non-digital cameras we found. One goon finally came to check, and saw they were empty of film. After that, I managed to sneak a digital camera in. For some reason, Zachary knew how to use it."

"I'll bet he did."

"For getting you this close to killed, I should set you free when we get back," Bronte said as she went to a giant old bed frame, its pieces stacked against a wall, unscrewed a thick-turned bedpost, reached in, and pulled something out.

"Without you, Bronte, I would wither and die, so do not consider condemning me to your notion of freedom."

"Right, because you can't be free if you're dead. We're both gonna die here, you know."

"I beg to differ." And he meant that for all deities in begging/prayer range.

At an ancient dressing table, she removed a drawer, slipped off the back to reveal a cubby with something shiny. She *click*, *clicked* the objects together and looked up at him. "Cartridges loaded. Can you shoot a gun?"

"There was a gun up here?"

She took a faded old jean jacket off the back of a chair, shook the dust off, and slipped it on. "There are lots of guns up here. Zachary Tucker, the elder, expected to die early and hard, so he hoarded some protection, little good the guns did him. Wanna see 'em?"

"The guns or the old man?" *Must stop picturing Zach-*

ary on his way to the morgue. I heartily regret reading about death on earth.

"Not the old man," Bronte said. "He's worm food."

"Worm's meat!" *Squawk.* The sound came from the round attic window. Through it, an upside-down parrot stared in at them. "The finished product of which we are the raw material: Worm's meat." *Squawk.*

"That bird's gonna get us in trouble," Bronte said, "and I don't think he'll be any quieter if we let him in." She went to the window and touched the gun to the glass.

"Puckin' A!" The bird squawked and disappeared, leaving his calling card on the glass. "Didn't poop on the girl . . ." they heard from a distance.

She set the guns on the table. "There's an antique machine gun in that corner. But Zachary and I never played with it."

"Played with? It's a wonder you didn't kill yourselves."

"Learning was a matter of self-defense."

"Scary self-defense. Do you realize what you just did?"

"Scared the noisy bird away? This is a matter of life and death. I had to do something so he wouldn't get us killed."

"Because that's how you were brought up. It's always a matter of life and death here, isn't it?"

She covered her heart with her left hand and raised her right. "Realizing that scares the daylights out of me, but I get it. I'm scared sick. I just held a gun to a bird. I wouldn't have used it, but I'm guessing that's how you get started in this game. You never plan to use it, but the day comes when you're forced to, and you do."

Both hands on her heart, she gave him a compelling look. "Do you still care about me? I wouldn't blame you if you didn't."

Darkwyn opened his arms, and she came readily into them. She couldn't love herself or her family, so she certainly didn't love him, but she needed him, he told himself. And he was okay with that. "You're not quite as ruthless as you think, because you figured it out on your own."

"When you pointed it out. What would I do without you?"

"You don't have to find out. We're married."

"Oh yeah."

"So, do you think you could grab that evidence so we can get the bloody hell out of here?"

"Right." She went to climb a table.

Darkwyn kept from reacting to her acrobatics, so he wouldn't distract her and make her lose her balance.

On her toes, on the rickety table, she felt along the top of a beam and pulled down a book she blew dust off of. After hocking up a lung, she slid the book into a zipperless compartment that formed a false bottom on Zachary's backpack.

Darkwyn admired her determination. "I take it you've been planning this?"

"Zachary has. His whole life. And I paid attention to his plans."

She jumped off the table like an agile monkey. He watched her approach, stop in front of him, raise his T-shirt, and shove a gun in the waistband of his jeans.

Darkwyn swallowed. "Uh, I don't like where that's pointing."

"I do. It reminds me how much power you have." She pulled down his T-shirt to cover the gun and wrinkled his shirt at his waist to cover the shape of it. "Don't worry, it's a prototype, but it's safe and shoots like a dream." She slipped a watch on his wrist. "That's the electronic safety."

"Did Zachary invent it?"

"No, the inventor sent it to Sanguedolce to get backing. But the old guy threw it in the trash. Zachary later got it out and brought it up here. We tested it on the roof. You can buy them anywhere now. Somebody must have backed the guy."

"How does it work?"

"The watch has a built-in electronic safety that disables the pistol when it's not within a few inches of it."

"So when I'm wearing the watch, the gun works for me only?"

"Right. If you're right-handed, wear the watch on your right wrist, and the gun picks up a signal from the watch, lights up green, here," she indicated, "and it's ready to shoot."

"If somebody grabs the gun, but I'm wearing the watch?"

"That little light goes red and the gun won't shoot. So Sanguedolce or one of his goons can take it away from you but they can't use it on you. Of course, they'll have guns of their own."

"Great."

She put a different kind of gun into her corset, neat between her breasts, and it didn't show at all.

"Can you get it out?" he asked.

"I'm betting I'll have time. Inhaling will help."

He chuckled. "I'd like to test your theory in a bed, without bullets, and with lots of time."

She sighed. "Me, too."

"Bronte, don't go taking any chances."

"Not here, I won't."

"You already did. You could have fallen off that table and alerted your stepfather to our presence."

He and Bronte turned on a dime to the unexpected chuckle behind them. "No need to alert Sanguedolce," said a raspy voice. "He is waiting for his daughter downstairs."

Three goons clicked their guns in sync.

What did the thugs do, fly in on silent wings? Eerie. They were not the same men as at Drak's, of course, but all goons looked the same to him. "How did you find us?" Darkwyn asked.

Goon number one stepped forward. "Lightning struck a circuit on our security system, and when it came back on, voila, every screen showed a picture of you two kissing on the roof."

Darkwyn knew then that they faced a double fight because Killian had alerted the mob to their presence.

"Such passion," the goon continued. "Good to know you care so much about each other. We, in the business, call that *leverage*. And we thank you for it." The thug bowed. "Miss Sanguedolce."

Ugly secret, Bronte communicated telepathically. *Sanguedolce adopted me. Do you wonder why I changed my name?*

Darkwyn grabbed her hand, squeezed, and answered silently. *We've already fixed that, Mrs. Dragonelli.*

Don't tell them.

Gotcha. "Whadda ya know?" Darkwyn said to the goons. "Cameras on the roof. You gorillas aren't as stupid as you look."

He got sucker punched for that.

That's it, boys, make my dragon mad.

FORTY-SIX

～

As if they mattered not at all, Enrico Sanguedolce barely glanced their way as he and Bronte were brought to the mob boss's inner sanctum, a room that might as well be papered and upholstered with hundred dollar bills. The man carried the stance of a powerful ruler, tall, straight, wide shouldered, if not robust, his hair a silver white, his heart as black as those of the Mighty Joe Youngs who worked for him.

Sanguedolce focused on stoking the fire in the hearth, probably with a solid gold poker, making the room about ninety degrees. That's where he showed his age, his craving for heat in October.

Ignoring them, well, that was part of his job, Darkwyn figured. Being boss had to be all about control.

His goons were sweating, either from the temperature, or fear. Both good reasons.

Darkwyn figured the man needed fire to prepare for a perpetual stay in hell. He knew only that if Zachary lost his life, this man had ordered the boy's execution. In the same way he'd ordered the death of the man whose name and soul Zachary carried.

Hit me again, Darkwyn silently begged, raising his arrogant chin. Get my dragon roaring. Even with his wrists bound, his dragon wasn't half mad enough to come out on its own. Darkwyn, the man, found himself too numbed by profound worry over Zachary to instigate the transformation alone.

He also needed a cool head in this life-and-death situation, so maybe remaining human for the time being would be best. Still he couldn't help poking the scum. "You live like a king, Sanguedolce. You're touted in your own newspapers as a smart and generous man. Surely you can talk to your stepdaughter without every brute in the house holding a gun on us."

Those guns went higher. The old man made a motion for his men to lower them. "At ease," Sanguedolce said, making another motion for them to put the guns away.

The thugs obeyed—of course they did—and stood looking from him and Bronte to their boss, and back, legs spread, hands at the ready, about ten watts of brainpower between them, and not a one "at ease."

"So, my daughter, you wear a mask? Why now?"

"Always. I wear it always to hide, because I'm ashamed to be your stepdaughter."

The old man clenched his fists.

The situation suddenly felt like a standoff, until a Monet flew from the wall to reveal a dumbwaiter behind it, open, and occupied.

"Zachary!" Bronte gasped.

"Don't move," the boy snapped, halting Bronte's instinctive step in his direction. "Don't turn your back on *them* and don't block my targets."

"Why didn't you stay out of sight?"

"For Mom." 'Nuff said. Zachary focused on Sanguedolce. "Hey grand-killer, did you miss me? Call your bozos off, or I'll show you everything I ever learned growing up here. I've got an arsenal, complements of Tucker, your old record-keeper, who personally showed me this rabbit warren and taught me its every secret. Yeah, I know, he died as I was born. Think about it. Meanwhile, if you hurt Bronte or Darkwyn, I have toys enough in here to make Castello Sanguedolce implode."

"You would implode with it," the old mobster said, paler and looking more fragile by the minute.

Zachary sneered. "I would go happily, if I took *you* with me, though I think we'll go in separate directions."

"You sound bold for a twelve-year-old."

Zachary said something that one of the goons identified as Italian and it made the old man gasp, stagger, reclaim his balance, and step back. His gangsters looked a little green around the gills, too.

"I didn't know you could speak Italian," Bronte said.

Zachary raised his eyes Bronte's way, straight and serious, and his take-no-prisoners look said it all. In those eyes, Darkwyn saw a hardened old man protecting the boy who shared his soul, the boy who shared his enemy. That had surely been old Tucker scaring the crap out of Sanguedolce by using his own language against him, and didn't the old man do a great job.

"Rico," Sanguedolce pleaded.

"I hate that you named me after you," Zachary said. "The thought makes me sick."

"You are only a boy, you don't know your own mind."

"You made a joke," Zachary said.

And quite funny, Darkwyn thought, considering the fact that the boy practically had two minds, his own and old Zachary's.

"No joke here, though," Zachary continued. "I've got stink bombs, tear gas, triple tasers, faithful *old* guns—my favorite's the machine gun—and bright, shiny high-techs. Every one you ever threw away."

"Rico," Sanguedolce said again, unable to mask his plea, faking a cool that the twitch of his fingers belied. "Why do you turn on your grandfather like this? Look around you." He indicated the room. "This is all yours. The purest of golds, marble from Italy, lapis lazuli and malachite from Russia's Ural Mountains, French bronzes, Japanese pottery, the riches of the world, my boy. It will all be yours, if you stay."

Zachary laughed as he pulled his Fangs backpack around to his lap.

One of the bozos made a move.

The boy grabbed something that filled his hand and held it out there like a threat. "Another move and I pull the cap."

Bronte caught her breath. "Zachary Tucker, are you playing with a hand grenade?"

"Zachary Tucker?" Sanguedolce's hands were stricken as if with a palsy.

Young Zachary looked amused, Darkwyn thought. As the boy flipped open his backpack, yellow smoke rose from inside, bright tendrils, a familiar whistle accompanying it, unmistakable.

"I think the kid's got a bomb," one of the thugs shouted, and four out of five gorillas hit the floor, though none of them saw the smoke.

The fifth remained standing and shook his head at their stupidity.

"The Sanguedolce dynasty ends here," Zachary said, as Jagidy flew from the backpack to smoke test the occupants of the room, invisible to everyone but the three of them.

Sanguedolce failed, of course. His smoke rose thick, and black as hell. The goons smoked black, too, except for the fifth, the one still standing. He tested yellow, which meant he was safe, aka not evil, aka on their side.

A plant. Probably, RCMP.

Darkwyn had never appreciated Jagidy's smoke testing more, until the pocket dragon got distracted by Bronte's cleavage and hit a wall. It made Darkwyn wonder, again, how Zachary got here, and Jagidy became the obvious answer.

Sanguedolce took another step toward Zachary, taking their attention from the pocket dragon.

"The hand grenade is the least of your problems," Zachary warned. "Not another step, old man. I changed my name. I disowned you. No family loyalty here, but plenty of brainpower."

"We will see how good the word of a boy is, shall we? Lorenzo," Sanguedolce said. "Take my daughter's backpack, give it to Guido, and you take her away. Lock her up, you know where, and stay with her. Don't touch her and don't hurt her, yet."

Darkwyn communicated telepathically. *Bronte, best behavior. We'll fetch you, soon. You still have your gun?*

I have the gun, but Zachary?

I'll take care of him. My dragon's ready to take over when the time is right.

Bronte raised her chin. *Take care of yourself, too.*

I will. I hope you'll be safer this way.

And more afraid, she admitted.

I know. He didn't dare tell her he was scared, too, that

he couldn't save Zachary. As long as Bronte and the boy ended up safe, nothing else mattered.

Lorenzo disappeared with Bronte while fury radiated off Zachary in waves. He must be listening to his soul memories not to protest. Or he waited until Bronte was safe away from here.

Meanwhile, after losing Bronte's escort, they were down to three gorillas and a good guy. The odds were getting better.

Guido, the tallest and dumbest of them, searched Bronte's backpack, as told. In half a minute the book of evidence came out. Sanguedolce took it, leafed through it, said something in Italian, and had the hoodlum drop the book in the fire.

All this way for nothing, Darkwyn thought, but Zachary didn't so much as blink at the destruction of his evidence. "Now what?" Darkwyn asked.

"Now, my men, they are going to beat the crap out of you. My daughter and grandson, they will sleep in their own beds, tonight. Tomorrow, they will agree to my terms, I promise you."

"If they do not, are you going to kill the boy? A child?"

"I wouldn't be the first," Zachary said. "Old Zachary's wife, Gina, died pregnant."

Sanguedolce straightened in surprise. "Gina? What do you know of Gina Fioranelli? She died years before you were born."

"Gina Fioranelli Tucker. How did you force her car off the road?"

"I never need to know the details. I am not a . . . how do they say . . . 'a . . . micromanager."

Zachary charged from the dumbwaiter—bad move—and beat on the mobster, likely for the sake of the old man inside him. "Murderer!"

The mobster reared back and slapped the boy across the face.

Darkwyn roared, his claws came out, his body weight shifted, and with one swipe, his tail took out the entire row of gorillas behind him. Strike!

FORTY-SEVEN

The old man's hands shook, his balance none too steady as he backed toward the door, and away from the dragon suddenly stalking him. "You're not real," Sanguedolce said.

Zachary laughed. "Why, what do you think you see, grand-killer? You look scared, like you've seen a ghost. Is it my mother? Or is it all of them? Every man, woman, and child, you ever killed. Now that *would* be scary."

Sanguedolce peeked around his dragon form and toward the room at large, focusing on his thugs. "Do you not see a dragon?"

Although they'd backed practically into the next room, so far back as to be laughable, they shook their heads in collective denial. The cop, however, wore a speculative expression, but he did stand with the thugs—as far away as he could get.

Dragon or not, Darkwyn had never wanted to laugh

and kill a man at the same time. Well, to be truthful—to himself, at least—he had never before wanted to do either, though as a Roman warrior, he'd had a similar job.

Zachary stood right beside him, Darkwyn noticed, and acted as if he didn't exist. *Smart.* "You doing drugs old man?" the boy asked.

Darkwyn had never seen Zachary's bitterness, then again, he might be radiating the bitterness of both man and boy.

"No drugs." Sanguedolce shook his grizzled head. "Nothing but an old man's medicine."

"So you admit to fallibility," Zachary said, "and hallucinations."

The mob boss raised his chin and stopped backing away. "I do not hallucinate. A reaction to my medication, this . . . aberration," he said in his fiercest mob voice. "Means nothing! I send the anomaly to hell."

I'm shivering in my scales, Darkwyn thought. *You keep telling yourself I'm not real, old man. Stand firm. Make this easy for me. I hate a moving target.*

Darkwyn approached the mobster, so slowly he wanted to yawn, while his claws came out, and he stretched his neck to tower higher over the killer, then his wings came up to add a further, satisfying bit of menace. His sneer revealed his hungry-dragon teeth, his smoke a bonus of torture.

Darkwyn raised a dragon hand and closed his claws around the mobster's surprisingly bony neck. He'd have to be careful not to squeeze *too* hard.

With his other hand, Darkwyn knocked the glass from a picture window, basked in the cooling air, and raised the old mobster off his feet.

A goon who thought the moment right lunged toward

Zachary, but as he did, Zachary produced a remote and aimed it at the dumbwaiter.

Zap! And welcome to the Fourth of July.

Fireworks came shooting from the dumbwaiter, breaking Ming vases, toppling French bronzes, annihilating priceless glass and dumb gorillas.

When the fireworks stopped, an energetic, ugly-faced, glow-eyed sizzler, like a fire-flashing head at the end of bungee-bouncing body—Zachary's name written all over it—chased goons in circles all over the room, into walls, over furniture, and into each other.

Still holding the old man off his feet, Darkwyn snorted; he couldn't help himself. How uncool for a black ice dragon to laugh, but when two bozos body-slammed each other senseless, what was a tickled dragon to do?

That's when Darkwyn noticed Zachary wielding a two-handed remote-type thingy full of buttons that he worked furiously, and Darkwyn realized that Zachary made the ugly-faced glow sizzler move in whatever direction he wanted it to.

The boy was chasing them without breaking a sweat, only one at a time, true, but whatever bozo the sizzler chased did all the damage while running from it.

Every time another goon approached, the sizzler turned on him, until they got it, steered clear, and let the scary thing torture one poor schlub until that one finally ran through the adjoining room and out a window.

Another thug down. Two goons and one cop left. Better and better odds.

"He's okay," one of the bozos announced, looking out the window. "Landed on an awning. Looks a lot like a beached whale, 'specially since he pissed himself."

The sizzler chose another victim, but for Zachary, this

torture must have seemed dull, because he picked up the other remote and clicked it for another, more powerful round of fireworks.

Finally, the gangsters ran for cover. The cop, he took a priceless painting off the wall and used it as a shield when he wasn't grinning and watching the show.

While the goons cowered, Darkwyn gave Zachary a wing wave toward the good guy, so he'd notice they weren't alone in the fight.

Zachary understood, followed Darkwyn's silent order to take cover, and when the boy got close, the cop pushed Zachary behind him, though, truth to tell, Zachary could have protected the cop.

Meanwhile, Sanguedolce, gasping for every breath and unable to speak while suspended, found himself outside, suddenly, with five or so floors drop beneath him, his legs kicking cold air.

Darkwyn turned and gave Zachary a nod.

The cop let the boy go.

Zachary ran to the window. "Where's Bronte?"

Sanguedolce, a powerful killing machine, nothing human about him, trembled with fear and swore vengeance and malice, and Darkwyn hoped he suffered triple for everyone he ever harmed. He even lessened his grip on the mob boss to scare him, and allow him a little more air in his lungs, so he could answer Zachary.

"I know of no Bronte," Sanguedolce said, after a terrified squeal at nearly falling.

"Damn," Zachary snapped. "Ysabelle? Where is Ysabelle?"

Good grief, Darkwyn thought. His wife's name was Ysabelle?

"Why?" Sanguedolce asked, too cocky by half. "Have you misplaced her?"

Darkwyn shook the old bastard just for the fun of it.

"I am keeping Ysabelle," he said, defiantly, "so you will behave, in trade for Raven Shadow, who you killed in Salem, as reported by the man you let live."

We let one of his men live? Darkwyn couldn't imagine who.

"We *let* none of yours live!" Zachary snapped. "If one did, it was an accident."

Two lifetimes' worth of anger and frustration coursed through Zachary.

"I am proud of you, my boy," Sanguedolce said. "You killed, and you are proud of it. You sound like me."

"I'm gonna try not to puke right now," Zachary said. "I want Bronte and Darkwyn, and I wanna go home . . . and wait for the day you fry."

FORTY-EIGHT

Raven Shadow had been Sanguedolce's. Hadn't Bronte said she was a regular? She'd been going to Drak's for months. That meant Sanguedolce found Bronte and Zachary long before he, Darkwyn, had mentioned his dragon past. He may have brought the media down on them, but he did not bring the mob.

One of the goons, taking advantage of his distraction, stabbed his side with the fire poker.

Darkwyn roared.

Zachary turned on his stabber. "Hurt him again and he'll drop your boss," the boy warned.

"Good," the stabber said. "Let him go. Give us all a chance to breathe easy." The poker entered Darkwyn's thigh again, a burning pain, as if to assure his attacker that the mobster would get dropped. *Dragons must have a lot of blood to lose*, Darkwyn thought, watching it pool around his feet.

He just might drop Sanguedolce, unintentionally on purpose.

Killian showed herself, or her vision of herself as young and beautiful, in a deadly sort of way. Almost appropriate, seeing her when he was at his weakest.

The sky grew black as doomsday. The clouds parted and the heavens pelted his dangly-toy with hail, fiery freezing hailstones that stuck to Darkwyn's arm scales and burned the mobster's skin.

Next up, Killian sent a twister, big and black and weaving a path of destruction across the property. Lightning struck, and the mobster became its conduit.

Darkwyn magick-cloaked his mind while he fought the energy trying to enter his body through the mobster, because the longer he fought, the weaker Killian and Sanguedolce would become.

Then he could send Killian's deadly energy back her way, and best both enemies at the same time.

True, he couldn't best Killian until he bested Sanguedolce for Bronte, but Killian's lightning was doing that for him.

Midzap, the lightning stopped, but the twister took out half the first floor. A chandelier fell and the floor beneath their feet dropped about six inches, which meant he dropped the mobster as much, and the weakened mob boss wept like a baby.

Killian must have realized she'd been working against herself with the lightning, so she'd stopped. *Scumduggers*.

Darkwyn brought Sanguedolce back inside, set the trembling puddle of mob boss on the floor, and realized he'd retained a great deal of energizing strength from the electrical power he'd absorbed.

Killian had actually done him a favor, though he hadn't bested her. *Yet*.

The poker-wielding, big-mouthed goon who had *wanted*

the mobster dead panicked and pretended to fight now *for* the boss, raising his gun toward Zachary, of all people, safe behind the cop, and the mobster managed to raise himself against a table.

A distracting thump echoed off the hall door.

Darkwyn heard a muffled "Ouch," then, "FBI. Open up or we come in shooting."

FBI? Wrong country. And that voice. Naw. It can't be.

A second thump, the "ouch," less noticeable. "FBI. Come out with your hands up. You're surrounded."

The goons pulled their leg-shaky, fast-aging boss to safety, held a gun to the traitor cop's head—the slow learners—yanked Zachary from the cop's hold, and tossed the boy's remotes against a wall.

Darkwyn's stabber shoved Zachary toward the door, so they could hide behind him, typical cowards. "Come in shooting," Darkwyn's attacker shouted. "That's the only way you'll get Sanguedolce."

Good thing Puck the cock would neither carry a gun nor shoot Zachary.

A third shout of "FBI, open up" came without action. Puck may temporarily have stopped the poker-wielder from stabbing, but the bird's lack of action after his announcements was going to get them killed, as soon as the idiots' cumulative brainpower caught up to the facts.

Rounding on them, Darkwyn roared, but he found them hiding behind sofas, chairs, a piano. He kicked each piece from here to the next room, tearing down walls and turning the inner sanctum into a double-wide.

Goons hit walls and forgot to bounce. *Goon football!*

Feeling himself shifting back into a man, likely due to his loss of blood, Darkwyn turned and slipped in a slick, sticky pool of it.

Zachary handed him Bronte's discarded backpack and led him to a corner.

Quickly, Darkwyn healed himself, more or less, and shifted while Zachary grabbed a remote in one hand and a gun in the other, wielding both as a warning. In that way, he kept watch so Darkwyn could have his privacy.

Zach went so far as to raise a hand to the cop to keep him where he was.

The cop gave Zachary a respectful nod but he watched as much of Darkwyn's change as he could see from where he stood.

A man again, Darkwyn put on his jeans and shirt fast. More than partially healed, he pulled himself up and made his way to Zachary while he gave the cop a nod of thanks.

From the hall, they heard footsteps. "RCMP, you're surrounded!"

Whoa, different voice, right country.

"That's what I've been saying." Puck perched on the exposed sill of the broken window and tilted his head Zachary's way. "Don't shoot."

The door flew open and a contingent of Royal Canadian Mounted Police flooded in.

"How did you know we were here?" Zachary asked.

One of the officers went to talk to the cop Darkwyn had pegged as RCMP, the one who'd protected Zachary, while the head man, addressed by his men as Commissioner bent to Zachary. "We got an anonymous tip, son. What happened here?"

Sanguedolce stood straighter. "My grandson came to visit me is all."

"Your grandson beat up your men?"

"No, the men, they were playing. Fighting it out."

"Considering the blood, looks like a couple of them

blew up. Sorry, but this 'playing to the death' has your name written all over it."

Zachary caught the commissioner's sleeve. "I'm his *step*grandson, and I hope you won't hold that against me. I can't help who my grandmother married. They were holding us against our will, and they're holding my . . . mother, probably in one of the cells behind the wine cellar. This is Darkwyn Dragonelli . . . my dad."

"Hey," one of the goons said. "He looks like that Vampire Dragon we saw on TV. And he acted like it, too."

Humbled at having Zachary call him dad, Darkwyn shook the commissioner's hand. "They *were* holding us against our will. And the boy's right, my wife is locked up somewhere in the house."

"Sam, Al, go look for his wife. What's her name?"

"Bronte. Bronte Dragonelli."

"She is my daughter, Commissaire," Sanguedolce said.

"It's not even legal to lock up your daughter, Sanguedolce," the commissioner said. "Find her," he told his men.

"Are you hurt?" the commissioner asked. "There's blood all over your hands and feet."

"I got stabbed with a poker by thug number three. Yes, that's the one," Darkwyn said as one of the officers lined them up.

A medic came over as if to examine him. "No thanks," Darkwyn said. "Just flesh wounds."

The medic looked entirely doubtful but he took his cue from the cop who saw everything, and nodded, and the medic closed his bag. "You can be transported to a local hospital, or you can see your doctor when you get home."

"I'll see my own doctor, thanks."

Bronte rushed into the room, embraced Zachary, then Darkwyn. "Oh, the blood. It looks like you slaughtered pigs in here." She looked around the room. "Whose blood is that?"

Nobody said a word.

"Darkwyn?" she asked. "Who died?"

"You'll have to check the body count on the pavement out back. One or two thugs went out the window."

She went to check. "Hey, that's Boris, down there. He's been coming to Drak's longer than Raven Shadow. A mob man . . . in my world all this time. This didn't all happen because you talked, Darkwyn."

"I figured that out," he said. "But I still should have kept quiet."

Bronte shook her head, relieving him of blame. "You were provoked."

"You got here fast, Mrs. Dragonelli," the commissioner said. "My men?"

"I met them halfway. They're getting the guy I tied up downstairs. I anchored him, arms, wrists, ankles, and legs, to separate cell bars; poetic justice and all that."

"You do like to do it up right," Zachary said. "Now give him my mother's jacket."

Bronte started to take it off, but stopped to focus on Zachary. "What happened to the book of evidence?"

Zachary shook his head. "Burned to a crisp."

Bronte removed her sister's denim jacket which she'd taken from the attic. "Officer, you might know Sanguedolce as a mob boss that you can rarely pin anything on, but if you look behind the crocheted rosebud in this pocket, you'll find a camera chip."

"There *was* an evidence book," Zachary said, "but it's ash in the fireplace, right there. Doesn't matter, this chip has a picture of every page and every picture. It pretty much tells you where all the bodies are buried, half a century's worth."

Sanguedolce shouted, "No," as if to the universe, but no one listened, except perhaps the growing hoard of angry spirits crowding him, half a century's worth. And they were not happy.

Darkwyn looked from Zachary to Bronte and wished that Sanguedolce saw the spirits of his evil work the way they could.

Darkwyn had never seen Zachary smile like he was now, and he suspected that old Zachary Tucker might be bolstering the boy's satisfaction.

Puck ruffled his feathers. "Happiness." *Squawk.* "An agreeable sensation arising from contemplating the misery of another."

Zachary faced his stepgrandfather. "You above all know that life ends in a blink."

The wind hissed a moan, as if agreeing, and the sun peeked out for less than a second.

Darkwyn knew he'd helped *Bronte* reach her goal: to best Sanguedolce and free herself and Zachary.

He would like to think that he had also bested Killian, except that she'd stopped torturing him on her own.

No, the evil one was not a sorceress to give up easily. For now, he must accept a partial victory. Bronte's victory.

The cop who'd been there all along took off his hat, scratched his head, and gave Darkwyn a questioning look. "Vampire *Dragon*?"

Darkwyn raised his chin. "Just another man in a costume."

The cop gave him a double take, scanned the blood on the floor, and turned to Zachary. "How about you, young man? What can you tell me about your stepgrandfather's crimes?"

"Hey." Zachary gave an exaggerated shrug. "I'm only a kid."

FORTY-NINE

"I'm only a kid," Darkwyn *mimicked, as they reached* the roof of Castello Sanguedolce several hours later.

Bronte put an arm around Darkwyn's waist, and squeezed Zachary's shoulder on her opposite side.

"I didn't want to be detained," Zachary said, "and with everything the old man knows, that could have been like a life sentence. No, the evidence *was* all in the book, or it used to be. Old Zachary always worried they'd find it and destroy it, so I got the idea to take pictures."

"Bronte, why didn't that cop ask you any questions at the end?" Darkwyn asked. "You're a mobster's daughter."

"Stepdaughter! I'm a woman; I played dumb and got taken away. Zachary, now he fought with old Zachary's emotions, so no wonder the cop asked. And you, Darkwyn, shape-shifting in front of him. I think he, like the goons, decided to shut up and not get put in a psychiatric ward."

Zachary grinned. "When they finally put that chip in a

drive and took a look, they were so happy, they just let us leave."

"Which we should do, and fast," Darkwyn said. "I need to shift again, before something—"

Killian appeared right there on the roof beside them, sending her ten-fingered lightning his way, up close and personal.

That fast, Darkwyn pushed Zachary and Bronte aside, knocking them to their knees, but he couldn't stop focusing on Killian to worry about that. Neither could Killian stop fighting him long enough to care that Bronte and Zachary now stood behind him, because the evil sorceress had grown weak throwing all her energy at him through Sanguedolce, and not pulling it back. Calculated error, there.

He had more strength than her, but which of them could outlast the other?

"I'll help you, Darkwyn," Bronte shouted.

"Crackle here, fire there.
Snap your heels; sizzle's fair.
Gone her strength, no one cares.

This my wish, harm prove ill.
Darkwyn's fight, aim to kill.
Banish Killian at his will."

The *hiss* and *sizzle, fizzle,* and *pop,* however powerless, broke Killian's concentration long enough for Darkwyn to turn back into a dragon, turn her power on her, so the evil sorceress screeched, glowed gold, then blue, then, *pffftt,* she turned to air.

"Has she disappeared to regroup?" Bronte asked. "Or did I get her in her Achilles' heel, pure fake distraction? Is she gone?"

"Yeah," Zachary said. "Did you win?"

One never knows with Killian, Darkwyn said telepathically. *Let's get the Hades out of here.*

After a satisfactory flight back to Salem, Darkwyn exited the woods near the fairgrounds dressed in his very last set of black jeans and T-shirt, and ruffled Zachary's hair. "Suppose Sanguedolce had taken that jean jacket, too?" he asked.

"Nothing of my sister Brianna's meant anything to Sanguedolce, except Zachary. The cop promised that when the jacket's no longer evidence he'll send it to us."

"That house will be released from evidence, eventually, too," Zachary said. "Our friend the RCMP said that Castello Sanguedolce is mine, so I'm gonna sell it and give the money to kids without mothers, or mothers who want kids. Whatever will please old Zachary."

Darkwyn shook his head. "I mean, what if Sanguedolce had found the chip *and* destroyed it with the book?"

Zachary flipped a thumb drive in his palm. "I have insurance, right here. And there's a world of dumbwaiters and getaway tunnels inside those walls. I left backup copies all over the house before I made my big entrance. I heard them take you from the attic, by the way."

"You could have let us know," Bronte said. "We were worried sick about you."

"You only had to wait a half hour more. Besides, if I'd shown myself, I would have been caught with you. Then I couldn't ply my tricks." Zachary rubbed his hands together. "I enjoyed that, except for the blood. No, it was best I stayed hidden. Anyway, I'm holding on to the pictures of the book, in case any of Sanguedolce's highly placed friends makes sure the one the authorities have gets lost."

"Smart boy," Darkwyn said. "I disliked that place. I'm

sorry you two had to grow up there. Zachary, what did you say to Sanguedolce in Italian that scared him so badly?"

"I'm going to send you to hell." Zachary released a heavy sigh. "Sanguedolce used to say that in Italian, word for word, before he killed someone—until he delegated the bloody dirty work to someone else. I got it from my soul memories. I don't think anybody alive could have known. *That's* what scared him. The words were like ghosts from his past."

"For a minute there," Darkwyn said, "I thought you were Zachary Tucker the first."

"For a minute, I think he took over. He was that mad."

"I looked into your eyes," Darkwyn said, "and that wasn't you."

"It won't happen again. The old soul is going into retirement."

That surprised Darkwyn. "Did old Zachary tell you that?"

"No, we don't communicate, as such, but I sense these things."

Darkwyn and Zachary laughed at that.

Bronte looked appalled. "Don't joke about your reincarnated soul. It already sc es me. On a lighter note, it was nice of the cop to look away, more or less, while we flew off."

"He was probably watching on the security monitors, but he did more than let us go," Darkwyn said. "He turned a blind eye to meeting a dragon, up close and personal. He saw me transform, half challenged me, and never said another word."

"There's more to him than meets the eye," Zachary said. "He's the grandson of old Zachary's RCMP contact, the one you talked to, Bronte. He arranged to get us out of

Canada, though he didn't do it personally. I'm betting he joined the mob as a plant after we were safe."

Darkwyn gave the boy a double take. "Are you sure?"

"Kind of. He not only looked familiar to my old soul, his name is the same as old Zachary's contact."

"Do you think he's reincarnated, too?" Bronte asked. "I mean, talk about your weird reunions."

"No, simply on the trail of vengeance. Wanna bet our step-killer killed the cop's ancestor?"

"What will he say," Darkwyn wondered aloud, "if somebody asks about Sanguedolce's dragon?"

"Sanguedolce won't make the same mistake twice. He won't mention a dragon nobody else admitted seeing." Zachary chuckled. "He's too proud for that, right, Bronte?"

"So true."

Zachary stopped when he saw the Phoenix. "I'm so glad you survived the fire, both of you."

"We can say the same." Bronte blinked her glistening eyes. "Darkwyn saved everybody. When we couldn't find you, we figured the mob got you, so we went looking."

Zachary waved a hand. "This is too emotional. I'm gonna see how the place looks."

"Be careful," Bronte called after him.

"Yeah, yeah." Zachary waved but kept walking.

Darkwyn took his wife's arm. "Relax, there's no more mob chasing him."

She sighed, watching the boy. "Remember how we felt when we thought we lost him? I'll always worry. There are other evils in this world."

"Just like a mother."

"A mother? Who's a mother?"

FIFTY

"*Brace yourself,*" *Darkwyn said.* "*Our boy introduced* me to the RCMP commissioner as his dad, and he said his mom—that's you—was being detained there in the house."

"Zachary did?" Bronte's eyes filled. "I'll never let him forget my sister, but, oh Darkwyn, he's been mine since he took his first breath. I'm beyond words."

"I can't pretend to understand the mother/son bond, but I know that he humbled the heck out of me when he called me his dad." Darkwyn took Bronte by her shoulders and turned her to face him. "Bronte Dragonelli, with you and Zachary, I am whole."

"About that. I have a confession to make. I married you under false pretenses. You *don't* have a green card."

"So?"

"So you thought I married you for your green card, but I learned from Vivica *before the wedding* that you don't have one. You think you helped me get legal, Darkwyn, but I'm not. You're not. We're not."

"So we'll be illegal together or Vivica will help us get legal. Bronte, I'm glad you married me. I wouldn't want to live without you for any reason."

"I don't think I'm very good for you. That was your blood on the floor, wasn't it?"

"Spilled dragon blood. No biggie. Look at me. All healed. Bronte, you're making excuses to deny yourself something you want. Me."

"Hah, you have some ego."

"Don't start an argument. You don't have the mob anymore to use as an excuse so you're choosing some other reason to deny yourself."

"I'm admitting that I lied to you by omission. Doesn't that bother you?"

"I entrusted you with my heart, with everything I am, man and dragon, forever. All I want is to walk this life beside you."

"Don't you see, I've given you further reason not to trust me."

"Trust is *your* issue, not mine. I trust you with my life."

"I envy you that," she said.

"Hey," Zachary shouted. "Come see. Home looks especially good, today." The boy ran over and grabbed Bronte's hand—Bronte the only mother he knew—and he tugged her through the fairgrounds.

He'd found home, a monumental event for a man dragon, never mind for a boy Zachary's age, especially considering where he was raised. Giving up a man to a death sentence, even Sanguedolce, couldn't be easy, for a boy or an old soul, no matter how cool the kid played it.

"Home," Bronte said, and laughed, stopping to embrace the boy. "We never had one before, did we?"

Zachary shook his head and turned away, probably so they couldn't see how much that mattered to him.

Finally, they walked together, Darkwyn grasping Bronte's waist, wanting her to sense his love without scaring her with the L word, especially with her saying she'd married him under false pretenses.

He wondered if this was too much change all at once for her, so much positive in their lives when they were used to expecting the worst. He'd have to keep her upbringing in mind and tread carefully. You could get hard and scared, living without love. He knew.

In the end, when he finally bested Killian—a goal that seemed so close, he might already have accomplished it—his win would be empty without Bronte by his side.

Unless . . . Bronte *wanted* to set him free. Could that mean she wasn't his heart mate, that his goal had short-circuited? If she left him, would he need to start over again, find a new heart mate?

No. He wanted only Bronte. Being with her was more than wanting to save Andra's magick and his brothers, though it was that, too.

"Does the Phoenix seem different?" Bronte asked as they cleared the fairgrounds and got closer. "I mean, besides people scurrying around the yard like worker bees."

"There's your answer," Darkwyn said. "Somebody on a ladder painting the back of the building. Can you paint brick?"

"Not well," Bronte said, "but people do paint windows."

"Darkwyn, pay attention," Zachary said. "Real vamps are working beside role players, beside regular Salem citizens. That *never* happens."

"How can you tell which is which? They all look the same to me."

"The real vamps are wearing sunglasses and probably

Daylight Allure. It's a potion we sell in the gift shop. Makes it easier for them to come out during the day."

"You're kidding, right? Besides, I know of one big difference. Real vamps and role players bicker, with each other and the general public," Darkwyn said. "It's what they do best, except that everyone here is getting along."

"Getting along and working together for a common cause," Zachary said. "Drak's."

Darkwyn ran a hand down Bronte's back, because touching her reassured him. "Now that we're home, I'll take care of you both," he said. "Oh, I know, Bronte Mc-Bride Dragonelli, Miss Independent, you can take care of yourself. You can do anything, yourself, except maybe fly without me."

"Flying is important," she said. "All kinds of flying."

That sounded promising. "I know you can take care of yourself, but let me help. Please?"

"I'm impossible to live with. Bossy is my middle name."

"She's right," Zachary said.

"I know you're rough on men, Bronte, but I'm your husband, and I can take it."

The boy pulled Bronte down to his level to whisper in her ear, loud enough for Darkwyn to hear. "Bronte, I think this one's a keeper."

"You are rather smart for your age."

FIFTY-ONE

Darkwyn and Bronte crossed the yard. "*I recognize* most of the construction workers. Look, Rory MacKenzie, a world-class carousel carver, is building our window frames."

"*That's* the difference," Darkwyn said, realizing it for the first time. "Every window frame is a different color. You said 'our.' So you do want to keep me?"

"I always wanted to do that, paint the windows different colors, I mean. Vivica and I talked about it. Hey, she must have started this. I'll bet she rounded everyone up and put herself in charge. Look, there's Jaydun and Bastian pushing wheelbarrows mounded with bricks, showing off their superior strength."

Bronte squeezed his hand. "You have great brothers. There, Melody, Kira, Vickie, and Bastian's McKenna are serving steaming mugs to the workers."

Darkwyn raised his head. "Hot cider. I can smell it in the air."

"I forgot about your acute dragon senses. Of course, hot cider on a crisp October day." Bronte leaned against his arm. "I feel blessed. They set mums and pumpkins on the porch and balconies. This *is* home," she said, her voice cracking.

From around the building came Scorch and Lila, both galloping toward them, and when they got close enough, the cats catapulted into their arms.

Zachary tilted his head. "They *do* have wings. Oh, gosh, that reminds me." He removed his backpack, and when he opened it, they heard a faint whistle from inside. "Whew, he's okay. Jagidy is still resting from his ordeal. Listen, he's snoring."

"What ordeal?" Darkwyn asked.

Bronte turned Zachary's chin her way. "Young man, what happened to you the night of the fire? How did the mob find you?"

"I got pushed out of the way and hit my head. That's all I knew for a while. Jagidy shape-shifted into a full grown dragon and flew me to safety. He's a really shiny soft green, like the sea on some sunny days."

Darkwyn glanced into the backpack. "*Jagidy* broke through the second-floor wall?"

"Yes, and he took me back to Mount Washington, where he healed me."

"I didn't think Jagidy had it in him. How did he manage in the blizzard?"

"Easy flying. No blizzard."

"Of course not, because Killian was focused on me. How is Jagidy after all those heroic deeds?"

"I've been nursing him back to health," Zachary said.

"He's really weak, and he compromised his recovery by flying me to Montreal, after we couldn't find you two, and then by smoke testing those thugs."

Darkwyn squeezed Zachary's shoulder. "He must *really* love you." Darkwyn wouldn't mention that Jagidy had also probably shortened his life, but hey, maybe on earth, he'd outlive them all.

Vivica left a group of window painters to come and meet them. "Oh, thank the Goddess you're okay," the owner of Works Like Magick said as she tested each of their arms for breaks before hugging them.

Bronte hugged her, hard. "Do we have you to beat, I mean thank, for the newscast that announced Zachary and I had died?"

Vivica stepped back. "You sound a bit sarcastic."

"We saw the news after Zachary went missing. Scared the heck out of us, except that I wasn't dead, so there was *some* hope."

"Oh no. I'm so sorry. I didn't think anyone would care, except the mob, and I figured they'd leave you alone once you were dead. You said to do what I had to."

"I did, didn't I? Okay, so pretending we were dead was pretty smart. But where did you think Zachary and I were?"

"Safe, hiding with Darkwyn."

Darkwyn put an arm around Bronte. "Thank you, Vivica, for believing in me, for trying to protect Bronte and Zachary, and for starting the repairs to the Phoenix. Bronte and Zachary's big threat is going to fry."

"A certain pissed-off dragon helped," Zachary added.

"A friendly dragon." Bronte kissed Darkwyn's cheek.

"Ah, um, 'scuse me," Zachary said, "but I'm gonna go paint with the vamps out back. I don't like the way you two are looking at each other. I mean I like it, but I don't wanna see it. Heck, you don't care what I'm saying, you're too busy looking at each other like you're both food and neither of you has eaten today."

"Zachary," Vivica said. "Take me with you. I want to introduce you to my niece, Gina."

Bronte squealed and followed them with her gaze.

Darkwyn smiled. "Let Zachary's fate take its course, and let me look at you any way I want, because I'll *never* let you go."

They kissed, hungry for each other, because they'd nearly lost everything. Darkwyn thought Bronte surely kissed like she wanted to keep him.

He lifted her in his arms and leapt up to the balcony, to a round of cheers and applause from their audience. "Scumduggers. *Caught*, stealing my own wife."

When he set her down, Bronte turned and welcomed him with a warm kissable mouth.

He pulled her against him, his heart in his throat. "You're mine," he said, raising her off her feet and twirling her in circles, her laugh a mix of all the good magick he'd ever known rolled into a sparkling crystal bubble of elation.

He slid her down his body, and grasped her face in his hands.

She sighed. "You deserve better than me."

"There is no better. I don't deserve *you*," Darkwyn said. "But I think I've figured out your ambivalent need to set me free. In the mob, they don't set anybody free, ever, right? And you need to prove you're different from the people who raised you?"

Bronte hesitated and then gave him a wide-eyed half nod.

"Well, see, here's the difference. In the mob, people beg on their knees to be set free. Me, I'm on my knees begging you to keep me. Do the right thing, Bronte. Prove you're not like them."

She bit her lip. "In that case, I'd like to keep you, please. I always wanted to."

"You are so stuck with me." He pulled her close. "I was never so scared in my life as when you said you should let me go."

She pulled a bit away. "Sure you were. You met Sanguedolce."

"That was nothing. Losing you would be worse." He ravaged her mouth and skimmed his hands over her body to make sure she was okay. But he found a bold new scar behind her ear. "You've been hurt? Are you all right?"

"No. Yes. That thug who brought me down to lock me up at Castello Sanguedolce, he tried to defend himself against me. Imagine!"

"How dare he. But you knew I would save you?"

"I did know. I . . . trusted you."

"Whoa, Bronte, you said the T word."

"I won't say I'm not scared."

"I can't promise never to let you down, but I do promise always to do my best by you and Zachary."

She tilted her head, her half smile an arrow to his heart. "Darkwyn Dragonelli, it's like you're proposing all over again, but better this time."

"Can we have another honeymoon?"

"We haven't had the first one yet, dragon man."

"Right," he said. "Besides, I want more. I want a lifetime where we adopt Zachary and give him brothers and sisters."

"That calls for a *lot* of trust," she admitted.

"You've got it. I know you have. You just have to practice by letting me have my wicked way with you."

The kiss they shared, sweet and tender, a rising of bound souls, became their ultimate release from darkness into light. She fulfilled him, healed his heart, took him from the brink of chaos to a splendid peace in her arms.

He would spend the rest of his life doing the same for her.

Lila, their white kitten, landed on the balcony, meowed, and morphed, in a sprinkle of light, into Andra, the Goddess of Hope, a beautiful sorceress dressed in stars. "My Darkwyn," she said, "you have done well."

He took Bronte's hand. "Andra this is Bronte, my heart mate. Bronte, Andra sent me to you."

"Thank you." Bronte curtseyed. Goddess, he loved her.

Andra raised her diamond wand. "May the hail in your life melt with ease, the sun shine long and warm, the good times become more numerous than the difficult, and may your family be loving, and as close, or far, as you want them to be. Thank you, Darkwyn, for returning my magick. Killian is out of your lives for good. She will plague the next Dragonelli, but not you. Meanwhile she *does* toy with Jaydun in the form of a leaf pixie."

Darkwyn chuckled.

Andra raised her wand. "Live long and happy." She disappeared in a burst of crystal sparks.

The wind screamed Killian's final lament, a shower of hail becoming violets that a white kitten with lavender wings tried to catch.

Bronte chuckled. "You have an unusual family."

"Thanks to Killian. However, if not for her curse, I would never have made it to earth to meet you and Zachary."

"Dare I say nice Killian?

"Oh, I wouldn't go that far."

Bronte stroked his lips with the tip of a finger. He kissed it, their eyes meeting, speaking volumes without words. "It's time," Darkwyn whispered, reaching for her mask.

She nodded and he removed it, saw her face for the first time. "As beautiful as your heart," he said, "the finest work of art." He adored the shape of it with his fingertips, his lips, and cupped her cheek in his palm. "I want you in every way. I love you enough for both of us."

Bronte turned her face into his palm and kissed it, then she looked deep into his gorgeous violet eyes. "I have never loved anyone the way I love you. Ultimate and forever."

"Bronte, we've learned the greatest of lessons. Love can't happen until the masks come off."

Keep reading for a special preview of

CHOSEN BY BLOOD

by Virna DePaul

Coming May 2011 from Berkley Sensation!

*Kyle Mahone, director of the FBI's Special Ops Tacti-*cal Division, quietly hung up his phone instead of slamming it down the way he wanted to. He'd expected Dex Hunt to be suspicious of the Bureau's job offer. What Other wouldn't be? The rest had certainly proceeded with caution, asking one question after another.

The werebeast, however, had done something the others hadn't.

He'd laughed his ass off.

Swiveling in his chair, Mahone looked out his window, clenching his fists until his knuckles were white. He'd gotten where he was by being smart, working hard, and maintaining his cool. But something about the werebeast's taunting had hit home.

Infuriating. Smart-assed. Cocky SOB. The epithets didn't come close to describing Hunt. Still, he was the best marksman in the nation, human or Other. He was also skilled in the martial art of Karakai, a combination of Karate and crazy-ass gymnastics the Others had come up with. That made Hunt lethal from a distance and in close quarters. Add the fact he could shift into something that would make Freddy Krueger look cuddly and Hunt would be invaluable to the success of Team Red, the FBI's first special ops team to recruit both humans and Others. In addition to Hunt, Mahone had already offered spots to a human, a human psychic, a mage, and last but not least, a wraith.

Wraith, as in ghost. The dearly departed.

A no-longer-living, d-e-a-d person who swore like a trucker, adored ABBA, wore four-inch stilettos, and unlike the other handful of wraiths that were known to exist, refused to take a real name. Instead, she'd sworn to answer only to "Wraith" until she discovered her true identity. Her surly attitude wasn't ideal, but she was a survivor to the extreme—incapable of being killed by any known methods. She also happened to be an expert in ammunitions and explosives.

Twenty years ago, Mahone would have checked himself into an insane asylum before admitting he believed in any of the Others, let alone a wraith. Now the future of the world seemed to rest in their hands.

Wearily, Mahone rubbed his hands over his face. According to the crazy dream he'd had two weeks ago, the fate of the world, or rather the fate of its inhabitants, actually rested more in *his* hands than anyone else's—on his ability to choose the right combination of six individuals, humans and Otherborn, to serve on a *new* type of special ops team—a Para-Ops team.

Talk about pressure.

If it had been up to him, a Para-Ops team would have

been formed years before, as soon as the President and all the Otherborn leaders had signed the Humanity Treaty. Instead, the U.S. government had left things up to local law enforcement agencies, which, while usually well intentioned, were simply unable to deal with the lingering prejudice and suspicion that naturally followed half a decade of civil war. Another five years had passed since peace was declared, yet the nation and its citizens were still recovering. Some days, Mahone doubted they'd ever find peace again. For that to occur, he knew the United States people needed help—a team dedicated to ensuring the rights of humans and Others alike, both domestically and internationally.

The dream had obviously been a manifestation of his growing unease and frustration with the President's unwillingness to step up to the plate. But in the end, the dream had also given Mahone the cajones to force the President's hand. Either give him the green light to form the FBI's first Para-Ops team comprised of humans and Others, or accept Mahone's resignation.

Now he had no one to blame but himself if the team turned out to be a disaster. Unfortunately, the call with Hunt wasn't exactly promising and he still had one more offer to make—the position of team leader to a dharmire. And not just any dharmire, but Knox Devereaux, the son of a vampire Queen and an infamous French revolutionist human, Jacques Devereaux.

This morning, Mahone had e-mailed Knox, his message concise: *Teleport to headquarters as soon as possible. Nora will buzz you in.*

Knox's reply had been even more concise. *Three.* For Knox, that was code for, "I'll be there at three o'clock, you bastard, just long enough to make you squirm."

Mahone checked the clock. Less than an hour away. Which meant Mahone needed to focus. It would be foolish to face Knox while he was still distracted by crazy dreams or a smart-ass were. Once again, he replayed the conversation with Hunt, trying to determine the point that annoyance had shifted into more.

Yes, he'd laughed at Mahone's offer, but the werebeast's laughter had barely died down before he'd gone for Mahone's throat. "A team to help both humans and Others, huh? Tell me, Mahone, how many Others do you call friend? How many do you drink a beer with when you're watching a game?"

Mahone's answer had been in his silence, just as Hunt had obviously expected. Even so, he'd persisted, giving Hunt both the parameters of the team's purpose, as well as a brief description of its first mission. When he was done, Hunt hadn't been laughing, but he hadn't jumped to accept Mahone's invitation, either.

No, he'd said he'd think about it.

Mahone snorted and shook his head.

Think about it. As if they weren't discussing one of the most elite teams in the world. As if riding a motorcycle to nowhere and back was half as important as things like justice or survival, or hell, even revenge.

But it was all bullshit.

Hunt didn't just want revenge, he craved it. What Mahone had proposed would give it to him in spades, complete with a "get out of jail free" card.

The werebeast could think about it all he wanted; in the end, he'd accept just as the others would.

Feeling marginally more settled, Mahone flipped Hunt's file shut and secured it. He swiped his hands over his face. When a spark of memory hit him, however, he froze.

How many Others do you call friend?

The question, virtually identical to the one posed by Hunt, drifted through his mind in a decidedly more feminine voice. Mahone frowned as he connected the voice to his dream.

How many Others do you call friend? The question played over and over, until he finally managed to form an image of the creature that had asked it of him in the dream. A creature he instinctively cringed away from remembering.

But he couldn't help remembering it, either.

Closing his eyes, he recalled how, in his dream, he'd dozed off at his desk. The sky had been dark. The building deserted. Then he'd been blinded by a flash of light and the sudden appearance of a creature at the light's center. A creature he'd never seen before nor ever wanted to see again.

She had hair that was comprised of colors both familiar and unfamiliar, floating around her in undulating waves, each strand a living, breathing entity.

A face that, instead of eyes, a nose, and a mouth, had hollow, cavernous sockets, bottomless and dark, terrifying and hypnotic, yet so beautiful it had made his own life force try to push itself out of his body to get to her.

A body that, underneath her diaphanous, flowing gown was neither female nor male, but both and so much more than he could understand.

After that first shocked look, he'd turned away from her and that's when she'd asked him, "How many Others do you call friend?" When he'd answered, "None," too scared even to think of lying, she'd told him her intentions and lamented the failure of an ancient prophesy. She'd listened when he'd told her about his idea for Team Red. And then she'd told him to form the team, explaining in shocking detail what would happen if the team failed to serve its purpose. If Mahone failed to deliver what he promised.

When he'd asked her who she was—*what* she was—she'd merely said "a divinity." In other words, she was a goddess. And a pissed-off one at that.

Thank *his* God it had been a dream.

Mahone opened his eyes, disgusted at the feel of sweat trickling down his temple. With a shaky hand, he grabbed a glass of water and chugged it down. Then he heard a voice, no longer in his memory but as if the speaker was standing directly beside him.

It wasn't a dream, Mahone. Thanking your God won't make it so.

You have one year to prove the team can do what you said.

One year and not a second more.

Whirling around to scan his empty office, Mahone dropped his glass and the traces of water within it poured out, staining the remaining files on his desk.

He knew instantly he'd been kidding himself. He hadn't dreamed the creature's visit any more than he'd dreamed the War. Instead, the living nightmare that had become his life was merely intensifying.

Falling back in his chair, he stared blankly at the water pooled on his desk, then slowly cleaned up the mess, stacking his files with precision before straightening his tie and smoothing out his jacket.

Minutes later, two raps on his door made him jump and curse. He knew immediately who was standing outside. He took a deep breath. Then another. The last thing he wanted was more drama, but he simply called, "Enter."

Simultaneously, he prayed, hoping that even though it hadn't been his God who'd visited him two weeks ago, and even though he hadn't prayed to Him in a very long time, God was still there and willing to hear him.

Special Agent Felicia Locke knew the minute she saw the willowy dharmire that there was going to be trouble.

She'd chosen the bar because it was as far from Pennsylvania Avenue and the J. Edgar Hoover Building as one could get and still be in Washington, D.C. With its spray-painted façade, dim lights, and ramshackle assortment of tables and chairs, the Black Hole was also light-years away from what a typical federal agent would consider reputable, let alone palatable. In its favor was the fact it served the best brandy in the state, strong and undiluted. That and some privacy was all Felicia wanted. She'd just locked her car and was walking toward the bar's back entrance when a dharmire, who couldn't have been more than sixteen years old, stumbled around the corner of the building and into view.

Felicia immediately recognized the female as half-Other; although she had a vampire's silver hair and black eyes, her skin was sun-toasted, just a shade lighter than a graham cracker. She clung to the arm of a stocky man with no neck, squinty eyes, and slicked-back hair. The man pushed her against the side of the building and covered her slim body with his own.

Felicia's prediction of trouble formed not because the man was ugly, but because he was unkempt and, considering the foul things he was saying, obviously uncouth.

She'd never met a vamp who'd willingly suffer the company of someone so appallingly unrefined. It would be like asking one to wear jeans or, God forbid, drive a beat-up old truck down a public highway. As a rule, vamps didn't do casual or tacky.

Even so, she tried telling herself that maybe the girl just looked young. There was no accounting for poor taste, after all. But the closer she got, the more apparent it became that the dharmire was under the influence. Her silver pupils were dilated and glassy, and she appeared to cling to the man out of necessity rather than affection.

The man shifted to the side just as Felicia walked within ten feet of them. She saw the fine gold chain and pendant around the dharmire's neck—a smaller, more feminine version of the one Knox wore and an exact replica of the one Noella had worn all her life. The same pendant Felicia's best friend had been wearing on the day she'd died, a gaping hole in her chest where her heart had once been.

Felicia came to an abrupt stop and blinked her eyes several times to make sure she wasn't imagining it. But no, it was real and it was a real bitch of a sign. Noella had died exactly one year ago today and it couldn't be coincidence that, before Felicia even had a chance to get rip-roaring drunk while avoiding Knox at the same time, a female appeared who was from Noella's clan—*Knox's* clan—and in obvious need of help.

Thoughts of Knox assailed her. Had Kyle Mahone gotten in touch with him? She'd been fully briefed on the Bureau's plan to add a new team to the FBI's elite, super-SWAT group referred to as the HRT, Hope Restored Team. She knew that team was the crucial step toward stabilizing relations between humans and the Otherborn races they'd once fought. And despite her preference to stay as separated from Knox as possible, she knew he was the right choice to lead it. Most civilians craved peace now, but it was a constant, often bloody battle given the insurgents, humans and Others alike, that resisted.

On the other hand, Felicia thought, still staring at the

man and the dharmire . . . There would always be individuals who just naturally preyed on those weaker than themselves.

Okay, okay. Message received.

No rest for the wicked.

Despite how shaken Mahone still felt, he didn't flinch when Special Agent Leonard Walker threw open his door and stalked into his office. Instead, he leaned back in his chair, crossed his arms over his chest, and waited calmly for the explosion.

He didn't have long to wait.

Even so, compared to an ethereal creature with the power to enter his mind and, oh yeah, the apparent ability to destroy the earth, Walker was hardly a threat.

The man planted himself in front of Mahone's desk, thrusting his face forward as if to compensate for his lack of height. "This is some kind of joke, right?"

It was obviously a hypothetical question. No sooner had Walker asked it than he thumped his fist on Mahone's desk.

"Ten years ago we were hunting these fuckers down, and now we're supposed to fight next to them?"

"Not too long ago," Mahone reminded him, "I wouldn't have been able to sit at the front of the bus with you, Walker. Now you answer to me. Times change."

Walker narrowed his eyes, making Mahone stiffen. Most of the time, Walker was an okay agent; what he excelled at was training exceptional ones. Walker had all the right moves, but only in theory. When it came to applying them in the field, where subtlety or quick thinking was required, Walker became set in his ways. He trained with all the special ops teams, but he wasn't going to train Team Red.

"Don't give me that ACLU, politically correct, we're-all-equal bullshit, Mahone. Regardless of the color of our skin, you and me, we share the same DNA." Walker jerked his thumb toward the office window. "These—these freaks are—are . . ."

Mahone cocked a brow, amused at the blustery man's red-faced loss for words but equally pissed at his lack of restraint. He allowed a hint of steel to edge his voice. "Don't let the fact that we graduated the Academy together make you forget your rank, Walker. Stay civil. And shut my door. Now."

Licking his lips, Walker searched Mahone's face, then quietly shut the door.

"Freaks or not," Mahone said a moment later, "the Others we've selected are half-human and they have special skills that no amount of training can duplicate."

"Our men are the best—"

"No question about that. But being fully human means they have limitations. The Others aren't aliens that just landed on Earth a decade ago. They're citizens. They live among us openly now. Hell, some of their ancestors roamed Earth before we did." He laughed at the irony. "We just didn't know it."

"'Cause they didn't want us to know. 'Cause they needed victims—"

"Victims like Manson's? Ng's? Dahmer's?" Mahone snorted. "Find me a species that hasn't been tainted by bad blood and I'll hand in my resignation right now."

"I'm not going to let you do this."

Mahone's brows lifted at the blatant threat in Walker's voice. Mouthy was one thing. Insubordinate something altogether different. "You might want to reconsider how you—" Mahone began, his voice low.

A commanding knock on the door interrupted him.

Walker spun around as Mahone got slowly to his feet.

Knox Devereaux was early.

Mahone couldn't say how he knew the half-vampire/half-human was standing outside. He just did. Mahone refused to attribute his racing pulse to fear, but it pissed him off anyway.

Mahone had known Knox for over ten years. The dharmire wasn't as overtly hostile as Hunt, but in some ways, his calm, formal mannerisms were twice as unsettling. Probably because anyone with an ounce of intuition could sense the passion boiling just beneath his controlled façade. Mahone had picked Devereaux to lead Team Red because his strategic skill, leadership ability, and calm under pressure couldn't be beat. Yet he knew there was so much more to the vamp. Mahone had seen for himself how dangerous the dharmire could be when his control gave way to blood lust, or straight-out lust—always for one particular woman.

Several more knocks shook the door.

Mahone's gaze found Walker's. "Team Red's a done deal," he snapped, hoping the decision wouldn't turn out to be the biggest mistake of his life. "And if you threaten me again, you'll wonder if we share the same DNA, after all." In a louder voice, he called, "Enter."

The door opened and Knox Devereaux stepped inside. He was, as always, impeccably dressed. Tall and grim-faced, his dark pants, expensive black duster jacket, and polished boots made him look like a *GQ* outlaw.

Yes, indeed, Mahone thought. The times had changed.

The right to life, liberty, and the pursuit of happiness no longer applied just to humans.

Wraiths had the right to vote. A court had just ruled that a mage's right to practice magic was akin to one's right to worship. And vamps, both full vampires and dharmires alike, couldn't be denied health coverage based on "malnourishment" being a preexisting condition.

The Others were demanding their due and making their presence known.

Soon, they'd be protecting some of the same individuals they'd fought just years before.

God bless the U.S. of A.

And just to be safe, the Goddess Essenia bless them all.

He'd done his best. By assembling Team Red, he'd either save the world or damn it. If Team Red failed, they wouldn't know the full ramifications of doing so.

Mahone, on the other hand, would take the knowledge straight to Hell.

Maybe, just maybe, Knox Devereaux could help make sure that didn't happen.